Ridout

CRASH

CRASH

KEITH HOUGHTON

THOMAS & MERCER

Published by Thomas & Mercer, Seattle

www.apub.com

Amazon, the Amazon logo, and Thomas & Mercer are trademarks of Amazon.com, Inc., or its affiliates.

ISBN-13: 9781612186528
ISBN-10: 1612186521

Cover design by Luke Bird

Printed in the United States of America

For Lynn,
the fizz in my pop.

Prologue

I remember coming to a point in my life where I thought I was invincible. Not quite in Superman's league, but hardier than most—you could say, more durable than the average joe. I believed no kind of suffering would dare to touch me, and hardship knew better than to come knocking at my door.

To anyone who passed through my world, I appeared focused and standoffish. A young inheritor of old money, racing through life on frictionless wheels, where no obstacle was insurmountable and the elasticity of my family's purse strings were all that held me back.

With favors called in, I never had to work hard in high school, and even less so in college. I was privileged, and I was protected. Breast-fed on capitalism at the teat of success. From the moment I came into this world, mine was a birthright to the big time, and no one was going to keep me from striding along my golden path.

Some people call it leading a charmed life.

But to me it was all I knew, and it shaped me.

At my pinnacle, I had my whole brilliant future mapped out in every detail. I knew where I was headed. I knew how to avoid the pitfalls, and I knew which shortcuts would get me where I needed to be. In short, I was aiming high, with the sweet spot clearly in my sights.

I thought I had everything.

I thought I was happy.

I thought I was invincible.

Then I met Cassie.

Chapter One

Hail clatters against the car, the wiper blades shrieking as they scrape across the windshield.

Every way I look at it, this is madness—sitting here in the crosshairs of the worst blizzard of the season, with a freezing gale threatening to overturn my car and screaming at me to flee to safety.

It's three o'clock in the afternoon in suburban New York, but it might as well be midnight at the North Pole. Shadowy clouds churn in a falling sky, and the streets are paved with snow. I ought to be at the office in the city, where no one knows the craziness wheeling inside me. Instead, I am out to prove a point, even if it gets me killed.

The strip-mall parking lot is all but abandoned, with just a handful of employee vehicles still on the frosted blacktop. I have been sitting here for seventeen long minutes, going over one doomsday scenario after another, trying to figure things out.

"Winners have well-ordered minds," a sociology professor once told me, during one of the few classes in which I paid a little more attention. "Structure, system, separation—these are the keys to opening life's doors."

But my mind is helter-skelter, my thoughts clashing and in torment.

Even with the heat on full blast, there is a coolness to my skin, and not for the first time, I ask myself if it's all worth it.

I want to believe it is.

I want to believe I am being paranoid and behaving irrationally, and that the events that have brought me here are nothing more than figments of my imagination.

But much of belief is based on faith, and right now mine is lacking.

Until Cassie converted me, I never believed in love at first sight. I was one of those pretentious people who snickered at mushy romanticism. Blindly, I thought I was happy leading a bachelor's life, coming and going as I pleased, with only myself to put at the center of the universe, convinced that I could sample the best of everything without ever committing fully to anything.

Smash and grab and never look back.

It was a surefire policy for going through life unhurt.

Then Cassie came along and opened my eyes. Cassie, with her cinematic smile and her passion for lost causes. She was a once-in-a-lifetime find. A keeper.

Although we haven't been together long enough yet to reach any significant milestones, we have connected on more than one level, and I'm the first to admit I am hooked. Like no other woman before her, Cassie has reached into my darkness and lit me up, and it's addictive.

Something blocks the streetlight coming in through the driver's window, and I turn to see gloved knuckles rap against the glass.

The fist belongs to a thick-cut police officer, his bulk framed against an illuminated storefront, his weatherproof poncho flapping and crackling as the wind tries to sweep him away.

He gestures with a finger, *Roll down the window.*

Even though it means letting out all the heat, I do as I'm instructed, and freezing air blusters in. Snowflakes melt on the dash.

I let him see me shiver. "How can I help you, Officer?"

I have nothing to hide, and yet I know there is a strong likelihood that a guilty look is broadcasting the opposite. The fact that I wear every emotion like a neon sign is one of the reasons I avoid playing poker.

"Sir, you're parked in a tow-away zone."

His voice is raised, gruff—it needs to be, competing with the gale— his breath misting from his mouth.

"I am? I didn't realize. Give me a second and I'll move."

But he gestures again. "Let me see your license and registration."

With numbing fingers, I fumble my driver's license out of my wallet and hand it over.

The officer inspects it, tilting the card into the storefront glow as he compares my image to real life.

This isn't the first time I have been asked to prove my identity to the police, and in not too dissimilar circumstances. You would think that a clean-cut thirtysomething white male wearing a Savile Row suit and sitting in a fifty-grand coupe wouldn't warrant much in the way of official attention. Then again, I suppose it depends on which part of town he's hanging around.

"What business do you have here, Mr. Allen?"

"My girlfriend is at the doctor's office. Last-minute emergency." I offer him a buddy smile to mitigate his suspicious tone. "You know how it is. One thing or another. There's always some kind of drama."

He nods, but I get the impression it's more of a reflex than a show of agreement. For a moment, his gaze focuses on the brightly lit Eastchester Urgent Care on the opposite corner.

When I first met Cassie, I thought I'd found perfection. She was everything I wanted in a woman: smart, sexy, sassy. She checked all my boxes and then some. Of course, I was deluded. There is no such thing as perfect. I can see that now. Some people call it being blinded by love. Falling in lust. The feeling descended on me over the period of a few hours, like heavy snowfall, until my world became unrecognizable, and it wasn't until it began to melt that I saw bits of my old life poking through.

"They have their own lot over there," the police officer says as he looks back at me. "Almost empty, as far as I can make out."

The comment is his way of questioning my choice to park at the strip mall across the street. It would mean my girlfriend having to cross the roadway in bad visibility. What kind of boyfriend would allow that? But that's not his point. A few yards behind my car, on the corner, is a Wells Fargo bank, and my car is running. My parking on the yellow cross-hatching isn't his primary concern. It's the slim chance that there could be something much more unlawful under way here.

Keeping hold of my license, he instructs me to kill the engine and to stay put, and then he battles his way to the back of the car.

I watch him through the rearview mirror as he checks my tags, another round of buckshot hail blasting at his poncho.

I know it sounds pathetic, but since I met Cassie, she is on my mind just about every waking moment. She's the kind of warmhearted woman that every cool-minded man wants to make his own, and when I think about her at length, competing feelings rise and fall with each breath. I picture the two of us building a future out here in the suburbs. One day getting married. One day having children. One day reminiscing about our wonderful life together. It's like I've been waiting my whole life for her to arrive, to reach inside me and shake me up.

It's something I've never had—a permanent relationship—and I think I'm ready for it.

A man can dream.

Until recently, I thought Cassie was equally invested, that she had her sights set on matching rockers and grandchildren running rings around us at our lakeside home in upstate New York. Then something happened. I don't know what exactly. Overnight, her behavior toward me changed. At first, it was subtle. Her smiles remained photogenic, but they soon slipped, as though they were too heavy to hold up. And her body language switched from approachable to defensive. I broached the subject more than once, but she refused to talk about it each time. And in the last couple of weeks, she kept rushing me off the phone, coming up with all sorts of excuses for us not to spend every second of our free time together.

I understand she has a life, and so do I. But I was led to believe that she wanted to integrate our lives.

The police officer stoops his way back to the window, one hand holding on to the peak of his hat to prevent the gale from snatching it away.

"Everything in order?" I ask.

"For now."

In other words, my ID has checked out and matched up to the registration of the vehicle, my taillights are all intact, and there is no whiff of marijuana wafting out the window. Even so, he's not satisfied that everything is aboveboard here.

He puts a gloved hand on the door and leans in a little. "What's with the camera?"

I glance at the high-end Pentax on the passenger seat, with its big telephoto lens, excellent in low-light conditions.

"It's my girlfriend's. She's a photographer. It just about goes everywhere she does." I look back at him and smile. "Anything else I can help you with, Officer?"

He straightens. "Just pay attention to where you park the next time you're up here." He hands back my license. "Safe driving, sir."

I keep the smile pinned to my face, waiting for him to move on before I back the car into a legal spot. Then I turn my attention back to the urgent-care center.

Of course, I could tell him the truth, that I'm spying on Cassie, but that would make him only more suspicious than he already is.

It won't matter one bit that I have good reason to be doing so, that Cassie's behavior lately has brought me to the conclusion that she is seeing someone else, that her increasing coolness has me questioning her fidelity, and that my following her has more to do with confirmation than intimidation. Of course, he'd be sympathetic to a point—men understand the need to protect their interests—but in the end his training would override his empathy, and the only thing he'd be able to see here is a stalker, even if I am the wronged party.

Movement in the glass entranceway across the street catches my eye. I pick up the camera, training it on a young dark-haired woman as she steps out onto the sidewalk, her raincoat clinging to her slim frame like a second skin.

As always, I am bowled over by Cassie's beauty, and my heart leaps at the sight of her.

The camera bleeps as it adds a photo to the stash I have already taken.

From the first moment we spoke, I never figured Cassie for a liar. Not that she has openly lied to me, as far as I'm aware. But each step of the way, she has avoided telling me what I'm beginning to see as the truth, which in my book is equivalent to lying.

I zoom in until Cassie fills the frame.

Hunched into the wind, she heads toward an SUV with its headlights on and its engine running. A silver SUV with New York plates that wasn't there a minute ago.

I track her with the camera, snapping images as she pulls open the passenger door and climbs inside.

The SUV is facing away from me, but I can see the back of a man's head in the driver's seat, and my suspicions harden.

With enough money, just about everything is obtainable. Material possessions, status, even people. When you're raised with a silver spoon in your mouth, wealth can act like emotional armor, shielding you from reality. Hardship happens to other people, and envy is only momentary. I know it sounds conceited, but I can't remember the last time I truly craved anything.

Then there's Cassie, turning my world on its head.

I put the car in drive and inch forward as the SUV crosses the parking lot. Then I pull out onto the street behind the vehicle, following it.

I don't want it to be true, that Cassie is two-timing me, but I can't ignore the evidence. It's here, in full color, billions of bytes stored on the camera's memory card.

What I will do with it, I have yet to decide.

The last thing I want is a confrontation, a showdown, that ends with me losing Cassie completely. But I'm not sure I can live with her cheating on me either.

The SUV accelerates through an intersection, its big tires spraying slush.

I follow, my wipers clunking and grating against the glass.

The road is marbled with hail, a crunchy glaze that inhibits traction. Even so, the SUV continues to increase its pace. As it moves beyond the speed limit, it starts crisscrossing the center line.

Oncoming cars swerve aside, sounding their horns.

With my knuckles white as I grip the steering wheel, I keep within a few yards' distance. All I can think about is Cassie's betrayal and what happens next.

A half mile later, a tight bend in the road comes up fast, and as the SUV cuts the corner, its red brake lights flicker. I am slow to react, distracted by my darkening thoughts, and I stomp on my brakes a fraction of a second too late—too late to avoid contact. The rear-ender isn't hard enough to cause any surface damage, but on the treacherous pavement the tap is more than enough to send the SUV into a fishtailing swerve.

It careens completely into the opposite lane, sliding sideways into oncoming traffic, its wheels locked.

There is no time to think, only to react.

I yank the steering wheel and stand on the gas pedal at the same time, and my car lurches around the stricken SUV, leaving it behind in a swirl of sleet.

Yet through the rearview mirror, I see the unimaginable unfold: cars crashing, metal twisting. The SUV is at the heart of the mayhem, bulldozing through it, and I know that the passenger side has taken the full brunt of the accident.

Cassie . . .

It's unreal, like I'm watching a scene from an action movie. The breath catches in my throat as I distance myself from the madness. But I am so transfixed by the shock of what I'm witnessing that I miss the fact that my own car has strayed and is headed toward the snow rimming the roadside. I try to take evasive action, but the car mounts the curb, jolting my hands off the wheel. A telephone pole appears as if from nowhere and buries itself deep in the grille, crinkling up the hood and throwing me hard against the seat belt. In the same instant, something like a giant snowball strikes me in the face.

Then the airbag is deflating, and I am blinking against dizziness and a cloud of settling powder.

Outside, steam hisses from the ruptured radiator.

Something is making a whining noise, and I'm not sure if it's the pulverized engine or me.

I take a moment to breathe, to assess my own damage, to taste the coppery blood in my mouth, amazed that I have survived the crash relatively unscathed.

The rearview mirror reveals the increasing carnage fifty yards down the road behind me, as each approaching vehicle brakes late and skids into the pileup.

Cassie . . .

With a trembling hand, I reach for the door and push it partly open. The metal grinds against the sidewalk, going no farther than a few inches. I lean into it, but there is no give.

I reach across to the passenger door, but my seat belt is locked, preventing me from moving.

Through ringing ears, I hear a loud creaking, which grows into the din of wood splintering as the telephone pole begins to break in two.

Fear takes hold, and panic slices through my chest. I grapple with the seat belt, but the latch is jammed.

A heartbeat later, the pole comes crashing down and the roof of my car collapses.

And the last thought I have as the windshield explodes is a selfish one: *Please don't let me die.*

Chapter Two

If you're reading this and it makes no sense to you whatsoever, that's because you're experiencing something called <u>intermittent amnesia</u>. The important thing is, don't worry. You've had it for months and it's not life-threatening. You need to stay calm, stay where you are, and let it take its course. It will pass.

The note is handwritten in black marker on a large Day-Glo-orange Post-it and stuck to the frame of a computer screen on the desk in front of me.

It's the first thing I see when I open my eyes, as though it has been positioned there to grab my attention.

Intermittent amnesia.

I reread the words over and over for several seconds; each time unable to fully comprehend their meaning.

My head is empty, the way it would be in those first few seconds when awakening from a deep and dreamless sleep. The only difference here is that I can't remember anything, including where I am and who I am. All I know is that less than a minute ago, I woke to find myself slumped over this desk, with an intense pain throbbing away in the back of my head and my entire body ringing like a bell.

Bewildered, I scan my surroundings.

I am seated in a rectangular office. The longer walls are composed entirely of glass—one looking through to a busy open-plan work space and people sitting at computer screens, the other providing a dizzying view of colossal skyscrapers, deathly still against a muslin sky.

Manhattan springs to mind. It feels right. All those beseeching buildings reaching for the unobtainable.

My eyes find their way back to the Post-it, and I mouth the words again, still at a loss to fully understand their meaning.

The computer monitor sits on a robust metal desk that could pass as a piece of modern art. Three overlapping circles meander around on the otherwise black screen—a white Venn diagram with the central region shaded gray. Aside from the usual office necessities, three items are within reach: a cell phone, an electronic car key fob, and a coffee mug with the words BELIEF IS A SUSPENSION OF REALITY stenciled on it.

Farther afield, a white leather couch sits against the internal glass wall, its cushions depressed from years of heavy lounging. And at the far end of the room, a pair of black file cabinets stand on either side of a 3-D printer on a metal stand.

Frameless pictures are hung on the shorter walls: computer-generated designs of futuristic buildings. Long curves and faceted domes. Images that could be concept art for a science-fiction movie.

A small flat-screen TV is mounted in one corner of the ceiling. The picture is on, but the sound is off. A local news channel is showing an aerial shot of FBI agents in blue windbreakers gathered next to trees painted with the coppery tones of autumn.

A clock in the corner of the picture says it's just after three in the afternoon.

I am still gazing at the TV when the door opens partway to reveal a man in a tweed blazer.

"Do we have a green light?" he asks.

A peppering of gray hair makes him look older than he is, but somehow, I know he's in his late thirties. My age. A trim mustache splits the length of his face, and a pair of designer eyeglasses complete his scholarly appearance.

"You were going to make the necessary arrangements," he says, "to secure the care package, for tonight's pre-meeting entertainment special." His tone is soft and as understated as a physician's, not much more than a whisper.

I feel I should know his voice, recognize his face, but I can't place him, and I have no idea what it is he's talking about.

He glances at the workers in the outer office, then looks back at me. "We can't afford any disappointments. You know the Chinese—they'll be expecting fireworks." He taps a fingertip against the gold watch on his wrist. "We have less than five hours to get our game faces on and our act together. So how about it, buddy? Are we good to go?"

"I. Don't. Know."

Each word comes out completely formed, able to stand alone and be unsupported by the others, but it's the voice of a stranger.

He sees the vacant expression that is surely fixed on my face and says, "Ah. I get it now. You're having one of your blank spells."

"I am?"

"Now that I think about it, you do look a little blurry around the edges. Like one of those life-sized cardboard cutouts. I should really make a point of learning to recognize that vacant look when I see it, especially since it's been happening more often lately. Just hang in there, buddy. It'll all come back. I take it you've got one of your humongous headaches as well?"

"Like I've been struck with a baseball bat."

He nods. "Well, that seems to be the pattern. You start with this monumental brain spasm, then the memory loss kicks in, and then . . . you have no idea what I'm talking about, do you?"

"Intermittent amnesia."

"Exactly. And bravo for reading the note you left yourself. I mean, it's okay—I can handle these brain spasms of yours, as long as you're not getting cold feet and thinking of reneging on me. Because you, of all people, know how much we have riding on this racehorse."

He sees my blank expression making an unwelcome comeback and says, "Since your brain is on vacation, let me jog your memory. Our big warm-up event with Xian Airlines is tonight. Eight o'clock, at Rafferty's. It's the reason you were arranging delivery of the extra-special care package. Remember?" He allows a few seconds for his words to penetrate and for me to think about them before continuing. "Either way," he says, "memory or no memory, I need you firing on all cylinders tonight. The future of this firm is counting on it. This is make-or-break for us. So do us all a favor and get your head in whatever space it needs to be in. We need a win here."

"Xian Airlines. Eight o'clock. Rafferty's."

"And I promise, once this deal is behind us, you have my blessing to take some well-deserved time off. I know these last few months have been difficult for you in lots of ways. I know I can be a real pain in the ass at the best of times. I know we've had our moments recently. But if anyone around here has earned an all-expenses-paid trip to somewhere exotic, it's you."

My expression remains robotic.

He draws a circle in the air with a finger. "Listen, about these mental time-outs of yours, I can see they're bothering you. Take my advice and don't let them stress you out, because that would be counterproductive. It's the stress that triggers them. All you need to know right now is that they come and they go. It's been this way since the accident. Your pills are in the drawer. Take them. They'll help with the headache, which should kick-start the recovery process. And before you know it, everything will come flooding back." He checks his watch. "Is that really the time? Listen, why don't you go home early, clean yourself up, and get your head together? I need you at your best for later. No excuses."

He turns to leave, then hesitates, glancing back at me as he hangs on the door. "It's Gary, by the way. We grew up together in Pleasantville, and we've been inseparable ever since. Just take your pills. Take them all if necessary. It'll come back."

Then he leaves, the glass door closing softly behind him.

And I am left with more questions than answers, and no recollection of my friendship with Gary, or of my role in this firm.

For at least a minute, I do nothing except stare at the Post-it and think. But my thoughts are sluggish and in disarray, as though I am concussed, and no matter how hard I concentrate, my head remains empty.

However, one thing is clear: I should have been more vocal with Gary, asked him to fill in my blanks. But it's like there's a disconnect between the parts of my brain that enable rational thought and those that deal with speech.

I pull open the desk drawer. Inside is an orange plastic pill bottle with a patient's name printed on the label.

"Jed Allen."

I speak the name out loud—apparently, my name—several times, frowning at its unfamiliarity. It fits my unfurling persona about as comfortably as a hat too small for my head.

The truth is, I don't feel either like a Jed or an Allen. Then again, I don't know what being anyone feels like right now. If anything, I feel slightly out of sync, as though I'm on some weird narcotic trip.

Experimentally, I pinch the skin on my arm—on the off chance that I am dreaming—but aside from a little pain, nothing changes. I do notice a small bruise in the crease of my elbow, though, with a tiny dot in the center, indicating I have given blood lately, or that something has been injected.

A warm panic starts to simmer in my belly.

If I am to believe Gary and what it says on the note, I have nothing to worry about. All I should do is sit here and wait for the intermittent amnesia to pass.

"But why do I have it in the first place?"

The pills have been prescribed by a Dr. Merrick, and the drug name might as well be in Finnish. I pop the lid and then pause to study my hand, as if for the first time.

It's an unfamiliar topography of peaks and valleys. Thin fingers with knotty knuckles and veiny ridges. The only redeeming feature is that I don't appear to be a nail-biter.

The instructions on the pill bottle say TAKE ONE, TWICE DAILY.

They look like aspirin. I go all out and shake two of the pills onto my palm, then a third, then a fourth, gulping them down and hoping for the best. Then I stuff the pill bottle in my pocket—next to a wallet, which I fumble out and examine.

The billfold is soft black leather with a red silk interior. Inside are several credit cards, each with the same JED ALLEN name embossed onto them, and a few hundred dollars. A couple of membership cards to various clubs, and what looks like a hotel keycard. One of the pockets contains a New York State driver's license, bearing a photograph of an ordinary-looking brown-haired guy with one eyebrow cocked slightly higher than the other, either playfully or arrogantly.

He looks like a rich kid.

I reach for the computer screen and angle it so that I can see my shadowy reflection in its dark surface.

The same guy from the license photo stares back at me with searching eyes—only this version looks less comfortable in his own skin. He wears a coating of brown stubble, like it's still the fashion, and a gray pin-striped business suit over an open-necked white shirt.

First impression is, I don't look instantly likable. Every way I look at it, mine is the face of a stranger, and it occurs to me that in robbing me of my memories, amnesia provides a unique objectiveness.

How many people get to look at themselves for the first time with the impartiality of brand-new eyes?

I rub my fingertips over my prickly jawline, along my slightly upturned nose, and through my curly hair, feeling the unfamiliar contours of my cranium, with as many bumps and craters as the moon.

It's all alien to me.

I look back at my reflection and frown. "Am I losing my mind?"

The Post-it note tells me nothing about the root of the amnesia, or if it's the precursor to dementia or Alzheimer's, or even a symptom of a terminal illness.

The panic in my belly heats up with the sudden thought that I might be dying, and it's an effort not to be consumed by it.

Instead, I draw a big shaky breath and blow it out, glancing toward the open-plan office as I do, fearing that somebody has seen my unnerved state. But no one is looking; everyone is intent on their work.

With my stranger's fingers, I slot the license back into the wallet. In the opposite pocket is another yellow Post-it note folded over a small photograph.

The photograph is a head-and-shoulders shot of two smiling people: a woman with long dark hair and high cheekbones, and possibly the bluest eyes in the world; and a man I now recognize as me, his face fuller, healthier than my reflection in the computer screen.

On the back of the photo are the words *Cassie and Me*, written inside a heart.

The sight of it pulls half a smile from my lips. "You don't look like the mushy, romantic type."

I study the picture again, this time absorbing every detail.

It appears to have been taken at a bar at Christmastime. Cassie and I are snuggled up and grinning at the camera. Christmas lights are hanging in the background, and one of the female partygoers behind us is dressed in a cute Santa outfit. I'm wearing a silvery open-necked shirt, while Cassie wears a knitted red dress, the same hue as her lipstick.

But if she is my love interest, I have no recollection of our relationship.

On the second Post-it note are the words *If you're thinking you've lost your mind, call me,* together with a phone number.

It stands to reason that if Cassie is indeed my partner, then I need to speak with her. If anyone would have intimate knowledge of my intermittent amnesia, she'd be the one.

The cell phone's screen brightens at my touch, requesting a password in the shape of a pattern. Nine white dots forming a square matrix.

I have no idea what it might be.

Swiping a finger across the dots in a random fashion causes the pattern to turn red, denying access. I try my initials, Cassie's name, and then several numbers, all ending in the same negative result.

The only app I can access from the lock screen is the camera.

Not to be outdone, I pick up the office phone and dial the number on the Post-it. A phone rings down the line, the call connects, and then a robotic voice answers, asking me to leave a message at the sound of the tone.

"Hey," I say. "It's me. I'm assuming you know all about this intermittent amnesia of mine? Well, it's happened again, and I need you to reassure me I'm not going crazy. I'm at the office. Call me back, the second you hear this."

Then, despite the first note's advice to stay put, I grab my stuff and head for the door.

I hesitate before stepping out into the open-plan office. My name—I have to accept that it's mine, even though it feels completely foreign—is stenciled in frosted letters on the glass door, followed by **SENIOR PARTNER**.

I still have no idea what kind of firm this is. The office suite seems spacious and busy. At regular intervals there are scale replicas of buildings, constructed out of white plastic and lit from within.

The firm's name is hung on the far wall next to the elevator. In big silvery backlit letters, it says **Q & A ARCHITECTS**.

Still, nothing stirs.

"Don't be late," a man's voice calls as I head for the elevator.

I pause at the open door to another glass-fronted office. It has the same impressive cityscape view as mine, but most of it is obscured by transparencies taped to the glass. Blueprints and technical sketches.

The name etched into the door reads **GARY QUARTUCCI, MANAGING PARTNER**.

"Taking my advice and heading home?" he asks.

"I think I need a cold shower. Either that or a stiff drink. Maybe both."

"Whatever it takes, buddy."

Gary is standing next to what appears at first glance to be an elephant's tusk, positioned upright on a table. But it's the mock-up of a building. A curving, twisting, tapering tower rooted in an island in the middle of a blue plastic lake. Judging from the scale of the miniature trees at its base, the real construction would exceed a thousand feet, which I know adds up to more than seventy-five stories.

"We certainly outdid ourselves this time," Gary says as he admires the replica. "You should be immensely proud of what you've done here, Jed. As a company, this is our crowning achievement. It's cost us—no doubt about it. We've had to make sacrifices to get here. I think it's all been worth it, though. Don't you?"

He claims he's my best friend, but I don't know him from Adam.

He glances my way. "The meds haven't kicked in yet?"

I shake my head, then wish that I hadn't.

"Go home," he says. "Get that girlfriend of yours to give you a head massage, or something else to make the blood flow. I'll see you later, at the club."

I ride the elevator nonstop to the basement parking garage, wondering how long my zombie state will last.

The elevator door opens into a dimly lit concrete cavern, and I linger, listening, before venturing into it.

The underground lot is warm, with a scent of exhaust fumes and rubber.

I press the key fob, and orange lights blink a few yards away.

My car is a sleek black Audi coupe with aerodynamic lines. I run appreciative fingers over the metallic paint before opening the door and slipping inside. The beige leather still has that business-class smell to it.

A yellow Post-it note is stuck to the dash, identical to the one I found in the office, reminding me I have no memory.

The engine starts with a purr, and then I pause before putting it in drive, realizing that I have no idea where my home is.

Forgetting, in my addled state, that I could just look on my driver's license, I check the glove compartment for clues. There are several torn-open envelopes stuffed inside, but I don't bother checking their contents; my whole attention is suddenly focused on the knife wedged into the tight space.

Cautious, I reach in and pull it out, at first holding it between thumb and forefinger, and then curling my fingers around the rubber grip.

It's a six-inch hunting knife with a jagged edge.

The blade feels unnatural in my hand, heavy, alien, and yet as oddly reassuring as a plaster cast on a broken wrist.

I glance at my stranger's eyes in the rearview mirror. "Why do you have a knife in your car?"

Then I place it back in the glove compartment and close the lid.

I notice that the car is equipped with an information console, so I tap through to the navigation system, bringing up a route list showing recent trips. The majority appear to be journeys in the city, with a few farther afield. Several for an address in Eastchester.

I say it out loud, three times, as if by doing so it will work a magic spell and conjure up an image of home.

But the name is as foreign to me as my own.

Still, I set the navigation system to retrace the route. A parking gate rises automatically at street level, and I pull out into a river of yellow cabs and messenger bikes, flowing between the monoliths of Lower Manhattan.

"Feel your way. Like a blind man in a maze."

It's weird that I recognize the city but not the shape of my own face.

It's equally strange that I can remember how to drive but not the last time I did it, and it's hard not to worry about what has happened to me in the interim.

"You need to speak with Cassie," I say to myself. "If anyone can clear up what's going on here, she's probably the one."

The West Side Highway is busy, and my car becomes part of a steady procession of traffic headed northeast, with the gray Hudson churning away on one side and stands of trees on the other, their leaves trading away their gold before the winter crash.

On the steering wheel, my stranger's hands are pasty white.

Amnesia hasn't robbed me of everything stored inside, I realize—just the window dressing. It has pulled down the blinds and locked the door, but behind the closed facade, information is still intact, still there, still accessible, enabling me to function.

A phone rings through the car speakers, startling me, and it takes a second to work out that my cell has connected automatically to the in-car infotainment system.

On the dashboard screen, the caller ID reads MOTHER TERESA.

I touch the TALK button on the steering wheel. "Hello?"

"Jed, it's Tess. What's going on? I've been expecting your call. The clock is ticking, and I need either a yea or a nay."

She sounds businesslike, her tone bordering on brusque.

Even though this woman is in my phone contacts, it goes without saying that I don't know who she is, aside from the fact that she isn't the real Mother Teresa, which leaves me with two choices: confess that I'm in the dark about the nature of her call and try to be a quick study, or go with the flow and fake it, without coming across like an idiot.

"Jed, is everything okay?" she asks before I can make up my mind.

"Listen . . . Tess . . . can I call you back, maybe later? I'm in the middle of something right now."

There's a noticeable pause, then, "Jed, you sound off. You're sure you're okay?"

"Just an infuriating headache. Otherwise, never better. How about you?"

"Now I'm worried. In the five years we've known each other, that's the first time you've ever asked how I'm doing. We all know empathy isn't your strong suit. In fact, you see it as a weakness. So level with me. You say you have a headache. Is it happening again? Are you having trouble remembering things?"

I glance at her name on the dashboard screen, as if she can see through it to my stupefied face.

First, Gary, and now, this woman nicknamed Mother Teresa. Both effectively strangers, and both with knowledge of my condition.

How many more people will I come into contact with who know more about me than I do?

"From your silence," she says, "I'll take it that I'm right and your amnesia is back in full swing, in which case it's crucial you take delivery of your care package ASAP."

My attention sharpens when I hear those words.

"You've got it, the care package?"

"Sitting right here on my desk. Will you be picking it up later? You did make a point of saying it was an important part of the soirée you have planned for tonight. Plus, it was just about the only thing that helped restore your memory the last time this happened."

"Great. But there may be a slight problem."

"Don't tell me. Even though you've been here a hundred times, right now you have no idea where I live."

"Right."

"Don't you love amnesia? Never fear. Maurice will text you the address. And I'll tell the boys downstairs to guide you to my door. In the meantime, try not to get too anxious. It will only exacerbate your problem."

I hear the connection drop, and her name disappears from the dashboard screen.

"Easier said than done," I murmur into the ensuing quiet—because trying to ignore the constant sensation of panic simmering away in my gut is like trying to convince a frightened boy that the monster he knows to be lurking under his bed is only imaginary.

Chapter Three

In the late afternoon traffic, it takes forty-five minutes to reach Eastchester. Plenty of time in which to collect my thoughts—what few I have.

I know my name is Jed Allen, and that there's a strong possibility I'm in a good place with a woman named Cassie. I know I'm a senior partner at an architecture firm in New York City and I drive an expensive automobile.

I know that, despite medication and wishful thinking, my memories have not come back, leaving me with a handful of facts in the redacted history of my life. It's disconcerting, with the only consolation being that the pills have taken the edge off my killer headache.

But maybe I will find the answers I need at home.

The navigation system guides me along quiet tree-lined lanes in residential suburbia. The kind of prime real estate high-flying professionals can afford. People with lofty offices in the city.

"People like me, it seems."

Home turns out to be a pretty two-story Colonial with beige clapboards and brown shingles, Georgian paned windows between decorative shutters, and a pair of white pillars guarding the roofed entranceway.

It's nice, quaint, and far too ordinary-looking for someone who designs futuristic skyscrapers for a living.

Worse still, it's not even remotely familiar.

I pull the car into the driveway and look at the house for several seconds, waiting for something to connect. But nothing about this place rings any bells. Even the life-sized reproduction of Rodin's *The Thinker* sitting in a gravel bed in the middle of the lawn seems an odd choice to me.

From the dashboard, the infotainment system bleeps, indicating an incoming text from Tess. It pops up on the display, revealing an address on Central Park West, back in the city.

"You have no idea what you're doing," I tell my reflection in the rearview mirror, "or what you're getting yourself into. This is madness. You should have stayed at the office and waited for everything to come back."

A paved front walk snakes across a leaf-littered lawn. I follow it to the front door, my heels clacking against stone.

Then I hesitate at the threshold, patting my pockets and realizing that I don't have a house key on me. Through the dimpled panes, a hallway and the foot of a staircase are visible, but there is no indication of movement inside. I press a finger to the doorbell, but nobody comes running.

Do I live here alone or with Cassie?

The truth is, I have no idea. What I do know is that it seems like a waste to have a house this big for just one person.

Optimistic, I try the handle, and the door opens at my touch. It's a surprise; the neighborhood seems nice, but even with my lack of memory, I know that nowhere is completely safe these days.

"Hello?" I holler as I slip inside. "It's me. Anybody home?"

The wood-floored hallway is silent, as though the wood itself is soaking up every bit of sound. Vanilla-colored walls stretch away from the entrance, vacant of any personalization. A wooden staircase with ornate balusters ascends to an airy landing and more empty walls.

I linger, suddenly feeling like an intruder.

"Is anyone here?"

I wait, listening, holding my breath. But there is no reply.

In the rooms on either side of the hall, an assortment of furniture is huddled in the middle of the floor. Chairs on top of tables. Cabinets and breakables sheathed in Bubble Wrap. Packing crates and cardboard boxes piled in the corners.

FRAGILE and THIS WAY UP.

"Am I moving in or moving out?"

There was no for-sale sign in the front lawn, but that didn't necessarily mean anything; everything's online these days.

The same scene is repeated throughout the first floor: a sense of transition and emptiness. Bare kitchen cupboards and no food in the fridge. Nothing on the walls except for the rectangular discolorations left behind after the removal of pictures or art.

I move from room to room, waiting for the vacuous house to pull my memory out of hiding.

None of it feels familiar.

The truth is, this could be anyone's house. It's as alien to me as everything else. I can accept that I don't remember it, but why doesn't it feel like home?

The only personalized item in the kitchen is a Post-it note on the fridge door. In black marker, it reads *Take your meds!*

Obediently, I shake a few pills onto my hand from the bottle in my pocket, washing them down with a slurp of tepid water from the tap.

"You need to get a handle on this," I say to my warped reflection in the faucet, "before you lose your mind completely."

My cell phone rings. I look at it, hoping it's Cassie returning my call. But the name on the screen is GARY.

"Just checking you got home in one piece," he says as I answer. "How's the headache?"

"Fading."

"Great."

"Not really. I still don't remember anything. And it's not like everything's still there and it's just murky. It's like my brain has been swept clean, and now it's totally empty."

"Scary."

"How long does this usually last?"

"As far as I know, minutes, normally. At first it was less than that. Seconds. You'd go blank midway through a conversation, like something had sucked out your brain, and only those who knew you would spot it. Then you'd come back, and it would be like nothing had happened. In fact, you've been getting good at hiding it. Winging it has saved your bacon a dozen times, especially at the conference table."

His breezy overview does nothing to dispel the panic tightening my gut.

"It's been over an hour."

"I agree—it's atypical. You need to have a conversation with your doctor, because the meds have always pulled you back. I don't know what else to say, other than don't be late for the party."

I hang up and return to the larger of the front rooms, even more desperate to feel anchored instead of adrift in my own life.

The cardboard boxes are an obvious starting point. Words are written in black marker on each box: *Pictures*; *Ornaments*; *Knickknacks*; and several saying *Books*. One has the word *Memories* on the side, crossed out with a big *X*.

My entire life is probably boxed up here. Dumped after a move, with good intentions to get around to unpacking it. Or waiting to be shipped to an undisclosed location.

Unlike the others, the Memories box isn't sealed with packing tape.

Anticipating a discovery, I pull open the cardboard flaps, only to find the box completely empty.

The irony brings a brief smile to my face.

A floorboard creaks overhead, and I look up at the ceiling to see a jagged crack running from one side of it to the other. I feel like I should recognize that crack, its angles, the way it zigzags, but it's just another absent memory.

Inside the Pictures box is a stack of photographs in black wooden frames of assorted sizes. One by one, I take them out, hoping that something will click in my head and my memories will come rushing back.

The photographs are all black and white, and appear to have been professionally taken. For the most part, they are portrait shots of ordinary people in exceptional places. Close-ups of time-traveled faces: ancient Indian men with wispy white hair and missing teeth, eyes sparkling with mischief; old Mongolian women with skin as rough as tundra, smiling through their hardship; teary African children under a scorching sun, drinking from old food cans, their big doleful eyes unable to see a tomorrow.

In every way, it's as though I am intruding on someone else's life.

Again, it hits home—my amnesia—exactly how much like a fish out of water I am. Disorientation is making me feel disconnected and out of step with my surroundings, like I've traveled through various time zones and been forced to stay awake. My brain is groggy, and there is a lag to each of my senses.

"So this is what it feels like to have amnesia."

I can't afford to dwell on it; right now I need to focus on fixing the problem, not the problem itself.

Another box contains photography equipment sealed in Bubble Wrap: professional cameras, various lenses and filters, a collapsible tripod.

Are these Cassie's? Is this what she does for a living: she's a professional photographer?

Above my head, the floorboard creaks again, followed by a single thud, and I return to the hallway, looking up the stairs.

"Hello? Anyone up there? Hello?"

The wooden steps complain as I ascend.

"Cassie? Is that you?"

The first two bedrooms are empty. No beds, no furniture, not even curtains at the windows.

The third, and what I assume to be the master, is the only room in the house that looks lived in.

Between two stylish armoires, a large wooden-framed bed occupies center stage. A red comforter is scrunched up on crumpled white sheets, and the pillows look like they've been beaten to a pulp.

I go to the first armoire and open it up, finding off-the-rack suits, white shirts with noticeable wear and tear, a few novelty neckties, and well-worn oxfords.

"Talk about living lean."

The other armoire contains a rainbow collection of women's clothing. I walk my fingertips across the silky shirts, the woolen sweaters, my fingers hesitating when they reach the knitted red dress I saw Cassie wearing in the photograph. The discovery confirms my hope that Cassie lives here, too, and it's the first time since waking at the office that I feel part of something bigger than my amnesia.

Facing the bed is a matching dresser, a vase of dead lilies on the surface. Crispy petals on dusty wood. The top drawer is crammed with Cassie's underwear. Skimpy briefs and lacy bras. Bright neon, stark against deep blacks.

Ignoring the screams of *Pervert!* in my head, I rummage through the contents, warmed by the touch of the soft materials and the faint fragrance of womanhood. Then my fingers find something papery at the back of the drawer, and my hand emerges holding an envelope bound with a red ribbon.

Inside is a single photograph, and my heart skips a beat when I see Cassie's wholesome smile beaming from the picture.

But my elation is momentary.

Cassie is not alone. She is with another man, their arms interlinked.

The photo appears to have been taken at a black-tie dinner, full of coiffed people, sparkling champagne, and crystal chandeliers. In the foreground, Cassie is wearing a clingy black evening dress, the camera flash sparkling in her sapphire eyes. She looks extraordinarily beautiful, and happy.

"But who is your date?"

He's shorter than her, and a few years her senior, with dark receding hair and an aquiline nose. He's wearing an unfashionable white tuxedo and a self-serving smile that I find instantly annoying.

We all have relationship histories—even people with amnesia. No one can reach their late thirties unmarried without first going through their fair share of dead-end dates, fair-weather flings, and impermanent partners. Although I can't even recall their faces, I have no doubt that I had a string of failed relationships before Cassie came along. Why, then, am I aggrieved to learn she had other love interests, too?

In a woman's handwriting, a location and a date are written in pencil on the photo's flip side, indicating that it was taken last December at a place called the Ambient Lounge.

It's the same time of year the picture in my wallet was taken—which leaves me at a loss to explain why Cassie has this particular photograph secreted away in her underwear drawer and not one of us together instead.

But there is one answer that makes perfect sense, and the excitement of my discovery returns. Only this time it's tinged with the fire of anger.

"Cassie is having an affair."

I am juggling jealousy and resentment when another thud sounds from outside the room.

The noise seems closer than the one I heard from downstairs, and I venture out onto the landing just as the thud sounds again, and I realize it's coming from the fourth bedroom.

The room is smaller than the others, with a window overlooking the rear of the house. A foldaway bed leans against one wall, and opposite is a vanity with a circular mirror. Bottles of lotions and potions crowd its surface, and its single drawer is filled with trays of makeup, creams, loose lipsticks, and various other beauty products.

I cock an eyebrow at my reflection in the mirror.

"What's the problem? You've got yourself a nice place here. A good life. A great job. So why would your live-in lover be cheating on you?"

Something moves at the edge of my vision, and I swivel to face the window.

A bird is perched on the inside sill, watching me with its shiny black eyes. It looks like a cuckoo. The glass behind it is smudged with grease where it has tried to escape.

I take a step toward it, intending to open the window, but the sudden movement spooks the bird, and it takes flight, swooping around the room.

Around and around it whirls, dive-bombing my head like a kamikaze pilot on a mission to take out my eyes. Stupidly, I try to catch it, but it's too fast.

It's like trying to catch a rapidly deflating party balloon.

With a sickening crunch, the cuckoo hits the rim of the bedroom door and ricochets into a wall, losing feathers and dropping to the carpeted floor.

Stunned, the bird tries to right itself, taking a few wobbly steps, one of its wings twisted upward like a fin.

I come out of my freeze and take a wary step toward it, hands outstretched, just as it launches into another mad spiraling flight, this time spraying dots of blood on the walls and making a god-awful screeching sound.

Now I'm panicked.

Before I can even think, the bird lunges at my head again, shrieking, claws scrabbling for my eyes. Instinctively, I shield my face, managing to bat it away with the back of a hand. Stricken, the cuckoo hurtles across the room, crashing into the window with a bone-crunching bang, and I look up to see it falling to the floor in an unmoving heap, its neck twisted at an awkward angle.

Blood spatters are everywhere, and feathers, falling like snowflakes.

My heart is in my mouth.

I take a clumsy step closer, just as the bird twitches and lets out a bloodcurdling shriek, and I realize with dread that it's not dead yet.

Without hesitation, I stomp my foot on it.

Chapter Four

Arnold Seltzer's hiccupping heart had him feeling queasy and light-headed, worsened by the motion of the bus and the fact that he was journeying into the unknown.

The medical name for his condition was arrhythmia, and he hadn't suffered with it in almost two decades—not, in fact, since he was a nineteen-year-old messenger for a local accounting firm. In those days, the malady had been an unrelenting torment. Day after day of discomfort and dread, with him thinking that each missed beat might be his last. Even after twenty years, there was no mistaking the characteristic palpitations. It felt as though a bird were flapping around inside his rib cage, about to break free at any moment, ripping him in half.

Back then, in Seltzer's late teens, when the condition had gotten so bad that he'd lie awake night after night believing he was on the brink of having a heart attack, the family physician had explained to him about interrupted nerve signals and healthier lifestyle choices.

"For starters, quit smoking," the doctor had said. "No use sugar-coating it, Arnie. Nicotine is a major player here. It's either that or we put you on beta-blockers."

Seltzer had been too young to understand the neurology aspect, but when faced with the prospect of a lifetime of medication, he had agreed that his sixty-a-day habit was something he should rethink.

After leaving the doctor's office that day, Seltzer hadn't smoked another cigarette since, not one, and his arrhythmia hadn't plagued him at all. But lately it had made several unwelcome comebacks, and his therapist had attributed its revival to PTSD, of all things.

Of course, he knew, it wasn't just his misbehaving vagus nerve that was messing up the signals being transmitted back and forth between his brain and heart. This last year, stress had become a prime factor in his arrhythmia's resurgence, and there was nothing he could do about it—not if he wanted to get the job done. And the trouble with Seltzer was that he was a stickler for finishing what he started.

On the other side of the grubby bus window, the brick buildings of Queens slipped by, forming an endless procession of gaudy retailers, supermarket delis, and auto parts warehouses, seemingly with either a laundromat or a liquor store bookending every block. He glimpsed a man smoking a cigarette in the doorway of a convenience store and recalled his conversation at the bodega in Soundview earlier in the day.

"Mama Butterfly's," Melvyn had announced after Seltzer had explained what he was looking for.

Melvyn was a rangy, greasy-haired man in his forties with features too big for his head and one of those wispy mustaches that looked like an ink smudge. Melvyn had worked at the bodega for as long as Seltzer could remember, the two of them sharing many an hour smoking in back like chimneys, when they were younger.

"That's where you'll find what you're looking for," Melvyn had said. "Mama Butterfly's."

"You're sure, Melvyn? I don't want to waste my time."

"Cross my heart and hope to win the lottery. Remember, Arnie, I *know* people. Some may think they're the wrong kinda people. But, personally speaking, I happen to think they're the right kinda people. You feel me?"

Seltzer did. It was the reason he'd made a beeline to the bodega for the first time since moving out of the Bronx. Melvyn and he didn't have the same kind of relationship they'd once had, but he knew he could count on him and his connections.

"So where can I find this Mama Butterfly's?" Seltzer had asked.

"Over in Jackson Heights. On Northern Boulevard. You don't drive, right?"

"I can. I just choose not to own a car these days. How do *you* know . . . ?"

"I don't miss a trick. I saw you hopping off the bus. Must be inconvenient for you, Arnie, especially in your line of work. Relying on public transportation, that is."

"No, not really. It's therapeutic. Gives me time to think." He hadn't added that the thought of driving a car terrified him.

"Anyhow," Melvyn had said, "you need to take the sixty-six all the way to the IHOP, and you'll find Mama Butterfly's right across the street. Even a blind man can't miss her—she smells sweet as a virgin. Between you and me, she's what the French call a *pâtisserie*. I'll let Charlie know you're on your way. Good luck, bro."

Now, two hours later, Seltzer was sitting in the bus seat with his briefcase standing on his lap, looking out for the blue peaked roof of a pancake house.

"Man in the suit," the driver called from up front. "This is your stop. Enjoy your all-day breakfast."

The bus came to a jerky standstill. Seltzer nodded his thanks and got off.

Although he'd never visited this exact part of town before, it looked familiar, right down to the car dealership on the corner. But it was a false impression, he knew, planted by corporate sameness. The truth was, this could be any major route running through any sizable city in North America. So much of the urban landscape looked the same these days. A blueprint for mass-market consumerism, with big-brand franchises undermining small business.

As the bus pulled away, Seltzer's attention turned to the strip mall across the street.

The shopping plaza was a jumble of color and competing signage; it was hard to tell where one store ended and the next began. Along with the obligatory laundromat and cheap liquor store, a total of five eateries vied for business here, offering an eclectic home-cooked dining experience of imported cuisines for ten dollars or less. Mounted above the middle establishment, a large cream-and-brown sign read MAMA BUTTERFLY'S – MEILLEURE PÂTISSERIE.

Melvyn had warned him to take care, reminding him that nothing was set in stone—not even his fate.

"You're the master of your own destiny," he'd announced as Seltzer had left the bodega. "It's never too late to change your mind."

But Seltzer's mind had been made up for a long time, and nothing short of divine intervention could make him change it.

With his heart flip-flopping in his chest, Seltzer waited for a gap in the traffic before crossing the street.

Chapter Five

Rain seems imminent, and so I hurry to the side of the house, intending to dump the dead cuckoo in the trash before the downpour starts. The bird tumbles from the dustpan just as my phone rings in my pocket.

I take it out and wedge it to my ear. "Hello?"

A woman's voice says, "Jed? Are you okay? I'm sorry I didn't return your call right away. I've had back-to-back appointments all day."

My heart races. "Cassie?"

"No. It's Sarah." There's a pause, then: "Jed, do you know who I am?"

It goes without saying that I don't recognize her voice even a little bit, or her name. Other than picking up on her Bible Belt accent, I am clueless.

"It's Dr. Merrick," she says into my silence.

Something clicks, and my brain makes the connection. "The doctor who prescribed my memory medication?"

"One and the same. We've been working together for months, trying to fix your intermittent amnesia."

"Yours is the phone number in my wallet."

"Yes. We put it there. For this exact situation."

"Great. So you know all about what's happening to me."

"And I've been with you through almost every step. We've been seeing each other regularly, trying to figure out a way for you to cope with these recall crashes of yours."

She doesn't use the term *memory loss*, and I wonder if it's a deliberate avoidance.

"You're a psychiatrist?"

"Of sorts. If you want to get technical, my professional title is professor of neuropsychology. I'm a medical specialist based at Columbia, within the Division of Cognitive Neuroscience. The wordy version is, I specialize in cognitive behavioral interventions for persistent postconcussion syndrome."

"That's some mouthful. Is there a concise version?"

"It's just as wordy, I'm afraid. I work with people with long-term and sometimes debilitating memory problems. Occasionally, I work on a one-to-one basis with special case studies, people in unique circumstances."

"You mean with people like me?"

"Yes."

I lean against the side of the house, conscious of my bloodless expression. "I must call you a bunch."

"Let's just say it's a new development. Until recently, we had your condition under control with medication. But lately, it's been having less of an effect. Hence the lifeline number."

I let out an expletive.

"Jed, I know this is scary for you. But please know that you will be okay. We're on top of this. Tell me—what's the last thing you remember?"

I tell her about my coming to at the office—my confusion, my unease—but my story is stilted and awkward.

Recounting the experience makes it feel like there's lead in my belly, and the empty windows staring at me on this quiet street reaffirm my sense of displacement.

"One of my work colleagues, he mentioned I was in some kind of an accident."

"That's right. It was a car crash."

I look at my new coupe sitting in the driveway with not a scratch on its sleek bodywork. "When?"

"Nine months ago, back in January, during the worst storm of the winter. There were multiple wrecks that day on the same stretch of road. You spent seven weeks at Presbyterian."

"Seven weeks!" My surprise is unmistakable. "How bad was I injured?"

"There were complications. And that's why I think it would be best if we talk this over in person."

"No."

"But—"

"Listen, Doc, right now my head's a mess. I feel like I've lost my mind, or, at the very least, I'm in the process of losing it. Everything's up in the air. I need to feel grounded. I need to know what happened to me."

"I'll tell you everything. I promise. But over the phone isn't ideal."

"It'll have to do."

I hear her draw a breath and then release it.

"All right," she says. "You sustained significant brain trauma in the crash. You had to undergo several procedures to prevent cerebral damage."

I touch the back of my head, feeling the lumps and bumps, imagining the surgeon's drill bit boring deep. "How bad was it?"

"For a while, it was touch and go. You were in a medically induced coma for most of those seven weeks."

I listen, stunned, as she proceeds to tell me how I spent a further month undergoing cognitive stimuli and intensive therapy regimens at a rehabilitation center in White Plains, under her care.

Of course, it's all news to me.

"Aside from being unable to recall the few weeks prior to the head injury," she says, "you were making good progress, too. You were responding well in your tests, and you were retaining newly formed memories."

"But there was still something wrong, wasn't there?" I can sense it from her lead-in. "I started experiencing these blank spells."

"The recall crashes. Yes. At first, we weren't aware of them, and neither were you. They lasted milliseconds. It was only as their duration began to lengthen that they became noticeable."

Dr. Merrick continues to tell me that repeated MRI scans showed no signs of structural damage, and various tests proved I was in possession of all of my motor skills and logic-making capacities. All of my faculties were firing on demand. I was able to understand and speak language as fluently and as disruptively as I could before the accident.

But the recall crashes were a definite hiccup hampering my progress.

"Strictly speaking," she says, "it's a kind of hysteria."

But not the uncontrollable emotional type displayed by excitable girls at pop concerts. Mine is a psychological stress induced by a physical pressure, the outcome of which is my intermittent amnesia.

"I'll fill in the rest of the blanks when we meet," she says. "Right now, it's best you don't fixate on the past. The only thing you need to know is that your present state is temporary, and that you will be all right."

"Except I've been going insane for nine months, on and off."

It explains why Gary is concerned about my focus and yet so blasé about my blank spells. Everyone who knows me has probably seen me go blank, time after time, while I wander around the office like a mindless idiot each time it happens, no doubt asking the same stupid questions and making the same puzzled faces, waiting for the real me to resurface so that things can get back to normal.

I wipe a cool sheen of sweat from my forehead with the back of my hand. "Just tell me, Doc. Is it fatal, this condition?"

As difficult to accept as the answer might be, I need to put it out there; it's been eating away at me since waking at the office.

"No," she answers, and I release a tense breath. "And I am being absolutely transparent about this. You aren't dying, Jed. As I said, we're on top of this."

"Not from where I'm standing." It comes out louder than it should, and I regret it instantly.

Dr. Merrick doesn't respond to my outburst. Instead, I hear the measured rise and fall of her breathing as she gives my temper time to dissipate. In all probability, this is how our conversation goes each time I experience this, and she's used to my behaving badly.

Even so, it's not her fault, and I know I shouldn't take my frustration out on her.

"Do you know what causes it?"

"We think there's an emotional trigger. A psychological component that shuts down your memory whenever your anxiety level reaches critical mass. Possibly a signal suppression in your hippocampus."

"In other words, they're stress-induced?"

"That, and maybe there's an anxiety disorder. But to be honest, we're dealing with a lot of unknown variables here, hence trying you on various medications."

"What's that saying? Science knows more about the dark side of the moon than it does about the brain."

"I think it's the moon versus the ocean floor, but it's the right idea. It's also quite rare, your condition, Jed. I can count on one hand the number of similar cases reported worldwide in the past fifty years. You're an exception."

She doesn't say *freak*, but I'm not comforted by the omission.

"So these pills I'm taking . . ."

"They're antianxiety meds. A stopgap and a preventive measure to help decrease your stress levels while we give you a break from the stronger drugs in our arsenal. Do you know if you've taken them today?"

"A few in the last couple of hours. I can't say for sure before I came to at the office."

"Okay. Good. Keep taking them. They'll speed up your recovery."

Her relaxed tone seems to confirm we've been through this same process previously, which makes me wonder how many times Dr. Merrick has had to explain the same things to me, maybe on a phone call like this one, over and over, without showing signs of frustration or even boredom. Always the same questions. Always the same answers. Both of us going around and around in circles.

"Jed, where are you right now?"

As though death had gravity, my heavy gaze is drawn back to the dead bird lying in the open trash can, and the hellish blood staining its angelic feathers.

"Home."

"That's good." She sounds relieved. "Listen to me. Stay there until it passes. Even though it's not familiar to you right now, you're in the absolute best place to ride out this storm."

Not if Gary has his way.

In just a few hours, I am supposed to be playing host to our business guests at Rafferty's, somewhere in the city. An event that I'm told is crucial to the firm's future, and blowing it off isn't an option.

Memory or no memory, I have to attend, and pretend if need be.

"Doc, the all-important question: Can it be fixed?"

"Honestly, it's too soon to say. We think there might be a workaround—one that will reduce the frequency and the duration—but we're not at that stage right now. The reality is, brain traumas like this can last for life, or they can disappear of their own accord. Most of the time, we're playing catch-up. We're still experimenting. We have discussed alternative treatments, and you are open to them."

"So, what are we waiting for?"

"Some involve quite radical procedures, and we need to discuss them further, face-to-face. I'll come over soon, before you leave for your business event."

"You know about that?"

"Jed, it's my job to know everything about you."

My gaze lands on the dead bird and its lifeless stare. "Not today. Tomorrow, if things don't improve?"

"Okay. As long as you think you'll be all right. In the meantime, however tempted you might be, don't mix alcohol with your meds. You don't want to be hallucinating on top of everything else."

Chapter Six

Arnold Seltzer pushed open the pastry shop's glass door, Melvyn's words of warning echoing in his head. He knew there was still time to turn back. He hadn't yet committed himself to anything he couldn't walk away from. If he wanted to, he could catch the next bus out of here and never look back. But since his world had fallen apart, there had been a kind of compelling inevitability about things, as though he were a passenger in his own life, where every route seemed to take him to the same destination, no matter which way he chose to go.

He'd once read something about cause and effect, and had wondered time and again if he had any real control over his life, or if everything he did would lead him to where he was supposed to be anyway.

Seltzer had never quite figured out if that kind of thinking was philosophical or defeatist.

"Welcome to Mama Butterfly's," said a man from behind the counter as Seltzer entered the cool shop. It was an automatic greeting; the man was busy boxing up pastries for a middle-aged couple standing at the illuminated glass display case, and hadn't even looked up to see who had walked in. "We have a special on cinnamon buns today. Sample bites at the end of the counter."

The pastry shop was deeper inside than it looked from the out-side. Dark wood and bloodred walls. Where the refrigerated display case ended, a seating area began. Wooden chairs with spindle backs, arranged in pairs around square tables covered in red-and-white check-ered cloths. On a large ornate mirror hung behind the counter, a list of delectable goods with their prices was handwritten in various neon inks.

The place smelled of cake and coffee.

Seltzer waited until the happy couple had left before approaching the man smiling at him from behind the counter. "Are you Charlie?" he asked.

"Excuse me?"

Seltzer repeated his question.

"I heard what you said." The assistant pointed to the end of the counter. "And I told you. Cinnamon buns. Buy two and get the third free. Today only. It's a good offer. You should take it."

Seltzer smiled uneasily; he hadn't much appetite for anything these days. "Thanks, but I'll pass. I'm here to see Charlie."

The assistant leaned his bony elbows on the counter. "Is that so? Charlie, you say? And exactly how is it you think you know Charlie?"

Seltzer's arrhythmia was peaking. "That's just it. I don't. Melvyn sent me here. Melvyn, from the bodega in Soundview? He told me to ask for Charlie. Said he'd let you know I was coming."

The assistant's gaze was unblinking, as though Seltzer was speaking a foreign language, and Seltzer experienced a sudden compulsion to turn around and leave the store.

But movement in the corner of his eye distracted him, and he turned to see a woman approaching from a doorway at the back of the shop. She looked to be in her sixties, with a fuzz of gray hair and a maternal resemblance to the assistant behind the counter. She wore a white chef's apron with the words *Mama Butterfly's* stitched on the chest.

"You say Melvyn sent you?"

"Yes. We go way back."

She stuck out a floury hand. "I'm Charlotte. Owner, chief cook, and bottle washer."

"Arnold Seltzer," he said, shaking her hand.

"May I ask what's in the briefcase?"

He glanced at it, at the worn tan leather and the scuffed corners. "Nothing. Just some documents. Personal items. Business stuff."

"What is it you do, Mr. Seltzer?"

"Do?"

"For a living, with your briefcase."

Seltzer's uneasy smile resurfaced. "I'm in the insurance business. But I don't see how it's relevant."

"Indulge me."

Seltzer glanced at the assistant, at his stoic expression, then back to the woman, his heart muscles performing a death-defying drumroll. "Look, I'm nobody. Okay? Maybe I made a mistake coming here. Why do you even need to know?"

"Because, Mr. Seltzer, I'm trying to figure out why someone who claims he works in the insurance business has a need to visit with Charlie. You got some ID on you?"

Seltzer fumbled out his wallet. The woman took it from his grasp before he could open it. Then she stepped back, out of his reach, while she removed his driver's license and studied his photo.

"I'm about as photogenic as roadkill," he said nervously as she looked it over.

She didn't react to his put-down, which made Seltzer feel foolish. Instead, she put the license back in the wallet and then examined the wad of cash. "How much is here?"

"Six hundred."

"Exactly?"

"Yes. It's all I have."

"Okay." She stuffed Seltzer's wallet in the pocket of her apron. "Come with me."

Then she turned toward the doorway at the back of the shop.

"When can I have my wallet back?" he called after her.

"After we complete our business. And five hundred dollars lighter. Are you coming?"

With his arrhythmia working overtime, Seltzer followed her into a kitchen of stainless-steel countertops and hot ovens, mixing bowls, and sacks of flour. In one corner, a beaded curtain screened a doorway. She swept it aside to reveal a rectangular hole in the floor and railed steps descending into an illuminated basement.

"Don't be shy," she said as she started down the steps.

The underground storage room was stocked with boxed ingredients and drums of dried foodstuffs. Metal shelving units crammed with jars and cans. It reminded Seltzer of a survivalist's underground bunker.

He followed her along a narrow aisle between two of the racks, to what appeared to be a dead end—a brick wall, painted white—and he slowed his steps with caution.

"No need to look so damn petrified," she said, pressing her palm against the wall. "Here comes the magic part."

All the same, Seltzer hung back, watching as a door-sized section of wall moved back an inch and then slid to one side to reveal a dark rectangular cavity.

She reached inside and switched on a light. "Say hello to Charlie."

The small room behind the basement wall was wider than it was deep, with a narrow countertop running along the length, above which was a wall covered in guns of all shapes and sizes. Bullet boxes and packs of cartridges were piled on the counter. Enough weaponry and ammo to wage a small street war.

And for the first time today, Seltzer's palpitations subsided. In fact, he couldn't contain his broad smile as the woman took a handgun from a peg on the wall and held it out to him.

"Go ahead. Take it. It won't bite."

Seltzer did, marveling at the coolness of the metal and the sudden sense of burgeoning power.

"It's a five-shot double-action .38 Special snubby," she said, "with a concealed hammer so it won't snag in your pocket. As you can see, Mr. Seltzer, it's a nice fit for those lily-white hands of yours. What do you think?"

Seltzer flicked the cylinder out and peered at the woman through the empty chambers. "It's perfect," he said. "Just perfect."

Chapter Seven

Y ou have suspicious eyes," I tell my reflection in the bathroom mirror as I shave, my wrist obeying a preset pattern of strokes. "Why do you have suspicious eyes?"

The more I inspect my stranger's features in the sobering light coming from the mirror, the more I realize that I have "the look." It's the shadowy pallor of a man who has experienced brain trauma. It doesn't involve misaligned eyes or a droopy mouth. No concave skull or visible train-track scars. Whatever it is that happened to me, it has left me with an overall blurriness, as though my skin no longer reflects the light properly.

It's been several hours since the amnesia took hold, and my mind is no longer a barren wasteland beneath a stormy sky. Not in the way it was when I first came to at the office. My head is full of fears. None more pressing than the thought that this—me, and how I am now— could be permanent.

I keep my distrustful eyes closed in the shower as I stand under the running water far longer than I need to, letting the jets chip away at the tension in my neck and shoulders. My headache hasn't completely gone, and at this rate I'm not sure it will. It remains a dull discomfort in the base of my skull, in close proximity to the larger of the indentations hidden by my hair.

In passing, Gary had mentioned an accident. Dr. Merrick had confirmed it and the seriousness of my condition. Stress feeds the amnesia. She made it quite clear. I need to relax, to stop fretting, to accept that fighting it won't help. It's hard, and I don't think I have ever felt this lonely in my life.

As the water flows, I try to summon even the smallest fragment of memory that might have slipped through the amnesia. Any freeze-framed picture of my world before today. But it's no use; the more I think, the further away it pushes the life I had up until a couple of hours ago.

It's like I'm treading water in a dark ocean, with my capsized boat remaining inches from my fingertips, the action of reaching out for it succeeding only in forcing it farther from my grasp.

Everyone is quick to reassure me that my normal programming will resume shortly, but I am not so quick to believe it. In my present state, my brain is like a TV without a signal.

After a while, the water runs cooler but I stay put, my thoughts centering on Cassie and what our relationship might look like.

Once or twice, I think I hear someone opening the front door, and each time I switch off the shower, listening, calling out Cassie's name, and each time I am answered with silence.

Not knowing anything about *us*, Cassie and I, as a couple, as best friends, as lovers, is not just disconcerting; it's paralyzing. According to Dr. Merrick, intermittent amnesia has been part of my everyday existence for months. It stands to reason that Cassie would be up to speed on my condition. She must be familiar with its every insidious twist, and how it leaves me a stranger in a strange land. Out of everyone, she must know exactly what to say to talk me down from the ledge, to walk me through my mental minefield, to allay my worst fears. Every way I look at it, Cassie is my best line of attack in combatting the amnesia.

As freaked-out by my missing memories as I am, I'm not as concerned about the lack of Cassie's presence. Although it would be a relief to see her before I leave for the meeting at Rafferty's, to speak with her, to get the real lowdown on how this intermittent amnesia of mine has interfered with our lives, I must have patience. And I have to remind myself that this isn't the first time I have been stripped bare, and I have come through each occurrence intact.

Amnesia isn't fatal; I can survive without Cassie for a few hours.

After all, it's Friday, early evening, and it's likely she's still at work, oblivious to the circus performing here at home.

It occurs to me that I ought to have asked Dr. Merrick or even Gary to let Cassie know.

I decide I will leave her a note, pinned to the newel post facing the front door, so that it's the first thing she sees when she enters the house:

CASSIE. CALL ME THE SECOND YOU READ THIS. I'VE BEEN WORRIED. JED.

At last, the water turns chilly and I leave the shower with a shiver. Night has fallen, and the house is in darkness.

Dried and deodorized, I grimace at the sparse selection of clothes available in the armoire, disheartened by the looseness of the shirts and the slightly baggy waistline of the pants.

"Stress is a great way to lose a few pounds."

I order an Uber, and then I sit in the car quietly all the way into the city, trying to convince myself that whatever difficulties lie ahead, I have the power to push through.

At least, that's the theory.

Manhattan is lit like a carnival, and the city is crawling with Friday night revelers.

The car pulls up outside the canopied entranceway of a large double-towered co-op building facing Central Park, and a uniformed doorman opens the car door.

"Good evening, Mr. Allen," he says with a smile. "Welcome back to the Majestic. Right this way, sir." With the sweep of his kid-gloved hand, he ushers me inside the building.

According to Tess, I have been here many times previously. I don't remember any of them. I would think I would; the art deco design here is something to behold, something an architect would not forget easily.

A baby-faced elevator attendant greets me by name and presses a button without my direction. "Looking dapper," he says as the elevator whisks us to the twenty-fifth floor. "Something special planned for tonight, Mr. Allen?"

I ask him, "Do we know each other?" And he just smiles, telling me to turn left when I hesitate on the landing.

"Miss Teresa's apartment is the last door down," he says. "You can't miss it."

I have no idea what I am walking into, or if I'm placing myself in a difficult situation.

From a distance, the black door at the end of the hall could be an aperture leading into another dimension. There is no sheen on its matte surface. It's as if the light itself can't escape.

Above it is a small plaque, with the words FROM A LITTLE SPARK MAY BURST A MIGHTY FLAME.

Even as my knuckles rap against the wood, the ominous door opens to reveal a man who stands no taller than the level of my hips.

"Bloody hellfire," he says in a British cockney accent. "Look what the cat dragged in."

"I'm here to see Tess?" It comes out as more of a question than a statement of fact.

He smirks. "No kidding, birdbrain. Why else would you be here? As wonderful as it is that you're gracing us with your presence—you and me, we don't exactly hang out and talk about cricket. Tess says your memory's gone AWOL again, so let me reintroduce myself." He sticks out a small hand. "The name's Maurice. I'm Tess's personal assistant. Some people have been known to call me Maurice the midget. It's a mistake they don't make twice."

I go to shake his hand, but he grabs my little finger instead and twists it back, sending pain rocketing up my arm. Instinctively, I try to pull free, but before I can, he exerts more pressure, bending my arm and pulling my face down level with his.

"A word of advice in your shell-like," he says in my ear. "Since you've conveniently forgotten everything, allow me to spell this out for you in words your peanut-sized brain can understand. Tess's greatest quality is her biggest weakness, and that's giving people like you the benefit of the doubt. She trusts you, and only God knows why. Maybe she has a soft spot for you. I don't. You've taken more piss than a urinal, but I'm on to your little game, my friend. If you think for one second I'll stand back while you take advantage of her goodwill, you've another think coming."

For a little finger, the pain is surprisingly intense, and I attempt to wrench it free again, but Maurice's grip is unyielding. His small blunt fingers are as tough as pliers.

His face comes an inch closer to mine, close enough for me to smell bitter tobacco on his breath.

"One more thing," he says. "My hands are the perfect size for reaching down your throat and ripping out your heart. Don't forget that."

He twists my finger some more, to emphasize the threat, and I manage to squeeze out the words, "Thanks for the heads-up."

Then he lets go, and I straighten, massaging my throbbing hand and wondering what kind of crazy business I've gotten myself into.

Maurice produces a small plastic bottle from his pocket, sprays sanitizer onto his hands, and rubs them together. "Don't just stand there, birdbrain. Tess is waiting for you in the living room. Remember what I said. Don't make me come looking for you, because it won't be pretty."

The décor inside the apartment is all black and chrome, including the furniture. It's tastefully done, but it wouldn't have been my first choice. I move through the dark foyer and into a dimly lit living room filled with trendy accent chairs and ebony figurines balanced on metal pedestals. A glass case, built into an interior wall, displays flint arrowheads and prehistoric battle-axes, making the place feel more like a museum than a home. Along two adjacent walls are big rectangular windows, each affording nighttime views of Central Park and its glittery backdrop.

I hear a woman's voice say, "One moment, Jed."

The comment comes from a skinny woman dressed in a loose-fitting black jumpsuit. She has one eye cupped to a big metal telescope, which stands on a tripod at the window, tilted downward, probably aimed at the park. Her hair is down to her waist, unnaturally straight, and jet black, contrasting with her snow-white skin.

The only splash of color in the room seems to be her bloodred fingernails.

Maurice comes past me and hops up onto the arm of a chair, his mocking eyes looking me up and down.

Inexcusably, I want to push him off.

"Has it come back yet?" the woman asks without looking up. "Your memory, Jed. Has it returned?"

"No, not yet."

She turns from the telescope, straightening to her full height, and I see that she's much older than I first thought, at least in her seventies and painfully thin, with the kind of Nordic bone structure that would have made her mesmerizing in her youth. Every bit the aged Snow Queen.

"What do you remember?" she asks. "Anything?"

"Crazily enough, nothing before this afternoon. I mean, I don't remember you at all, *this*, even myself. It feels like I didn't exist before today."

"You must be fit to scream."

"To tell you the truth, I don't even know why I'm here."

Maurice shakes his head. "Now isn't that a convenient way to forget you owe us? If you want my opinion, Tess, I think this wanker's trying to pull another fast one. Just like he did the last time."

Her eyes narrow. "Are you, Jed?"

"Am I what?"

"Trying to deceive me?"

"No. At least, I don't think so."

She wants to believe I am a man of my word—whatever word it is that I have given her previously—and that her faith in my character is sound. But I am not yet there myself, which doesn't exactly instill confidence either way.

I raise my hands. "The truth is, I have no idea what kind of arrangement we have going on here or what this care package is all about. But if it helps bring my memory back, like you say it did the last time, then I'm in. It's only been a few hours, but I've had my fill already of being a stranger in my own life."

Tess studies me for a moment before nodding. "You made the right decision coming here."

"So you can help me, with my memory problem?"

"Indirectly, yes."

Maurice snickers. "I'm telling you, Tess, this is a mistake. Look at him. He's taking the piss and buying himself an extension. I say we send him packing. Or better yet, let me wire his nipples to a car battery."

I hunch my shoulders. "Listen, guys. I promise you there's no hidden agenda here. I have amnesia. That's it. I'm not lying. I'm the one who's disadvantaged. I know we have a history, but I have no idea what that is or why there's so much animosity coming from this little dude."

"Maurice has my best interests at heart," Tess says, her gaze searching my face, as if she'll find something more than the blank expression that has moved in and taken permanent residence. "He's paid to be protective. You, on the other hand, are one of my best customers, who doesn't deserve being treated like a bad debtor. Isn't that right, Maurice?"

Maurice emits a snarl and glares at me.

"Jed, we all know how much tonight means to you, how much is at stake. Unquestionably, this is the biggest night of your life so far. It's going to change your fortunes forever. It's pointless pretending that we won't benefit as well. All that wealth will filter through. And for that reason alone, I am happy to support your tab. Now don't move a muscle. I'll be right back."

She floats away, disappearing into an adjoining room, and leaving an awkward vacuum behind her.

I clear my throat, looking everywhere except at Maurice, wondering how many times I've stood here, and how many times Maurice has assaulted me.

I point at the telescope. "May I?"

"Knock yourself out."

I go over to it and cup an eye to the lens piece.

At first, I am unable to make out what it is I am looking at. The round image is dark and blurry. Adjusting the focus makes everything clearer, however, and I am presented with a view along one of the park's poorly lit pathways. All but one of the visible bench seats are empty. Central in the image is a seated young woman, busy texting.

"It's Tess's latest obsession," Maurice says from behind me. "The Vigilante Voyeur, I call her. You've heard about this Central Park Slasher character and the bodies they found near Armonk?"

"No. Well, maybe. I think I saw something on TV. I just don't remember the specifics."

"It's all everyone's been talking about. The cops found a dozen dead women, sliced like melons."

I spin around and stare at him. "In Central Park?"

"No, you idiot. They *disappeared* from Central Park, hence the name. The press reckons he's been abducting women from here for years, dicing them up into little pieces, and then burying them in the mass grave they found."

I look back through the telescope. The woman is no longer in the image. But at the top of the field, half in shadow, I can see a man in a hoodie walking away into the dark.

Tess reappears from the adjoining room and sashays across the black-carpeted floor toward me. In her hand is what appears to be a leather cigar case.

"Your care package," she says, placing the travel humidor in my hand and curling her cool fingers around mine. "This was the only thing that jump-started everything the last time your memory crashed. Let's hope it will do the same this time. You need every synapse firing on target for tonight. Just save the Cubans for your after-dinner celebration."

I leave the lofty apartment feeling no less confused than I was before entering.

Discovering more about my contacts, my history, and my relationships seems to only add to my perplexity.

At least I have the care package, with its promise of reviving my memory, in whatever shape that takes.

Chapter Eight

By implying that he was gainfully employed, Seltzer had lied to the woman who called herself Charlotte. Partly to save himself from embarrassment, but mostly because he couldn't stand the fact that he had destroyed his own life.

Working in the insurance industry had never been high on Seltzer's list of preferred jobs. He'd always considered it in the same league as used car sales or politics—with the same amount of credibility—and so he'd entered into it with caution, more through desperation than choice.

The accounting firm he'd worked at for years after leaving school had been involved in a book-cooking scandal, and Seltzer had found himself laid off overnight. Worse still, in the months following the IRS inspection, he'd been unable to secure any job interviews with other accounting firms, and he soon arrived at the conclusion that they viewed him as tainted goods. Guilt through association. Not just unemployed, then, but also unemployable.

Martin, a friend since they were kids, worked in insurance and had done so for years. He'd told Seltzer about the firm taking on new reps. No experience necessary. Better yet, no one at the firm knew anything about the stain on his career. After several months without an income, Seltzer signed up, regarding the move as a means to an end.

That was ten years ago.

What had been intended as an interim job had turned out to be the best career move he'd ever made.

To his surprise, Seltzer had excelled at insurance sales.

Clients had warmed to his humility, to his self-effacement. They bought into him, with his downtrodden humor and his human touch.

"It's so much easier selling policies to people who feel sorry for me," he'd told his wife.

Within five years, Seltzer was earning an income unimaginable to him when he was slaving away at the accounting firm. Enough to put down a sizable deposit on a property in a classier neighborhood, and to allow his wife to pursue her own career dreams.

For a while, they had enjoyed a comfortable lifestyle and a deeper kind of happiness.

But then Seltzer's jealousy had gotten in the way, and he'd sabotaged everything.

And that was why he couldn't bring himself to go home right now, not with the loaded gun weighing heavy in his briefcase. His wife would never have approved of him bringing a lethal weapon into the house. For as long as he'd known her, she had celebrated life in all its glorious manifestations, condemning anyone who practiced violence of any kind.

Her undying motto was: Never wait for life to come to you. You need to chase it down, tame it, make it your own.

It was a great philosophy to live by, but it was also one of the reasons they had begun to drift apart.

At first, Seltzer had been happy to act as the main load-bearer in the home they'd built together, selflessly supporting his wife's fledgling career, both financially and emotionally. He'd been happy to provide the space and the means for her to give her dream wings, to help it take off, to see it fly. It was worth it, too. Seeing her so full of spirit and determination had made him feel more connected to her than ever.

Like a loving husband should, he'd encouraged her to aim high, burying himself in his own work when hers took her elsewhere, sometimes away from him for days at a time. It wasn't an ideal arrangement, but he'd never complained. Not at first, anyway. He'd learned to live with it, accepting that everything came at a price, nothing more so than happiness. And as his wife's career blossomed, he'd kept his growing concerns to himself, aware of the fact that her work made her happy. To him, his wife's happiness was paramount.

But as her business trips grew in frequency, sometimes separating them for weeks at a time, the stress of maintaining a long-distance relationship had begun to cause fractures, and Seltzer started resenting her. He hadn't wanted it. He hadn't invited it. The resentment snuck up on him before he'd realized it, changing him for the worse. He became picky, touchy, grouchy, deliberately obstinate. If the least little thing bugged him, he'd throw his weight around like a spoiled child. It wasn't like him. But it *was* him. And over time, his resentment escalated to the point where nothing his wife could do was ever good enough anymore—even though it always was, and he knew it.

But once things start sliding, the slope soon becomes slippery.

And the more she'd tried to fix it, to pander to his tantrums, to reassure him that he was the center of her universe, the more he'd rebelled and pushed her away. When she was home, he'd avoid being there—his way of making her feel his loneliness. And when they had to be together, they were either arguing, living in tense silence, or worst of all, debating.

God, he'd hated those soul-searching debates.

The here's-what-we-need-to-do-to-fix-this discussions that flew in the face of his reasoning, that made him see himself for what he was: inadequate, juvenile, but most of all, petty.

And so it had come as no surprise that the weight of his jealousy finally crushed their relationship, and the load-bearing wall came crashing down, triggering a domino-like collapse.

Not only had he lost his wife, but he was now jobless, almost penniless, and quickly on his way to being homeless. Seltzer was lonely, lonelier than he'd ever been, and for the first time in his adult life, he couldn't abide living with the emptiness.

Yet he was no longer hopeless.

He'd spied a glimmer of light at the end of the tunnel. A guaranteed way for him to be reunited with his wife.

The briefcase, with the gun inside, was a comforting hand on his lap as he rode the bus back to the Bronx.

Chapter Nine

Although it's a temptation, I wait until I'm in a taxi and on my way to Rafferty's before investigating the contents of the cigar case.

The travel humidor has four cylindrical slots, arranged side by side. Only the outer two are home to sweet-smelling cigars. The middle pair contain glass test tubes with red rubber stoppers.

I glance at the back of the driver's head, then to his face in the rearview mirror, before examining the vials in more detail.

The first test tube contains what looks like yellow candy pieces—little round shapes with an imprinted smiley face on one side. The second tube is filled with a fine-grained white powder. I give it a little shake and a flick with a fingernail.

Tess isn't just a voyeur, I realize. She's also a drug dealer. And she's on my speed dial.

I stow the tubes back inside the cigar case and bury it in my jacket pocket.

The driver's eyes are still on the road.

My name is Jed Allen. I'm an amnesiac. I'm apparently also a cokehead.

As far as I knew, aside from prescribed medication, I didn't do drugs. Then again, how *would* I know? A lack of current cravings wouldn't exonerate me. The proof is right here, next to my heart. Is this why the discovery doesn't sicken me and shock me more than it does? Is it because, somewhere deep within, on a fundamental level, my subconscious already knew the contents of the care package from previous transactions and eased me in?

It seems the more I find out about myself, the less I like.

The taxi drops me off on a busy street in the Theater District.

This is Midtown, in the city that never sleeps: droves of people moving in every direction; excited theatergoers hurrying to their shows; hungry diners following the scents of their favorite cuisines; bright-eyed tourists taking selfies and souvenir snapshots of just about everything, including the unsmiling bouncers in their monkey suits.

I am ten minutes early.

The club is all blacked-out windows, with spotlights running the entire length of its black canopy, angled in such a way as to transform the windows into smoked-glass mirrors, in which I can see a reflection of a man I barely recognize.

Above a roped entrance, **RAFFERTY'S** glows in neon crimson.

I join the end of a short line of men waiting to show their IDs at the door. Men drenched in cologne and wearing clothes that make mine look like I picked them up at a yard sale. With a disinterested frown, a bouncer examines my driver's license, checking my name against a list on his phone, and then lets me pass.

Inside, the machine-gun rat-tat-tat of dance music assaults my ears, and it's clear that this is no ordinary nightclub.

The velveteen booths and the subdued lighting don't give it away, nor do the rainbow-colored mixers behind the mirrored bar, or the fact that all the patrons here appear to be men. It's the raised stage and the topless dancers cavorting around the brass poles that reveal its true nature.

This is a strip club.

I wonder how often I come here, ostensibly wining and dining business contacts, and if I am a regular.

More importantly, does Cassie know?

Most of the clientele are in groups—laughing, cajoling, back-slapping—probably here to celebrate the end of bachelorhood or the beginning of midlife freedom. A handful of loners are scattered throughout, their unblinking eyes glued on the performing girls.

I hear someone calling my name, and I turn to see Gary—I have already forgotten his last name—working his way toward me. He is dressed in a black blazer and a white shirt, open at the neck, red pants, and black loafers. One hand is waving at me while he nurses a cocktail from the other.

I nod in acknowledgment. It's the only confirmation I give him, the most interaction I can muster, and I don't know why it should be this way. When I think about Gary, the word that best describes my feelings toward him is *lackluster*, which has an immediate effect on how I interact.

I wonder, where Gary is concerned, am I missing something or sensing something?

He snakes an arm around my shoulders and we share a fashionable bro hug. I come away smelling of his designer cologne.

"Mocha?" he shouts, frowning at my suit. "Really? That's so 2000, and not a bit like you. I thought you were going to wear your purple Brioni tonight?"

"My . . . what?" I'm having a hard time hearing him, and understanding him, it seems.

"Your suit with the . . ." He sees my bafflement and shakes away his frown. "Look, never mind. Luckily for us, the lighting around here leaves a lot to be desired. Plus, a little alcohol blurs everything. If we keep our Chinese guests suitably distracted, we might just survive your catwalk calamity. Now let's get you a drink. God knows, you look like you could use one. The usual?"

Again, I nod, vaguely hoping that my "usual" doesn't come with a paper umbrella and an annual club membership.

Gary's smile is fixed as he guides me to the bar, where he waves at a bartender. "Bourbon on the rocks for my best bud. And another one of these splendid daiquiris for me."

Gary seems tipsy already. His words aren't slurred and he isn't swaying, but he hasn't stopped smiling at me like a crazy person since he spotted me. There's no way of telling how long he's been here or how many daiquiris he has already downed.

He points a finger. "Make no mistake—you're the reason we're here, Jed. And I don't mean *here*, specifically, although this was your suggestion. And a super one at that—God knows, we've had some fun in this place. But I mean where we are as a firm. You and me. Coming from nowhere and giving the big boys a run for their money. We've come a long way since Pleasantville." He squeezes my shoulder. "Incidentally, how's the old memory doing?"

"Still AWOL."

"You're kidding!"

"I wish I was. I'm beginning to think I'm stuck like this."

Gary lets out a long and dramatic sigh, then he takes a consolatory slurp of his cocktail. It's the first time his smile slips. "This isn't good, Jed. I need my human supercomputer to be able to do more than simply add and subtract. The medication hasn't had any effect?"

"Not so far."

"Okay. We can still pull this off. This brain blip of yours is a hurdle all right, but it's not going to stop us. They know us. We know them. It's not like we haven't already forged one or two firm relationships along the way. Just be yourself and let me deal with any sticky points. More than anything, be accommodating."

Gary wants us to appear irresistible to our Chinese guests, to make them want to jump into bed with us. But I'm beginning to think amnesia is the best libido killer.

He squeezes my shoulder again. "Now don't forget. Tonight is all about entertaining. It's time to let your hair down and forget about your amnesia. We can do this."

Yet despite his upbeat statement, he looks worried, any concerns about my fashion sense blown away by the thought that I might under-perform tonight and leave us looking like amateurs.

Our drinks arrive. Gary drains the daiquiri in his hand, then swaps it for the new one, telling the bartender to put everything on his tab.

"But first, a toast," he says to me, raising his glass. "To us, to success, and to hell with the competition."

It's a bold sentiment, and I'm not sure I share it. The little I have learned about Jed Allen isn't exactly inspiring. Already, I have a pretty bad impression of someone who is solely driven by success, someone who could well be cutthroat. Even so, I clink my glass.

His grin reemerges. "Bottoms up, buddy."

The bourbon is an explosion of fire on my taste buds, like bleach clearing out a drain. The buzz is immediate.

Gary smacks his lips. "So did you retrieve the care package?"

I tap my hand against my breast pocket.

His eyes light up. "Excellent."

And it occurs to me that Gary knows all about my speed-dial drug dealer and the arrangement I have with her. More so, that Gary and I are not just best friends; we are also coke buddies.

"There's just one thing," I say. "Do we really want to entertain our guests *this* way? I mean, it's a little, I don't know, over-the-top."

"It's their way," he says without hesitation. "They started the tradition back in Shanghai."

"Still . . ."

"The care package was their idea, Jed. It's the way their top brass like to do things. Luckily for us, we play by the same rules." He sees my frown and adds, "What do you want me to say? They like to party like the best of us. Now come on. Let's head to the private lounge. Chaz is already there, and our guests will be here any minute. We need to bring you up to speed."

The VIP lounge is a dimly lit world of purple velvet and black-buttoned leather couches grouped around a low glass table, and, thankfully, it's fifty decibels quieter. There's a private bar, neon-lit, with dancing girls on tap.

"You've known each other for years," Gary says as he introduces me to a rotund man with curly ginger hair and a mouthful of nibbles. "But for the sake of clarity, this is Chaz. He's our hard-nosed legal counsel. He sits in on all our negotiations. Isn't that right, Chaz?"

"Exactamundo," he says, crumbs raining from his lips.

Gary playfully punches Chaz's arm. "Just for the record, Chaz is part of our usual gang, so he's fully aware of your momentary memory blips."

Chaz nods. "I don't mean to overshadow the importance of tonight, but do either of you know what's on the menu? I could murder for a New York strip."

Gary laughs. "Chaz, think about your heart, for God's sake."

"I am. Otherwise, I'd be ordering the rib eye." He gives me a wink.

Chaz the lawyer: one slab of steak away from a heart attack.

Gary spends the next couple of minutes pacing and watching the clock while filling me in on the broader details of tonight's schmooze-fest. He's nervous, hence the cologne overkill, and I suppose I would be, too, if I had any real emotional connection to what's at stake here.

I study his movements, his mannerisms, waiting to see if anything familiar jumps out. He doesn't say so, but I get the impression he is barely tolerating my condition. Like a man who is staying in an unhappy marriage for the sake of the children. How many times has Gary had to cover for me at the office? How many allowances have been made, how many excuses given for my condition?

It isn't a leap to wonder if I am a liability.

"Honestly, buddy, you could at least do me the dignity of paying attention."

I blink, realizing that I have zoned out, and that Gary has stopped pacing so that he can direct the full force of his disapproving stare at me.

Chaz, our mountainous legal eagle, is snickering and almost choking as he inhales the complimentary peanuts.

"This is the crux of everything," Gary says, then proceeds to reveal that the Shanghai Tusk—the building I saw a replica of in Gary's office—has been the firm's sole project for the last year and a half. It's a huge building, not to mention a massive undertaking, investment, and risk. We have poured all our resources into its development, used up every bit of capital at our disposal, working night and day to build the dream.

I take another taste of the bourbon and hunker down.

Apparently, Gary and I have traveled to Shanghai several times during the past eighteen months, brokering a groundbreaking deal to put us on the architecture map for good. We have done everything in our power to romance our Chinese clients into a long-lasting relationship. Until now, we have dealt with delegates, intermediaries, and go-betweens to convince Xian Airlines that our design is the only one that will win them global respect, taking them one step closer to Asian market leadership. This is the first time they have returned the favor and visited us, and tonight marks our first face-to-face meeting with the big boss himself, Chang, here to sign contracts on what will become his flagship hotel and our defining moment.

In my present state, it's all news to me.

Then Gary drops the final bombshell. "Without this deal, we'll be in danger of going bankrupt, and we won't be in any position to repay our creditors."

He doesn't say, *And the firm will go under,* but he doesn't need to. Even Chaz has stopped his locustlike decimation of the bar snacks and is looking solemn.

On his gold-plated smartphone, Gary shows me a 3-D aerial view of an East Asian cityscape with a full-feature rendering of the Shanghai Tusk superimposed, plugged into its designated plot. He's got good reason to feel excited, proud. From every angle, the tower is breathtaking, awe-inspiring, majestic, and I can see why he's so passionate about it.

I try to muster the same amount of enthusiasm, but it falls short. Worst of all, he sees it.

I force a smile, wishing I could be warmed by his passion. But I am as cold as a ghost.

"Exactly how much in debt are we?" I ask.

"Enough," Gary says.

I look at Chaz.

Chaz wipes his lips. "To the tune of ten million and counting. Basically, if this deal falls flat on its face, you guys will be regulars at Saint Paul's soup kitchen."

I am surprised by the amount of debt we are in, and I ought to be a quivering wreck, but the news isn't emotionally crippling. It's not that I don't care. I *can't* care. Amnesia has limited my ability to relate to my normal life.

Both Gary and Chaz seem disappointed when my jaw fails to drop, and I realize that they still don't fully understand that everything is brand-new to me: this, my world, my job, my friends, my life—all handed to me fully packaged, already formed and developed, expected to fit snugly and seamlessly into what has become an uneven worldview.

Gary says this design project is my baby. But the truth is, I feel like a sperm donor who learns that his remote creation learned to walk. How can I be expected to gush with paternal pride if I have zero emotional attachment?

"Screw it," Chaz says, clapping his meaty hands together. "It's decided, and there's no changing my mind. I'm going all out and ordering the rib eye."

Chapter Ten

The Xian Airlines party of five turns up late, and I am unable to read from their expressions if it's a deliberate tactic and a power play or the result of traffic. Either way, no apology is given.

"Acts of contrition are considered a weakness," Gary whispers as we watch the Chinese contingent remove their shoes and file them in a neat row along one wall. "Keep smiling, be amenable, and agree with everything they say, even if you don't."

The Xian Airlines team is made up of four men and one woman, all dressed conservatively, the men in dark-blue suits and the woman in a long figure-hugging black dress with a high neckline. They are all equally unsmiling and inscrutable, the opposite of how Gary expects us to appear. Three aides orbit a gray-haired man, who looks to be in his late sixties. Gary addresses him as Director Chang. The woman is the youngster in the group, in her early thirties, slim, with dark, evading eyes and black hair cut in a slanted bob.

She seems vaguely familiar, like someone I have seen in passing—on a billboard or in a foreign film. But it's just a feeling and impossible to confirm.

During the formal introductions, she lingers in the background, her deep-brown eyes never quite meeting my gaze.

Gary is a master at making people feel at ease, and I imagine in other circumstances he makes a great party host. His outwardly friendly behavior suggests he has met Chang's underlings in previous engagements, probably during video conferencing and our trips to China. He and they seem genuinely pleased, eager, to rekindle relations. I follow his lead, smiling on cue, speaking softly and giving nothing of my present state away.

Even though she wears a wedding band, the woman is introduced as *Miss* Chang Song, the boss's eldest offspring, and our gazes meet for the first time.

Her eyes are like portals to the blackness of space.

Respectfully, we shake hands and bow. Then we go through a strange gift-giving ritual that sees both parties politely refuse several times before eventually accepting. Neither gift is then opened. I have no idea what Gary has picked on our behalf or what they have chosen for us. Formalities.

Finally, Gary clasps his hands together and says, "Welcome to wonderful New York. Truly, it is our honor to have you here as our guests, on what is a momentous occasion in the fortunes of both of our companies. How was your journey?"

"As expected," says one of the aides.

"And your rooms at the Mandarin Oriental?"

"Acceptable."

"Wonderful. Let's eat."

And we spend the next ninety minutes sitting around the low glass table, dining on a fusion of Asian and American dishes, chitchatting about everything except business, which suits me.

My thoughts are elsewhere. I keep going over my conversation with Dr. Merrick, wondering if there's more to my intermittent amnesia than she told me today, maybe for my own benefit. I think about Cassie, visualizing us at our home in Eastchester, wondering how long we've lived together and how we first met.

Several times, I check my phone, thinking I hear it ring. But there are no missed calls.

Throughout the meal, Gary remains fully immersed in his sales routine, laughing gently and keeping his comments positive, while I smile on cue, feeling like a fraud.

Between serving up our food courses, the topless waitresses snake themselves around the metal dance poles, slithering to the rhythm of the mind-numbing music. To our guests, they are a distraction, a talking point. But they are invisible to me. My eyes are on Song Chang, with her tapering fingers and her ghostly complexion. All the while, she sits facing me, nibbling at her food, her spine straight and the tight cut of her dress forcing her small knees together.

But she never speaks. Not once. Just the occasional enigmatic smile.

I can't take my eyes off her.

I eat less than I should and drink more than I should. It doesn't hit me at first, but as the dinner gives way to brandies, I begin to feel strangely disembodied, realizing belatedly that on my medication even a moderate amount of alcohol would be enough to get me drunk.

Gary instructs the bartender to lower the lighting level and crank up the music, and our plush environment becomes dusky dim, womb-like, with half-naked girls cavorting in the shadows.

"Time to get this party started," he says, indicating the slight bulge in my breast pocket.

I get out the cigar case, still apprehensive about what it contains and yet unable to prevent my stranger's hands from handing it over.

I can't deny Gary his moment in the spotlight, or risk disenchanting our business partners.

As Gary removes a glass test tube from the humidor, I glance around at the faces of those present, at the eagerness of our Chinese guests to partake in tonight's special festivities, and I wonder how badly the other version of me has behaved in their country.

Gary clears a space on the glass table. Our Chinese guests gather close, as though we are about to play an exciting board game, their eyes alight as he tips out a small mound of white powder and uses his corporate Amex to chop it into eight neat lines, which he arranges in a star.

He offers Chang a short metallic straw. "Director Chang. Please."

And Chang doesn't hesitate.

He's done this before.

We all have.

Chang snorts a line of cocaine, and his eyes roll up in their sockets. He pivots back in his seat, falling slowly, as though he has been stunned with a blow to the head. Then his aides go for the kill, vultures ripping apart the carrion, sniffing up the coke and yapping in appreciation.

Gary chops more lines and then dives in. When he surfaces, his face is filled with a childlike glee.

Despite the alcohol suppressing my inhibitions, nerves begin to claw at my belly.

Song Chang takes her turn, swooping to inhale, swift and graceful. Then her black mirror eyes are on me, and in them I see infinity. Licking her lips, she holds out her straw in my direction. Anyone observing would think that she is urging me to join her, but her stance is challenging, like she's daring me to try.

Everyone is watching, waiting—even the topless waitresses.

It's ridiculous of me to think that this kind of mindless partying is not my scene, because it's obviously part of Jed Allen's lifestyle. To me, it's crazy. But the other me, the one I was before today, thinks it's a blast.

Even so, all I want to do is to run.

Song thrusts the straw at me, and I take it, knowing that to back down now could damage our credibility.

"Home run, buddy," Gary says, slapping me on the back.

I close my eyes, praying for salvation. Then I snort, nearly gasping for breath as nuclear fire erupts through my veins.

Gary claps his hands, and more drinks arrive: bottles of fancy French wine and chilled Dom Pérignon. The pole dancers drape themselves over the arms of the couches, over Chang and his juniors, laughing and flirting.

The music is crashing, the lights are strobing, and there's glass after glass of bubbling champagne. Line after line of chopped cocaine.

I begin to lose all sense of time, of identity, caught up in the whirlwind of alcohol and excitement and the runaway chain reaction as the drug crashes through my blood-brain barrier.

At some point, the ecstasy pills are handed out like after-dinner mints, as if the practice is not only routine but expected. Chang's aides swallow theirs first—reminiscent of food tasters rooting out poison for their king—and then it's our turn. With challenging eyes, Chang watches Gary swallow his down.

"Whatever it takes," Gary had said before the Chinese delegation got here. "It's all about saving face."

Chang's dark-brown eyes find mine, and all at once my bladder feels fit to burst. I murmur, "I need to excuse myself," but the words are lost in the music and my cocaine buzz. Chang swallows his pill as I push to my unsteady feet. Then, blood whistling through my head, I retreat to the sanctity of the restroom, where I splash cool water on my face.

Everything about this situation feels wrong, forced. I can accept that the other version of me is a cokehead, but that doesn't mean that I have to be one now, too. Amnesia has given me a clean slate. I can make new choices, change. I don't have to be what I've always been.

I stare at my stranger's face in the mirror, my vision pulsating, warping his pained expression. My head feels ten times bigger than normal, and the lights seem too bright. I guzzle water from the faucet and splash my face again. But the world around me remains a bright blur, and there's no altering the fact that I have overdone it on the alcohol and drugs.

The door opens and Song enters, holding a glass of merlot. I turn to face her. She doesn't ask if I'm okay. Instead, she descends like a dark angel, her lips pressing against mine before I realize what's happening.

Her mouth tastes of something exotic, and I'm not sure if it's the ecstasy or her natural flavor. Her hand cups the back of my head, steering me deeper into the kiss, but I pull back, gasping and holding her at arm's length. "Song. Wait. Please. This isn't right. I can't do this."

Her big brown eyes fill with confusion, and one of her eyebrows tilts. "I do not understand."

It's the first time I have heard her speak this evening, and her voice is like a charming spell. It would be the easiest thing in the world to let the moment take its course, to let my drunkenness direct me, to surrender to those bottomless eyes. But what would that make me?

I snap out of it, maneuvering around her toward the exit. "Song, I'm sorry. We can't do this. I'm with someone."

"But what of Shanghai?"

Her question brings me to a stop, one hand pressed against the door. At first, I have no idea what she means. The toxic mix of alcohol, coke, and prescription meds is making me dumb, spaced-out, and it takes a couple of seconds to permeate, to register. But when it does, I realize the meaning of her words: Song and I have been together before today.

"Look, Song, I don't know what happened between us in Shanghai. But whatever it was, it wasn't real. Okay? It should never have happened. I'm sorry. It's not you. It's me. I have a lot on my plate right now, and it's too complicated to get into. This . . . this can't happen. Not now. I have to go. It was a mistake."

For a second, she is as still as a statue, her face blank. Then she flicks her wrist, and the contents of her wineglass curve through the air, hitting me square on the chest. Cool merlot drenches my shirt.

"This was the mistake," she says.

I give her a cheerless smile and then make my escape, rushing through the strip club and out onto the street, my brain suddenly ablaze.

All I can think about is distancing myself from the scene of the crime, getting home to Cassie, and the pathetic words I will conjure up to explain my infidelity.

Some people might say, *No harm, no foul—a kiss is just a kiss,* and let it go at that. But to me, a passionate kiss is the height of intimacy, and I can't ignore the feeling that Song and I went much further in Shanghai.

I can't believe my other self has been unfaithful to Cassie. Even with the alcohol cushioning my senses, it's a hard blow, right on the chin.

Heart thudding, I push my way through the crowds of happy theatergoers finished with their shows. It's mayhem on the streets, with people blocking the sidewalks and no available taxis in sight. Even so, I keep searching for a ride back to Eastchester, and before I realize it, I'm at the north end of Seventh Avenue, facing the wall of darkness that is Central Park.

My headache has returned in full form, chiseling away at the insides of my skull, and the peace and quiet of the park is a big draw.

Without slowing, I cross the street, glad to put some space between myself and the chaos behind me.

On clumsy feet, I follow a dimly lit pathway as it snakes through the darkness. The bright lights of the liveliest metropolis in the world lie all around, yet here at the heart of the city, it's dead, the park feeling more like a cemetery than a social space.

A bench appears out of the dark, and I drop into it.

My senses are diluted, turning them wishy-washy. No doubt, I have indulged far too much, and I'll regret it in the morning. I lean back on the bench, breathing hard, hoping the cool night air will clear the fuzziness shrink-wrapping my brain.

Few people are in the park at this late hour: the occasional after-hours jogger; groups of noisy teens using it as a shortcut from one side of Manhattan to the other; solitary night strollers, hunched into their coats and actively avoiding eye contact.

I check my phone.

No missed calls.

I've been out all evening, and Cassie hasn't tried calling. Not once. I don't know if I should be worried or less controlling. I left her the note asking her to call me, but it's possible that she's used to me staying out late like this. It's not unreasonable to assume that she wouldn't interrupt me during a business dinner. All the same, I can't help but wonder why she hasn't even sent a text, even to wish me good luck with cementing the deal.

Does she know about Shanghai?

If not, how have I hidden this side of me from her?

The thought that I have been cheating hurts my brain, and I am forced to ask myself if my dalliance with Song in Shanghai was a one-off, a result of alcohol and cocaine and peer pressure, or if I am a serial scumbag with a string of indiscretions here in New York.

I know the answers lie with Cassie. Whether or not I like them is another matter.

My phone rings, the noise drilling through the dark, and I see Dr. Merrick's name glowing on the screen.

"Doc, this is unexpected."

"Jed, I realize it's late. I just wanted to check up on you, that's all." Her voice is hushed, as though she's settling down for the night.

I lean back on the bench, letting my gaze drift. "This is quite the personal service you've got going here. Following up with patients around midnight, and on a Friday. If you're calling to find out if my memory has come back, I've got bad news for you."

"I know."

"You do?"

"I could tell from the second you spoke. Plus, you've been drinking."

"Guilty as charged on both counts."

To me, my words don't sound slurred. But right now, I know my gauges are askew and can't be relied on.

"How much have you had?" she asks.

"Doc, you don't need to worry about me. I'll go home and sleep it off. I'll be fine."

"I'm more concerned that your recall crash hasn't ended. It's been eight hours, Jed. That's the longest it's ever lasted. This is a major development. If your memory doesn't return by morning, we may have to consider introducing more radical measures sooner than anticipated."

I wish I could reassure her that everything will be okay, that I'll wake up tomorrow with my mind fully reinstated, that the new me will be swallowed up by the old me, and that everything will go back to normal. But I'm not hopeful. And I'm not sure I want to lose what the new me has learned.

"I'm at meetings all morning," Dr. Merrick says in my ear. "I'll come over afterward, and we'll discuss strategies."

"Call me first," I tell her. Then I hang up and let out a long sigh.

I know Dr. Merrick's intentions are good, but I also know I'm her prized case study and that she'll probably write a career-defining paper about me, and I can't help feeling like her personal lab rat.

Something squawks in a nearby tree, and I look up to see the upper floors of the Majestic in the distance.

Is Tess watching me though her telescope, curious as to why I am sitting here alone, wringing my hands?

What am I doing here?

I fumble the bottle of pills out of my pocket and gulp a bunch of them down.

Then I close my eyes and pray for the world to stop spinning.

Chapter Eleven

The bus decelerated sharply, jarring Seltzer awake, and he stretched a kink from his neck, looking around through bleary eyes.

Where was he?

He squinted at the yellow streetlights, at the graffitied shutters lining the roadside, wondering which replicated neighborhood he was in.

As was so often the case these days, he'd been dreaming about his wife, of the two of them messing around in the garden in the summertime, skipping through the sprinklers and chasing rainbows. Acting like the happiest couple alive, destined to be together forever.

Of course, it was all just so much baloney.

People like him weren't meant for happiness. Maybe a little taste, just to make the loss of it more painful. But no long-term stroll down easy street.

This was what grated Seltzer's gears: knowing that some other people seemed to breeze through life, everything coming easy to them. He'd sold insurance policies to people like this, poking fun at himself while they looked down their noses at him. People who had had wealth and status handed to them on a silver platter. People who never encountered any hurdles, their passage from birth to death seemingly greased with good fortune.

"We're all born equal," he'd told himself time and again as he'd come away with policies signed. "Just some of us more equal than others."

The bus jerked again as it set off, and Seltzer closed his eyes, letting the vibration of the engine lull him back into slumber.

Chapter Twelve

I have no idea how long I sat on the bench in Central Park, trying to figure myself out.

As it stands, I'm still a blank canvas. It's up to me to decide what kind of picture I paint of myself. Will I be a Renaissance masterpiece with perspective and light, or a dark Hieronymus Bosch with otherworldly themes?

Will I get enough time to find out?

At four in the morning, Lakeshore Drive is as quiet as a tomb as the taxi drops me outside the house in Eastchester, and I linger on the threshold of the property for a long minute, shivering, while cowardly thoughts seek cover in my head.

Is Cassie curled up in our bed right now, half asleep, safe and secure, waiting for her faithful boyfriend to find his way home?

Is my selfishness about to destroy her world?

On heavy feet, I advance past the bronze sculpture and up the front walk. Monstrous trees hunch over the fairy-tale house, their bony branches reaching for the dark windows. I pause before opening the door.

"Is this who I am, a cheater? What's wrong with me?"

Fear feeds the twisting in my belly. My mouth tastes of copper, and my headache is coming back with a vengeance.

Inside the house, it looks like nothing has been disturbed, but deep shadows lurk in the corners.

The note is still pinned to the newel post.

Did Cassie miss it or decide to ignore it?

Could this be the reason why I haven't heard from her: We've been fighting, and now our weapon of choice is silence?

I draw a deep breath and trudge up the stairs. Then I hesitate before entering the master bedroom, unable to figure out a way I can off-load my guilt without crushing her.

Confess or lie. Either choice is selfish.

The glow of distant streetlights is creeping in through the window, and in its lugubrious glow I can just make out that the bed is as I left it: neat and tidy, and not slept in.

Half of me is relieved. But the other half is condemning.

I look toward the bathroom and call out, "Cassie?" and go inside, switching on the lights.

Everything appears as it was when I left for the party: the damp towel heaped on the sink top; the razor in a puddle of foamy water; the cologne I couldn't bear to wear, simply because it reeked of materialism.

I catch sight of my disheveled reflection in the mirror—the gray-circled eyes and the leery gaze, the hollow cheeks and the white powder stains on my lapel—and shy away from it, retreating to the bedroom.

I check out the whole upstairs, but there is no evidence of Cassie coming home. I find myself drawn to the windowpane in the smallest bedroom, where the ghostly impression of angel wings was left behind by the suicidal cuckoo. Through the grubby glass I can see the backyard. A leafy lawn slopes down to a stand of skeletal birch trees and a fuzz of wild undergrowth, beyond which lies a body of dark water.

The house backs onto a lake.

I squint, trying to see how far it stretches, and that's when I notice something moving down at the shoreline.

In the dark, it's hard to make out exactly what it is.

I have no idea what kinds of wild animals might roam the neighborhood at night. But it looks like it could be a person moving along a wooden dock that juts out from the backyard.

It occurs to me that it could be Cassie, and I shout her name, rapping my knuckles against the glass. My breath fogs the pane, and I rub it away, erasing part of the bird tattoo.

The indistinct figure is barely a smudge behind the charcoal trees. It moves to the end of the dock and disappears into the dark.

My reaction is instinctive, stoked by a sudden fear heating up my lungs. It sends me racing downstairs, through to the back of the house, and out into the cool night air, shouting her name as I go.

The lawn is slick with dew, and my feet slip as I rush toward the water. Panic burns in my chest. I duck and twist as tree branches scratch at my face. I crash through the thicket onto damp planks that creak as I thunder along the dock. I come to a juddering halt on the last board, almost sliding into the water. Heart racing, I peer down through the quicksilver surface.

There is no sign of Cassie or of anyone falling into the water. Not even a stream of bubbles to signal where someone might have gone under.

"Cassie!"

It's hard to tell for sure in the poor light, but this part of the lake seems to be no deeper than six feet. Bunches of black fronds reaching up from a muddy bottom. All of it undisturbed.

"Cassie!"

I scan the shoreline and then out across the glassy water, spotting a black shape rolling under the surface a dozen yards out. And without a second thought, I shuck off my jacket and dive in.

◆　◆　◆

The cold water punches me in the face, as hard as a blow from a heavyweight boxer, and it's an effort not to cry out and inhale water. It's much colder than I'd foolishly expected, and within the first few seconds of being submerged, the heat is sucked out of my lungs, replaced with a crushing chill.

I have no idea how good a swimmer I am, or that I can even swim. Worst of all, I am fully clothed and still wearing my street shoes.

People drown in six inches of water, I think.

Panicked, I drag myself hand over hand, kicking and keeping my mouth clamped shut.

From the dock, the lake looked relatively clear. But underneath that deceptive surface there churns a blackness as unforgiving as the vacuum of space.

Even so, I strike out for the shape I spotted from the dock, ignoring the penetrating chill and my own survival instincts urging me to resurface, to breathe.

I have no precise memory of an example, but I know I've heard about those ordinary people who risk their lives to save people and animals being swept away in floodwaters, those unsuspecting heroes who sometimes drown trying to save something they love.

My muscles are weakening at an exponential rate, the biting temperature sapping my energy.

A rumble of panic tries to squeeze through my sealed lips.

Then my fingertips touch something that feels foreign to the natural lake-bed flora, a man-made material wrapped around a soft lumpy mass. I hook my fingers onto it, kicking downward and pushing upward, my lungs pancaking.

I break the surface, gasping, shaking water from my eyes, the body-sized mass following a second later. It bobs up and rolls over, and I expect to see the worst:

Cassie's lifeless eyes, her lips turned blue.

But it's just a garbage bag, no doubt filled with household trash, and I push it away with frustration, scanning the choppy surface all over again.

"Cassie!"

I turn full circle, creating waves, desperate to locate her, my breath steaming.

"Cassie!"

Now I'm fearful, aware of a heavy sense of failure pressing down on me, all sense of direction gone.

My foot snags an aquatic plant and pulls me under. Bitter water floods into my mouth before I can thrust myself back to the surface to cough it out.

Lack of stamina, stupidity, and clinging clothes are weighing me down.

Finally, I see the dock emerge from the dark, and I splash toward it. I haul myself out, flopping onto the rough wood, exhausted, the world spinning and black dots pricking my vision.

Then I reach for my discarded jacket, just barely aware enough to pull it on before digging out my cell phone. I select the emergency option from the lock screen and dial 911.

"It's my girlfriend," I gasp into the phone after the operator asks what my emergency is. "I think she fell into the lake. I can't find her. I'm at a house on Lakeshore Drive. I don't know the number. There's a bronze statue on the front lawn. Please hurry. I think she drowned."

Impressively, the police arrive less than ten minutes later, in which time my panic has subsided into a sullen resignation.

The lake is calm again, and has been the whole time I've been waiting for Cassie's body to float to the surface.

But it hasn't, and neither has any shred of grief.

I should be an emotional wreck at the thought of losing the one person with the power to stabilize my life. But amnesia is paralyzing, and what ought to be a seismic event is nothing more than a slight tremor, mostly brought on by the cold.

"Mr. Allen? Mr. Allen. Eastchester PD."

I look up to see a pair of police officers jogging down the lawn toward the dock, one male and one female, their flashlights probing through the trees and throwing ghoulish shadows across the lake.

I raise a weak arm in confirmation.

The female officer remains at the shoreline while her partner continues across the dock. He's big and burly, with the air of someone who can handle himself in any situation.

"Mr. Allen?"

"Yes."

"Officer Davis." The beam from his flashlight passes over my face. "Sir, are you injured?"

I scrunch my eyes against the glare. "No. I don't think so."

I must look a mess, though, standing here on the end of the dock, soaked to the skin and cuddling myself for warmth.

"Sir, can you step back away from the edge?"

Mechanically, I obey.

The flashlight shines in my face.

"Can you tell me what happened?"

"It's my girlfriend." My voice is a defeated monotone. "She went in the lake. I went in after her. I searched, but I couldn't find her."

Even with amnesia, I know that no one can survive this long underwater. The officer knows it, too, hence the reason he's not kicking off his shoes and leaping to her rescue.

Instead, he sucks in a big breath and runs his flashlight across the lake, illuminating phantoms in the tangled trees leaning out across the water. In every way, it's like a scene from a horror movie.

"And she definitely didn't come out?"

"I don't think so. I mean, I haven't seen or heard anything. Please, you have to do something."

But he doesn't jump at my request. Instead, he peers out across the dark water. "Is your girlfriend a good swimmer, Mr. Allen? There's a lot of lake back here. Is this something she often does—swimming in the middle of the night?"

I can't provide an answer, but it wouldn't surprise me if it's something we both do, or have done, in the summertime especially, and maybe in the nude. This is the kind of secluded location that wouldn't have it any other way.

The flashlight beam skips across the surface, throwing a pale disk across the reedy shoreline. The garbage bag is nowhere to be seen.

"So," he says, "let me get this straight. The two of you were out here swimming?"

"No. I was up at the house. I saw her from the bedroom window."

I point, and the officer follows my direction, dipping his head as he tries to see the second-floor windows through the trees. His flashlight casts webbed shadows across the backyard and up onto the rear of the house.

"That's some good eyesight you've got there, Mr. Allen." His gaze finds its way back to me, and even in the poor light I see more than a trace of skepticism in it.

"I know what I saw, Officer. Someone was down here. They jumped right in."

"Other than you?" He doesn't wait for me to bite back. "And you're sure it was your girlfriend?"

"Who else would it be?"

It's a dumb question, because the truth is, I have no idea who else might have access to the lake; I haven't seen any fences dividing the properties.

"Mr. Allen, I have to ask. Were the two of you arguing tonight?"

"No."

"How about earlier this evening?"

"No. Look, I haven't seen her all day. I've been in the city. I just got home about fifteen minutes ago. Check with the taxi company if you don't believe me. I went straight upstairs, and that's when I saw her."

"Through the window?"

"Yes."

"Jumping in the lake?"

"Yes."

"Not falling or slipping? You're sure? Definitely jumping?"

His gaze roves my face, waiting for a reaction, something to confirm he has caught me in a lie.

I don't give any, and the flashlight is blinding.

"Sir, is that blood on your shirt?"

I look down at the stain, as if noticing it for the first time. Even under the glare of the flashlight, it's barely visible—just a pale pink patch, diluted by lake water—and the officer has done well to spot it.

"It's red wine. I was at a party."

"In the city."

"Right."

"Sir, how much alcohol have you had tonight?"

Now I can't help but flash a nervous smile. "What's that have to do with anything?"

"It's just that you're slurring your words. Do you have a medical condition to explain it, Mr. Allen?"

"No. And I don't appreciate you insinuating I'm drunk, Officer."

He disregards my weak deflection, shining the light right in my eyes instead.

"But you are under the influence of something—unless your pupils are naturally this dilated." He peers a little closer. "Sir, have you taken any nonprescription drugs tonight?"

"What?" Now I flap my arms in an attempt to appear inconvenienced, but I'm sure it only makes me look foolish.

"I'm specifically referring to recreational drugs."

"I know what you mean." I rub a finger under my nose, even though there are no traces of cocaine to wipe away. "I was at a party. Okay? Like I said, I had a few drinks. So what? It doesn't mean I hallucinated my girlfriend leaping in the lake. I wouldn't get you guys down here under false pretenses." I let my impatience show, but it doesn't even dent his skepticism. "Look, Officer, I don't want to tell you how to do your job, but you need to do *something*. I saw somebody go in the lake. I'm pretty certain it was my girlfriend. You need to call for reinforcements."

But he still isn't in any rush to go into the water. I sense his stance switch from concerned to cautious.

"Sir, I'm going to have to ask you to turn around and put both hands on the railing."

"What?"

"Both hands on the railing."

"You've got to be kidding me."

He waves at his partner to join us. She steps up onto the dock, the heel of one hand resting on the butt of her gun, her flashlight picking out my face.

"Hands on the railing," he repeats.

"Why, am I under arrest?"

"No. But I have reason to believe you may be in possession of a controlled substance."

"Now wait a minute. I called you here because my girlfriend is—"

Before I can finish, he reaches out and spins me around, effectively putting an end to my objection. A booted foot taps my feet apart from behind, and I am pushed forward so hard that I have no choice but to grasp the wooden handrail to stop myself from falling.

Then he proceeds to pat me down. Quickly, expertly, the action making wet slapping sounds against my sodden clothes. His hand reaches my jacket and hesitates over the bulge in the inside pocket.

"It's my phone," I say. "Is this really necessary?"

The officer reaches in the pocket and pulls it out.

"Please turn back around, Mr. Allen."

I do.

The object in his hand isn't my phone. It's the travel humidor that Tess gave me. And a flame ignites in my stomach.

"You a cigar smoker, Mr. Allen?"

All at once, my thoughts are plowing through my drunken haze and picking up speed, accelerated by the fear of being found with a pocketful of cocaine and ecstasy pills.

Before I can answer, he pops the lid, and the flame in my stomach erupts into an inferno. I glance at his partner and see her eyes narrowed and her hand still resting on her gun.

The officer puts the humidor to his nose and sniffs. "Cubans?"

"I. Have. No. Idea." My expression must be one of sheer panic, underpinned with red-hot guilt. "They were a gift."

He nods, seemingly satisfied, and then closes the holder, handing it back. "Let's continue this conversation at the house."

"What about my girlfriend?"

He glances back at the lake, but not with searching eyes. "We'll get to that." He motions for me to start moving, and we head back along the dock, with me in the lead, breathing a secret sigh of relief.

At this point, any concerned boyfriend would be protesting, shouting up a storm, and insisting that the lake be dredged. But the urgency has gone out of me. I know Cassie is probably the most important thing in my life. I know I should be more distraught than I am, devastated at the thought that she might have drowned.

But, insanely, I feel nothing.

Has amnesia stolen my soul?

On heavy feet, I lead the way into the kitchen, switching on the lights and the heat as I go. The furnace rumbles to life, feeding hot water through the pipes and into the radiators.

As we head into the living room, the female officer peels off, climbing the staircase.

"Routine check," Officer Davis tells me.

I switch on the living room lights, revealing mounds of furniture and stacked packing crates.

"Do you have a photograph of your girlfriend?" he asks.

I take the photo of Cassie and me from my wallet and hand it to him. He scrutinizes it for a few seconds, then hands it back.

He motions to the packing crates. "So are you moving in or moving out?"

"Yes. No. It's complicated. Honestly, I don't know."

He turns his gaze on me, his eyes widening, as though seeing me for the first time. "We've met before, you and I."

"We have?"

"Give it a second. It'll come to me. What is it you do, Mr. Allen, for a living?"

"I'm an architect."

"They pay well?"

"Excuse me?"

He spins a finger at the room. "You designed this house, for instance?"

I glance at the rough wooden beams and the uneven plaster walls. "No. At least I don't think so. This place looks ancient and badly in need of a renovation. As far as I know, I specialize in blobitecture."

He looks at me like I'd just chewed off my own tongue.

"It's a postmodernist style," I say for clarification, "involving organic curves. I take it you've seen New York by Gehry in Lower Manhattan?"

His baffled expression stays put for a second, then he wags a gloved finger at me. "January. Now I remember."

"Excuse me?"

"When we met before. You were in your car outside the Wells Fargo on White Plains Road. I remember because it was the biggest snowstorm of the season. Took down power lines across the county. You said you were waiting for your girlfriend."

"I was?" Of course, it's news to me.

"You said she was at the urgent-care clinic across the street." He waits for me to elaborate. When I don't, he asks, "Was everything okay back then?"

"I don't know."

He raises an eyebrow.

"It's not what you think."

"Oh? And what would that be, Mr. Allen?"

"That I mistreat my girlfriend. That I roughed her up last January and she ended up at the clinic. That tonight we had an argument and I pushed her in the lake."

"Your words. Not mine."

"The truth is, I don't remember because I have memory issues. Okay? And I don't mean I'm forgetful. I experience periods of complete amnesia, where I don't even remember my own name." I lean against a radiator, letting the intensifying heat take away my chill.

He nods, as though he can relate. "They got you on medication for that?"

"It doesn't change the fact that I saw what I saw."

Again, my words are met with a nod, but I don't think he believes me.

"Must be fifty yards from the house to the dock," he says. "It's the middle of the night. There's a bunch of birches in the way. And then there's your partying to take into account."

"You won't let that go, will you, my reckless partying?"

"All I'm saying is maybe it's not the smartest thing, mixing medication with alcohol."

"Thanks for the lecture."

His partner rejoins us, announcing that there's nothing unusual to be seen upstairs. And then they both stare at me like I'm an escapee from the asylum.

"I don't think I was hallucinating," I say.

"But you're not sure."

"Even so, you need to take me seriously, Officer. Dredge the lake. Bring in your divers, your sniffer dogs. Do whatever it takes to find my girlfriend. Do *something*."

Officer Davis sighs. "Frogmen? Well, that would cost the town a heck of a lot of tax dollars, Mr. Allen, and I'm not sure they'll find what you're looking for. You see, here's what we got. You're on medication for amnesia. You've been out partying all night. And there's a possibility that this partying of yours involved some recreational drug use." He holds up a gloved hand before I can protest the charge. "Again, you've already admitted you're on medication. The way I see it is you've come home, maybe still a little bit high and intoxicated, maybe with one or two questionable chemicals floating around in your bloodstream, and you believe you saw someone jumping into the lake, which you then go on to assume is your girlfriend, who you say you've been looking for all day. Then we show up, and there's no indication that anyone other than you went in the lake."

I'm about to speak, but he holds up the hand again.

"Now, here's what I'm thinking, so please bear with me. Between these forgetful periods of yours, you're normally an intelligent guy. Rational, too, no doubt. You've got to be a smart cookie to be an architect, right? So something like this, a missing persons report, under different circumstances, we'd be all over. But couple your condition with mind-altering substances and, well, I'm guessing there's some pretty weird side effects going on here. Wouldn't surprise me one bit if one of those turns out to be visual peculiarities. You see where I'm headed?"

My mouth is a hard line.

"So here's what I suggest you do, Mr. Allen. Once we're done here, you take yourself to bed and sleep things off. Then, if your girlfriend hasn't come home in the morning, and you're unable to contact her through the regular channels, by all means come down to the station and we'll be happy to take another look at things. See how everything stacks up in daylight and with a clear head. How about that?"

"Thanks for your time," I say. "You can see yourselves out."

Chapter Thirteen

Wired, I am convinced I won't sleep. But I do. And I wake with a tacky mouth and a splintering pain behind my eyes, as though somebody is sledgehammering walls in my head. Just as depressing is the realization that my historical memory hasn't returned, and neither has Cassie.

Her side of the bed is cold and empty.

Aside from the blur that is the party at Rafferty's, I can recall everything that my brain has stored since my awakening at the office yesterday. Everything before that is blank.

A pair of muddied pants is draped over one end of the dresser, bringing clarity to the overnight events.

Despite the police officer's advice, I spent the rest of the time before the emergent dawn investigating the reeds hemmed up against the shoreline and under the dock, convinced that I was right about seeing someone falling into the lake. But the more I looked, the less confident that conviction became until I was left with the conclusion that the police were right about at least one thing: mixing alcohol and cocaine with medication was a dangerous concoction.

I fumble my phone from the nightstand and scowl at the time. It's one o'clock in the afternoon. Luckily for me and my blossoming hangover, it's Saturday, and I don't need to go rushing into the office.

There are no missed calls from Cassie.

I close my eyes again, letting the weight of my headache pull me back down into sleep. Then I open them just as quickly as I hear a sudden crash coming from downstairs, and I sit up to listen. It's then that I notice the smell, and it takes a moment for my reawakening senses to recognize it as the scent of cooking.

I pull on some clothes and make my way down the stairs, the unmistakable smell of pancakes and bacon and freshly brewed coffee drawing me forward.

"Cassie?"

Strangely, the daylight seems brighter here, warmer, the colors more vivid, as though a freak autumn heat wave has arrived.

"Cassie? Is that you?"

On quickened feet, I cross the hall and then pause at the kitchen doorway, all of my concerns about Cassie's welfare falling away.

The room is saturated in sunshine, and Cassie is at the stove, working pancake mix with a spatula, her hips tilted as she hums a happy tune to herself. She's wearing a short floral dress, black flowers on white fabric, and I can't imagine a more beautiful sight.

"Hey there, sleepyhead," she says as she glances at me over her shoulder. "I hope you're hungry."

"Cassie. You had me worried. I thought you were never coming home. When did you get in?"

"Not long ago. Pull up a chair—I'm almost done."

But I go straight to her, wrapping my arms around her from behind and holding her close, relishing her warmth, her presence, her shape.

I nuzzle her neck. "Do you know how much I missed you?"

Cassie turns her face to mine and pecks me on the lips. "Someone's not so sleepy anymore. Don't make me burn the pancakes."

I back away, sliding onto a stool at the breakfast bar, happy just to watch her cook. Cassie has laid out plates, silverware, and two mugs of steaming coffee on the countertop. Plus, crispy bacon on white china.

"Where were you?" I ask, picking up a bacon strip and biting it.

She turns from the stove with the pan in hand. "Don't play games. You know where I was."

"Remind me."

She eases two pancakes onto my plate. "Are you being serious? It was your idea."

"That's just it. I don't remember."

"But it's all we've talked about in ages. You know we had this planned." She sounds puzzled, and a little kink has popped up on her forehead.

"Honestly, Cassie, I had no idea where you were. I even called the police."

Now she pauses to give me a bewildered look. "I don't understand. You called the police?"

The kink on her forehead grows into parallel lines, and I realize that I have made an error in assuming that she knows about my intermittent amnesia.

"Have you been using again?" she asks, her question taking me by surprise.

"What? As in doing drugs? No!" I laugh it off, but it comes out like I'm trying too hard, which is always the telltale sign of a lie.

All at once, I'm not thinking about the coke and the ecstasy, the mindless cavorting in the strip club. I'm not even wondering why I've kept my amnesia from my girlfriend, or how. I'm reliving Song Chang kissing me in the bathroom and the exotic taste of her lips.

It was my intention to come clean with Cassie about my unfaithfulness. But now that her questioning has put me under the spotlight, all I want to do is to shy away from the exposure.

"We had an agreement," she says, her jaw tightening, her whole demeanor on the brink of hostility. "You said this would stop. You promised. Quitting the drugs was the only way for us to be together."

I slide off the stool. "Cassie, just hear me out. Okay? I have amnesia. I'm on medication for it. I can show you the pills." I start to reach for them in my pocket, then realize that they're upstairs.

"Amnesia?" Her expression isn't one of concern or even surprise; it's that of someone who has heard one lie too many.

I reach out a hand, but she evades my grasp, as though I am contaminated.

"Cassie, I don't know why I've never told you. Maybe I was thinking I was protecting you. I don't know. But I'm telling you now. My behavior, my forgetfulness. It's not the drugs."

Instead of opening the lid, my confession acts as the final nail in the coffin, and Cassie's disappointment is palpable.

"You know what?" she says, her posture stiffening. "I refuse to do this anymore. You had your chance, and you blew it. This isn't the kind of life I want."

I start to formulate another weak response, but she hefts the frying pan over her shoulder and swings it at me like a tennis racket.

And I am too slow to react. In fact, I don't. I just stand there with a mindless look on my face as, with a resounding clang, the metal strikes me on the head, hard enough to unleash lightning bolts in my brain, and I crash out of the world into a pit of unfathomable blackness.

For a chaotic moment, everything is untethered—my thoughts, my feelings, my grip on reality, my whole persona, swept up in a whirlpool and shattered into a million pieces—and then my eyelids snap open again, banishing the darkness and flooding the world in light.

And I find myself back upstairs in the master bedroom, sprawled on the bed, with sweat pooled in the hollows of my skin and my head ringing like a bell.

For a moment, I am out of sync with my surroundings, everything overlapping—until I realize that my encounter with Cassie in the kitchen was nothing but a bad dream, and that her side of the bed is still cold and empty.

Worse yet, my memory isn't back, and the same warm panic as yesterday starts to spread through my stomach.

I take a deep breath, holding it in, closing my eyes and pushing down on the anxiety until it lessens.

Despite my unease, I am not totally devastated to find the amnesia still in residence. Half of me was expecting as much. If anything, I am on the fence where my condition is concerned. Sure, it would be great to feel less like I popped into existence only yesterday, to have my memories fully restored, but in a weird way I am already getting used to being the new me, acclimating, fascinated by the unique opportunity for an unbiased introspection.

In spite of our natural resistance to change, it's amazing how quickly we adapt when push comes to shove.

On the nightstand, my phone rings, growing louder by the second and adding to the pain behind my eyes.

The call is from Gary. I decline it and put the phone in silent mode.

Until I come to terms with the night's events, I am in no mood to suffer his criticizing my early exit from the party.

Beyond the din in my head, the house is silent. No sounds of bacon sizzling in the pan. No indication that Cassie is downstairs, humming tunefully and cooking up a Saturday treat. The dominant smells are my own musky stench and the dry lake mud staining the sheets.

I sit up with a sigh. "Just a damn dream. You need to get a grip."

Even so, and to remove any doubt, I pull on some clothes and venture downstairs, calling out Cassie's name as I go.

In the dreary October light, the kitchen is a place of mausoleum stillness, with no indication that anyone has been here while I slept.

A clock on the wall confirms it's after one.

Outside, the autumnal air nips at my skin. I head down to the lake, scanning the backyard and the bare trees for any trace of Cassie.

Everything looks different in daylight, safer, transforming the horror movie set into a picturesque scene straight from a real estate brochure.

As far as the eye can see, nothing out of the ordinary.

In the sobering aftermath, it seems even less likely that I saw what I thought I saw, and I have to concede to the possibility that I was mistaken. The lake is calm, innocuous. A flat panel of cobalt beneath a gunmetal sky. No lifeless bodies floating facedown or chopped up in garbage bags. Just some muddy footprints on the weathered planking.

Shoulders rounded, I return to the house, where I take my meds, and a couple of Tylenol for my hangover.

I ought to shower away my nightclub veneer and the flakes of lake mud, but the need to find out why Cassie hasn't come home is overriding everything else.

Sitting cross-legged on the floor, I go through the packing crates in the living room one by one, looking for clues.

Aside from what I have already seen, most of the boxes contain miscellaneous stuff: ornaments, a CD collection, paperback books, tableware wrapped in newspaper. Each item has been handpicked with personal taste, giving an insight into Cassie's and my preferences, but none of it provides any specific information. There are no diaries, no address books, no official documents. Nothing to lead me to where my search should go from here. And after a while, my head is splitting again.

Dehydrated, I guzzle water from the kitchen tap, then let it spray over my head and face.

Finished with the packing crates, I go through the bedroom closets and the dressers, looking for anything that might clue me in on my relationship with Cassie.

The truth is, in my present amnesic state, I know nothing about her. I have no idea if she's an only child or if she has family living nearby. What school did she attend? Who is her best girlfriend? If she is indeed a professional photographer, which publications have bought her amazing photographs?

I come across the hidden photo in her underwear drawer and can't resist another look.

This second time around, Cassie doesn't seem to be quite as happy as I thought. At first glance, her beaming smile overshadows the rest of her face, and it's easy to misinterpret the mood in the picture. But a closer inspection reveals an emptiness in her eyes I didn't notice before. The suppressed tension of someone uncomfortable in their surroundings. Someone forced to participate, either through obligation or necessity.

My instinct was to think that Cassie is having an affair. But it's clear she's faking it for the camera, and I wonder why.

Behind the man's smile, a similar strain is present. And now that I reexamine the photo in brighter daylight, I can see that even though their arms are linked and they are obviously posing as a happy couple, they are both leaning slightly away from each other, their body language sending mixed messages. On one hand, they want to be seen together, but on the other hand, they don't want to be together.

I take the photo from my wallet and compare the two.

Although the setup is similar, my photo is a completely different picture. There is no awkwardness between Cassie and me. If anything, she is draped over my arm, clinging, giggling, and if she were sitting any closer, she would be on my lap. My smile seems genuine, too, and even my suspicious eyes seem to have a friendlier sparkle. Cassie's smile is effusive, and the sight of it tweezes one from my own lips. But her eyes seem dull in comparison, glazed, almost as though there is a film over them, her pupils so big that her irises are reduced to thin blue circles.

Otherwise, she looks like she's having a ball, like *we're* having a ball, and for the first time since losing my memory, I feel a twinge in my heart that isn't founded in jealousy.

I look again at the photo from her drawer, with the words *The Ambient Lounge* written on the reverse.

I take out my phone, intending to find a number for the venue, then realize I still haven't cracked the access pattern on the lock screen. I try a few random patterns without success.

I go to the kitchen and call the operator from the house phone, who then patches me through to the Ambient Lounge. A man answers, and I begin to explain that I'm looking for information on an event held there last Christmastime, when he interrupts midsentence to inform me that the venue is closed.

"You need to call back later," he tells me, "preferably after five. Someone might be able to deal with your question then."

I thank him and hang up.

Then something occurs to me, and I grab the car keys, heading out to the driveway, where I start the car and wait until my cell phone links with the infotainment system. When it does, I instruct it to call Cassie.

The number connects. I begin to get a little excited, and then the call goes straight to an out-of-service tone.

Frustrated, I am about to turn off the ignition, and that's when I notice a warning light illuminated on the dashboard screen.

One of the tires is flat, and I have no idea if I'm a member of AAA.

A quick rummage in the glove compartment turns up no membership card, but once again, the sight of the hunting knife is startling, and I am still in the dark as to why the old me put it there.

I go around to the trunk, hoping to find a spare tire or, better yet, an inflator kit.

Instead, I find a black garbage bag.

Curious, I ease apart the loose knot and open it up. Inside is a garment of clothing. A woman's dress, white with a green floral pattern, most of which is obscured by a large red stain running its full length. Not only that, but there are tears in the fabric, and the zipper on the back has come away from its stitching, as though by force.

It's one of those moments when the brain stutters, and it takes longer than it should for me to realize what it is I'm looking at.

Then I slam the trunk lid, glancing up and down the street as I return to the house.

Chapter Fourteen

With its spongy tire disintegrating, my car limps to the Eastchester Police Department on Mill Road. By the time I arrive, the rubber is in shreds and the wheel hub has cut through. I park between a police cruiser and a Prius, and then go around to the trunk to collect the garbage bag with the bloodied dress in it.

"Mr. Allen?"

I look up to see a burly police officer standing on the other side of the Prius. At first, I don't recognize him in his street clothes. Then I realize it's the same officer who called at the house in the early hours of the morning.

I acknowledge him with a nod. "Officer Davis."

"Your girlfriend didn't come home?"

I shake my head. "About to make it official, like you said."

He nods. "I hope she turns up okay. In the meantime, do you need assistance with the tire?"

I glance down at the tattered rubber and the shiny hub poking through. "No. It's okay. I'll take care of it. Thanks anyway."

"No problem. Just don't try and drive it home."

"I won't."

"You have a good day, sir."

"Yeah. You too."

I wait until he has driven out of the parking lot before crossing toward the stone-clad police station.

Surrounded by stately trees, the building looks like it used to be a country club, with stone steps leading to a pillared entranceway.

"My girlfriend is missing," I tell the clerk at what looks like an antique reception desk. "I need to speak with a detective."

In a monotone, he informs me that everyone is busy, and hands me a form to fill out.

I take a seat on a bench positioned between two vending machines and stow the bag between my feet.

Right away, the form asks questions I can't answer: When did you last see the person you are reporting as missing? Was anything different about his or her behavior prior to their disappearance? Is the person on medication? Has the person disappeared for any length of time previously? Does he or she have a reason to disappear? Does he or she pose a danger either to themselves or to somebody else?

I chew the end of the pen, frustrated with my lack of recollection and the amount of white space I am unable to fill in.

Even so, I do the best I can and return it to the clerk. Then I spend the next ninety minutes browsing last year's real estate magazines, glancing up every time the main doors open or somebody walks past.

My mind wanders, and I go over what I know so far about my life before yesterday, about my brain surgery nine months ago, about my time in the hospital and then in rehab, about my career as an architect, and about my friendship with Gary and my relationship with Cassie.

From every perspective, my world contains all the elements for a beautiful life. I'm successful, I'm comfortable, I'm in love, and I'm on the up-and-up. But there's an ugliness behind the facade, a hideous condition threatening to blemish my world forever.

And there's no hiding the fact that I'm a mess inside.

If my mind is like a computer, then my amnesia is a virus corrupting my programming and denying access to my data store.

How soon before everything is deleted permanently and all I am left with is a blank space? What will happen then? Will I begin my life afresh each day, with no recollection of anything that's gone on before? Can I live like that?

Dr. Merrick seems confident she can keep my condition at bay with various as-yet-untried treatments. But even she admits they're temporary solutions, and I'm not sure a Band-Aid is good enough to stem the hemorrhaging.

I need to get a handle on my condition.

Eventually, I hear my name being called out, and I look up to see a dark-haired man of about my age leaning out of a doorway farther down the hall. He looks like he's been sleeping in his suit.

"Mr. Allen? I'm sorry for your wait. I'm Detective Westfall. Would you like to come with me?"

We go to his desk, located in a corner of an open office space that looks like it was once a large meeting hall. Old wood-paneled walls rub shoulders with contemporary fiberboard. We are the only people here.

"So, Mr. Allen," the detective says as we sit down, "how can I help you?"

"Did you read my form?"

"I gave it the once-over, and I have to say it was a bit on the vague side. You say your girlfriend's missing?"

"That's right."

He glances at the report on his desk. "You didn't fill out all the questions."

"That's because I don't know all the answers."

His eyes come back to me. "You don't?"

"It's complicated."

He leans back in his chair, pressing his fingertips together, almost as if in prayer, with his index fingers against his upper lip, and studies me. From the way his eyes narrow, I can tell he's already thinking I'm a flake.

"What's your address, Mr. Allen?"

"It's right there, on the form."

"It says Lakeshore Drive."

"That's right."

"What number?"

I try to visualize the front door of the house, the beige wood, the four-digit number on the plate next to the doorbell, but it's all foggy. "I'm not sure."

"You don't know your own address?"

"It's not what you think."

"You say you're an architect. Where's that at?"

"Q and A."

"In the city?"

"Yes."

He nods, as though he's heard the name. But I'm sure he hasn't.

"And how about your girlfriend?"

"She's missing."

"I get that. I'm asking what she does for a living."

"She's . . . a photographer. I think. Look, are these questions absolutely necessary?"

"They are if you want me to take your report seriously, Mr. Allen. On the form, you say your girlfriend's name is Cassie, right?"

"Right."

"What about her last name?"

"I don't know."

He leans back in his chair, his eyes narrowing again. "You see, there's the problem. Seems to be a bunch of basic stuff here that either you don't know or you don't want to share. And neither is helpful. If you want me to take your report seriously, Mr. Allen, you need to be more forthcoming. What makes you think your girlfriend is missing?"

"Because she never came home last night."

"Was she supposed to?"

"We live together."

"Okay. Let me rephrase. Is there any reason to think your girlfriend might have felt she couldn't come home last night? For example, did the two of you have a fight?"

"No. At least, I don't think we did."

Again, his eyes narrow, as though he's deliberating how much of my hot air he can collect in a jar and quantify.

"I have amnesia," I say before he can close me down.

"You do?" He sounds skeptical, as though I've plucked an excuse out of thin air.

"It's why I can't answer all of your questions. Because I don't know the answers myself."

"And you're under a doctor's care for this?"

"I can even give you her number if you need to check."

Westfall's stance seems to soften a little. "No, Mr. Allen, that won't be necessary. Why didn't you just mention this right at the start?"

"I was getting to it. Besides, it's not the first thing you blurt out to everyone you meet. I'm still trying to wrap my own head around it."

"So it's something new, this amnesia?"

"Apparently. I was in a car accident earlier this year. They had to operate on my brain. It's left me with intermittent amnesia."

"So it comes and it goes?"

"Yes."

"Do they know what triggers it?"

I shrug. "Stress. Anxiety. That kind of thing."

"And it's happening to you here, right now?"

"Yes."

I can see where Westfall is headed with this. He's thinking that Cassie and I have had a dustup and she stormed out. A fight of such magnitude that it sparked my amnesia.

I'd like to think he's wrong, but the truth is, I honestly don't know.

"Okay," Westfall says, sitting up. "Let me get this straight. Your girlfriend has gone missing since this latest episode began?"

"As far as I know, yes."

"So you don't know when was the last time you saw her?"

"Correct."

He nods. "Then it's pointless asking if you remember any other times she didn't come home as expected. Or if she said anything to you before she left this time, presumably yesterday morning."

"Now you can appreciate where I'm coming from."

Westfall is quiet for a few seconds, presumably to mull over my comments. From any angle, my predicament is an obstacle. When he speaks again, it's in a somber tone. "Mr. Allen, what I'm about to say may be difficult for you to hear. But please bear with me. Is it at all possible that your girlfriend is with someone else, romantically speaking?"

"Like she's having an affair?"

I visualize the photograph I found in Cassie's dresser, the picture of her with another man, and I am powerless to stop the jealousy from flaring up in my face. Heat prickles around my neck, and I loosen my collar.

"I'm sorry," Westfall says. "I always hate asking it. But you'd be amazed how many wounded husbands sit right where you are now, pouring out their hearts, only to learn later that their missing wives turn out to be runaway brides." He picks up the report and slots it in a tray on his desk.

"So that's it? You're not going to look for her?"

"I wish I could say we have the manpower and the resources at our disposal, Mr. Allen. But we don't. Besides which, we only consider a person as officially missing once they've been off the radar for more than forty-eight hours. The reason we do this is because you'd be equally amazed how many of those absent people suffer an attack of conscience and come rushing home after the first night away. People have their reasons for behaving erratically. It's not always a police matter. More than likely there's a reasonable explanation for your girlfriend's absence. I see it all the time. My advice is, if she doesn't come home by Monday and you still don't hear from her—"

I slam my hand on his desk. "Detective. I wouldn't be here if I wasn't seriously concerned for her welfare."

Now he sits forward. "You think that's the case—that something has happened to her, maybe something bad?"

"I'm just putting it out there."

All the same, Westfall can't help but eye me with suspicion, and suddenly I'm wondering if I have shot myself in the foot by coming here. Amnesia isn't just making me come across as incompetent; it's making me sound like I have something sinister to hide.

Westfall draws a big breath. It's one of those reverse sighs that people do when they think you're giving them the runaround. "But you don't know for a fact that your girlfriend is even missing. For all you know, she could be staying with friends, or visiting a sick relative. If she's a photographer, she could be away on a shoot, and you just don't remember her leaving."

"You're right. I've thought about all that. Then I found this, and that's why I came right here."

I put the garbage bag on his desk, knowing that its contents can say more about my concerns than I can vocalize.

Westfall frowns. "What's this?"

"I found it in the trunk of my car. You need to take a look at it. I'm not sure, but I think it could be Cassie's." I open the bag, flattening out the edges so that the bloodstained dress is plain to see.

Westfall perks up, seemingly drawn by the prospect of discovering a serious crime. He takes a pencil from his desk and lifts up a section of the dress. In the fluorescent lighting, the dried blood has a coppery sheen to it, and there's a noticeable odor of rust.

Westfall looks up at me. "Why didn't you tell me this right away?"

"Because . . . I needed you to understand my situation first. Like I said, it's complicated. I didn't want you getting the wrong idea and jumping to a conclusion."

"Which is what exactly?"

"That I hurt her." My words come out no louder than a whisper, and Westfall's stance hardens again.

"Did you?" he asks, staring at me. "Did you hurt your girlfriend, Mr. Allen?"

Then he waits for my rebuttal, waits for me to convince him that in spite of my amnesia and my unreliable testimony that I am a credible character. But I can't put up a defense, simply because I don't have one, and it leaves me looking anything but innocent.

Chapter Fifteen

Seltzer paused, his hand inches from the door handle as his eyes tracked from the fake wood grain to the nameplate: **DR. ARIANA VARGAS.**

The nameplate was one of those slide-in types that made replacing it easy. Seltzer had no idea how long Vargas had occupied the office, but he suspected it was quite some time; the black cardboard plate had faded to gray in the sunlight from a nearby window.

Seltzer knocked on the door and then quickly let himself inside without waiting for permission to enter.

Vargas was working on a laptop at her desk, her long dark hair spilling over one shoulder. When she saw him enter, she closed the laptop's lid, took off her reading glasses, and smiled.

"Arnold? This is a lovely surprise. I didn't expect to see you again."

Vargas was in her midfifties, but Seltzer thought she looked ten years younger. Probably, it was down to a combination of being childless and the fact that she'd done what he had: fallen in love with someone younger.

"I was in the neighborhood," he said with a shaky smile.

"You missed your last few appointments."

"I know."

She rose to her feet. "I tried calling, and I left several messages."

Seltzer continued to smile uneasily; it was an expression he'd grown used to wearing lately. "I've been burning the candle at both ends. No time for anything else."

She nodded, but it was a slow nod, like she was deliberating. "Why don't you sit. I want to hear all about how you've been and what's been keeping you so busy."

He did, settling onto the big couch reserved exclusively for people like him. A comfy couch with floral-print cushions and a potted aspidistra on each side. A couch that knew a secret or two. After his life had imploded, Seltzer had visited Vargas on a weekly basis for months, sitting here in this same spot, at first resisting the pull of the plush upholstery and then letting it suck away his tension as Vargas's words massaged his mind.

But then his financial situation had taken a tumble, and even Vargas's modest fee had been an expense he couldn't justify continuing.

"So, tell me, how have you been?" she asked as she sat down in the chair facing him.

"Physically, just the usual aches and pains. People say forty is the new thirty, but it's wishful thinking."

"How about emotionally?"

Seltzer's shaky smile resurfaced. "All things considered, okay, I guess. Getting my act together one day at a time. Still breathing."

"That's good. Along with introspection, I definitely encourage breathing."

Seltzer didn't respond to her subtle humor. He might have, at one time, taken the bull by the horns and run with it. He used to consider himself the king of banter at the office. But these days it was a challenge even to speak at all.

"I see you have your briefcase with you," Vargas said. "Did you find a job? I know you were looking so hard."

Seltzer dropped his gaze to the briefcase on his lap, with its handle flattened against his waistline. When he was here last, he'd lied to Vargas about the extent of his job hunt. He'd told her he was distracting himself by looking for work, night and day, and that he'd registered with employment agencies across the state. But it had all been a ruse to redirect her from striking home.

"I lost the house, by the way," he said, unable to stop himself from deflecting again. "The mortgage lender foreclosed. They served a notice of eviction. They want me out by the middle of next week."

"I'm so sorry to hear that. I know you loved it there."

Seltzer shrugged. "It was inevitable, I guess. There was no way I could keep up with the payments. Not after losing my job. And savings only stretch so far, you know?"

"All the same . . ."

"It's just bricks and mortar. That's what my mom used to say. When I was little, our family home burned down to the ground. I don't remember the fire, but I do remember my mom's blackened face and the streaks where her tears had dried. I can still feel her clutching me to her shirt, the drumbeat of her heart, the stink of the smoke, and her saying, 'A house is just bricks and mortar. You can always replace a house, but you can never replace a life.'"

"Your mother sounds like a wise woman."

"She was." He didn't add that the life she had referred to was his father's, who had saved his family from the fire, only to go back inside the burning house one last time, never to come out again alive.

"So, tell me, Arnold, what have you learned about yourself, with all this intense thinking you've been doing?"

Again, Seltzer looked at his hands on the briefcase, feeling the dampness of his palms bonding them to the leather. The last time Vargas had tried to debug his brain, he'd still been a wreck, unfocused, and it had taken only a gentle nudge to get the words pouring out of him. He'd been that way for a long time, floundering. Then he'd come across something by chance. Something that had reset his focus, sending him off on a different path and giving him a new direction. One that he knew would lead him to a place where, finally, the balance in his life could be restored.

"I can't talk about it," he said.

"You can't, or you won't?"

"It's too close to home."

"And yet something brought you back here. If not to talk, what then?"

Seltzer stuck out his lower lip, suddenly feeling cornered. "I think I made a mistake."

He went to rise, to leave, but Vargas held up a hand, halting him.

"Arnold, I can't help you if you don't let me in."

All at once, strong emotions were throttling his throat, and he wanted to get up and run, to distance himself from everything he associated with the pain. But fear was paralyzing him, pinning him to the couch, and he was at the mercy of Vargas's penetrating gaze.

"Coming here, it reminds you, doesn't it?" she said. "It brings it all crashing back into the present, as though you're there again, right at the heart of all the pain."

Somehow, he managed to nod.

"Would you rather forget?"

Seltzer swallowed, suppressing his anguish. "There's little chance of that ever happening!" He had to squeeze each word out, each one barbed and dripping with hurt. "And I know you've said it's better for me that I do remember everything, that I talk about it, that I get it all out in the open, that I share it, analyze it, quantify it, and understand it, because that will negate its power. But coming here . . ." He shut his mouth to stop the pain from spilling out.

"It makes it real," Vargas said.

Seltzer felt his heartbeat stumble and sweat prick out on his hairline. He peeled his hands off the briefcase and wiped them on his pants. "It's nothing compared to living with the self-recrimination. It's killing me."

"Even though you know, and in the past you've agreed with me on this, that not all of what happened was your fault?"

"That's just it. I've come to realize that some of it *was*, and that's the part I can't live with."

Vargas leaned forward, her fingers knitted. "But that's not the entire reason you're here, is it, Arnold? You weren't just in the neighborhood. I can sense it. There's something else, isn't there? Something you have to get off your chest. It's okay, Arnold—you can tell me."

Seltzer swallowed the thorny lump in his throat. "I bought a gun."

"You bought a gun?"

He saw Vargas withdraw, leaning back and crossing her legs, her whole posture turning defensive.

"Do you have it with you?" she asked.

"It's not what you think. It's for protection."

"Against what?"

"Everything." A nervous smile twisted his lips. "These are crazy times, you know?"

She nodded, ostensibly in agreement, but her expression and her body language told a different story. She seemed to study him for a moment, and he wondered if she could see right through his skin to what lay beneath. What would she say if she could see the ticking time bomb inside him? Her sense of duty as his therapist would compel her to try to defuse him. Did he want his anger neutralized?

After all, these days, his anger was all he had. It was his drive, his reason for being. He didn't need a therapist to tell him that hate flourished in the absence of love. He was the living, breathing proof.

"You do know, Arnold," she finally said, "that statistically you're no more likely to come to any harm now than you were before? With people experiencing PTSD, it's not uncommon to feel like your life is in danger. But it's a warped perspective. It's scary, for sure. But not everybody resorts to buying a gun. Can you tell me how you felt when you bought it?"

Now he stared at her, anticipating what she was thinking, that she was concerned he might use the gun on himself. How could he begin to tell her that the second he'd laid his hands on the revolver all he had felt was an unburdened sense of elation?

Vargas wouldn't understand. Who could, unless you were living with the torture, day after day, like he was? And if he told her he was *this* close to finding the man responsible for his wife's death, he knew Vargas would say everything she could to talk him down. There was also the strong possibility she would warn the police, and then where would he be?

"Don't worry," he said, getting to his feet. "I didn't come here to settle my psychological account."

"Then why did you come?"

"Because I never got the chance to say thanks."

He offered her a grim smile, then opened the office door and left before she could say anything to change his mind.

Chapter Sixteen

Fifteen minutes after being grilled by Detective Westfall, I am sitting in my car, still feeling the heat.

My cheeks are hot enough to glow.

In light of my big revelation, I answered every one of his questions as truthfully and as honestly as I could. I shared what little I know about my life, and none of it helped explain the presence of the bloodied dress in the trunk of my car.

To make matters worse, I am convinced that Westfall suspects foul play, by my hand.

I can't blame him; it's a possibility I can't rule out myself.

Although I am the new custodian of his body and mind, the reality is that I know hardly anything about Jed Allen, the high-flying architect, the drug user, the womanizer. Everything I have seen so far points to him having a questionable moral code, and I have to accept that I have no perception of how deep his imperfections run.

The question is, is he capable of harming someone?

And more to the point, am *I*?

I look away from my reflection in the rearview mirror, sick to my stomach. Westfall has told me to remain available, reachable, while he looks into my situation—while forensics puts a rush on the bloodied dress—and I can't help feeling a little disconcerted with the thought of what he might uncover.

Even so, in the meantime, I need to be proactive. I need to keep searching for Cassie, to return to the house, to go through everything with a fine-tooth comb.

With my car out of service, the clerk at the reception desk has called a taxi for me, and while I wait for it to arrive, I make yet another startling discovery.

The opened envelopes in the glove compartment aren't junk mail, as I'd assumed. A few are final notices from utility companies, and one is a past-due letter on a mortgage made out in my name. But none have been sent to the lake house. Instead, they correspond with an address in the city, an apartment on the fifth floor of the Majestic on Central Park West.

It's the same building I visited yesterday to pick up the care package from Tess.

"Why is my mail going to *this* address?"

It's a puzzle, and at first I am confused. Then one damning conclusion comes to mind: I own the apartment, using it either as a means to save on travel time during the workweek, or for more clandestine purposes, such as a place in which to hide my transgressions from Cassie.

Either way, I need to find out.

Instead of returning to the house, I give the taxi driver the new address, and then I ride into the city with a cool hollowness growing in my belly, knowing that there is a greater chance of learning more about the real me from my Manhattan hideaway than from my picture-postcard life out in the suburbs.

Against the overcast sky, the double towers of the Majestic rise with cathedral grandeur.

"Good afternoon, Mr. Allen," a doorman says with a smile as I head inside.

The apartment is located halfway along a hallway on the fifth floor. I stop short at the door, lingering like a nervous youth on the threshold of picking up a girl for a first date. On either side, the hallway is deserted, quiet, and I wonder how many of my immediate neighbors know more about this place than I do.

The keycard from my wallet works the first time, the electronic lock disengaging with a clunk.

As I enter, I hear voices coming from within, and I holler, "Hello?"

But no one answers.

The apartment has a pigeon-gray décor with black floorboards throughout. Walls littered with the kind of random knickknacks picked up in home stores, to fool a visitor into thinking the owner has educated taste.

But it's all bland, cheap.

Following the sound of the voices, and hardly breathing, I move deeper inside, scanning the setup as I go.

The layout is similar to Tess's den of iniquity twenty floors above: a square foyer with two exits—one leading to a short hallway, a bedroom, a bathroom; the other opening out into a rectangular space split into a living room and a kitchenette. But there's only the functional furniture of a bachelor pad. And no impressive views of Central Park. The windows here face the building across the street. Brick and glass and prying eyes.

The voices are coming from a big TV screen mounted on the end wall. It's tuned to a local twenty-four-hour news channel, where a man and a woman are talking over footage of FBI agents in a wooded area, flashing police lights, and crime-scene techs in white coveralls. It's a scene similar to the aerial footage I saw on TV back at the office yesterday. A red-and-white caption reads CENTRAL PARK SLASHER, with a smaller banner scrolling underneath: MULTIPLE BODIES FOUND IN GRAVE AT KENSICO RESERVOIR.

I pick up the remote and turn the set off.

Stuck to the bottom of the TV screen is a yellow Post-it with the same amnesia warning I saw in the office and in my car. Underneath the TV is a table with a video game console and a rack of games next to it. The games appear to be of a similar theme: end-of-the-world-survival horror and zombie apocalypse. No design simulators and no city-building games, which I would have expected, given my profession.

Framed pictures line the side walls. A dozen in total, each depicting an iconic New York building or bridge in high-contrast black and white. Each taken at a trendy angle, using sun and shadow to define features. The only exception is the picture hung above the faux fireplace. It shows a great white shark leaping out of the sea, suspended in a cloud of water droplets, its terrible teeth bloody.

Unlike the kitchen at the lake house, this one is stocked with snacks, beers, and mostly microwavable meals-for-one. In the cupboards, breakfast cereals for sugar cravers. Peanut butter and jelly in the fridge. Overall, a sad impression of a solitary existence.

On the breakfast bar is a laptop, its screen blank. Another yellow Post-it is stuck next to the trackpad, bearing the now-familiar amnesia warning.

Curious, I press the power button, but nothing happens.

I make my way to the bedroom, wondering how many women have been here without Cassie's knowledge.

The answer is at least one; half the drawers in the dresser contain women's clothing, all in earthy tones and much less flashy than the neon in Cassie's wardrobe back at the lake house.

I feel around and under the garments, checking for hidden envelopes with photographs secreted away. But this search comes up empty-handed.

I tell myself to stop overthinking.

In the bathroom, a collection of designer toiletries is lined up on the vanity, with bottles of cologne pricier than Scotch. A group of feminine products is huddled in one corner, including a bag full of makeup with a color palette of bronzes and greens, nothing like the blue tones in Cassie's cosmetics.

It looks like I have a regular guest, and the discovery weighs heavily in my stomach.

"What kind of man are you?" I ask my reflection in the bathroom mirror.

My stranger's face scowls back, refusing to give anything away.

In the medicine cabinet are several pill bottles, each prescribed by Dr. Merrick, with dates spanning the previous six months.

A small walk-in closet lies beyond the bathroom, appointed with an assortment of men's designer clothes. Expensive garments hung in color coordination or folded in neat piles. Italian leather shoes that I can see my shadowy reflection in.

Right away, I can see from the labels that this darker side of me has a leaning toward luxury, with probably little consideration of price. Stylish shirts and thousand-dollar tailored suits.

There is nothing here like the off-the-rack clothes I found back at the lake house, and it occurs to me that I must lead two lives: a less gaudy one with Cassie out in the suburbs, in which I am a loyal partner, devoted and happy with my lot, and a much flashier one in the city, in which I am a well-heeled playboy, with dark desires and no moral fiber.

"But which life is the facade?"

Something on the floor at the back of the closet catches my eye, and I drop to my haunches for a closer look.

A corner of a piece of white card is jutting out of the baseboard, stark against the black floor tile. I tug at it, trying to work it free, but it seems to be stuck fast. Then I notice a hairline groove scratched into the corner floor tile, a curve extending out from the angle of the wall, invisible from even a few feet away.

Testing, I knock my knuckles against the drywall. It sounds hollow behind, but that's no surprise. What is surprising is that it gives a little under the pressure, as though it's loose.

I stand straight, examining it.

The wall is an eight-by-five panel, painted dark gray and otherwise featureless.

Experimentally, I run my fingers around its edges, pushing and gauging the bounce-back. And as I press a seam at the level of my waist, I hear a soft click. I push a little more to release it, and the whole wall angles away from the corner.

We all harbor secrets. We all keep things to ourselves. We've done it since we were children. Usually, it's stuff we're too embarrassed to admit, to share, to hear out loud, and we do it for any number of reasons: to protect ourselves from ridicule, to fit in with our peers, to survive. Sometimes, our secrets are of a nature we'd rather no one else knew about, because it would change their opinions of us for the worse forever. These kinds of secrets exist in dark places.

And it's dark behind the false wall.

With a careful hand, I reach inside, feeling for a light switch. My fingers locate a dangling cord, and as I pull it, a solitary bulb banishes the dark, but not the darkness.

The hidden space at the end of the closet is a few feet deep and as big as the secret door. The same size as a personal elevator. But this is no such thing.

There are several parallel shelves on the side walls, with seemingly random small objects on their surfaces, but it's the rear wall that draws the eye. It's covered in photographs. At least a hundred pictures in various print sizes, forming a colorful mosaic.

Cassie is the focus of each photo.

At first, the word *shrine* comes to mind. But this is no place of worship. And as I begin to comprehend the true nature of what it is I am looking at, my lungs begin to burn.

I am about to take a closer look, when I hear a woman's voice calling my name, and I turn, the fire expanding up my throat, as I realize someone has entered the apartment.

Mind whirling, I close the concealed door with a snap. Then I suck in a deep breath to cool the flames in my chest, and venture out into the hallway.

A woman is slipping out of her coat and closing the apartment door behind her. She's a small redhead in a green skirt suit, her long hair pulled into a ponytail. She has milky skin and a hint of freckles. She seems to be my age or maybe a little older.

"Thank goodness you're here," she says, breaking into a smile. "I've been trying to reach you for hours. Is your phone off?"

"I . . . I don't think so." With fumbling fingers, I take it out to confirm. It's still on silent. I increase the volume, offering her an apologetic smile and hoping she doesn't notice the heat in my face.

"No wonder you're unreachable," she says, coming toward me. And before I can say anything, she kisses me on the lips.

Her touch is warm and full, and it would be easy to be seduced by it, find comfort, and lose myself in it. But I pull back instead, startled by the bold physical contact. I push her to arm's length, saying, "Stop. Please."

My heart is beating much too fast—for the wrong reason, it seems. Unquestionably, she is pretty, and there is something attractive about her, but I can't continue to cheat on Cassie.

"It hasn't come back, has it?" she says, her expression circulating through confusion to comprehension.

"If by that you mean my memory, no, it hasn't."

"Awkward." She takes a step back. "This is embarrassing. Dang it, Jed. I was hoping it would have by now. As you can see, I assumed it had." She looks me over with concerned eyes. "You have no idea who I am, do you?"

"You're Dr. Merrick. I recognize your voice."

Her smile returns, although this time it's a little less radiant. "Please don't look so terrified. I said I'd come over."

"You just took me by surprise is all." I put my back to the short hallway leading to the bedroom and the stash of photographs.

"If it's any consolation," she says, hanging her coat on a peg behind the door, "I'm surprised, too. This is a first for both of us. None of your recall crashes has lasted this long before. I know it's weird for you. But trust me, it's weird for me, too." She motions to the living room. "Can we sit down and I'll explain everything?"

"Lead the way."

We sit on opposite armchairs, facing each other, a black ash coffee table and a tangible tension between us. Dr. Merrick perches on the edge of her seat, elbows on knees, her hands keeping each other company, while I sit back, arms folded, trying to figure her out, trying to figure *me* out.

"So . . . you're Dr. Merrick."

"Please, call me Sarah."

"Is that how you greet all your patients, Sarah? Intimately?"

"I think there are some who would like me to." Her smile makes a brief appearance, but it's shaky. "However, let me be clear, before you go jumping to any conclusions here. Please remember you're not in possession of all the facts right now."

"There's only one thing I need to know. Are we having an affair?"

It's the obvious question, given her overfamiliar greeting. But I have to ask it.

"Let's not focus on that right now."

"Just tell me the truth. I need to know. Are we having an affair?"

"No, Jed, we're not having an affair."

I let out a nervous breath. "I don't understand. The kiss . . . ?"

"It's not what you think. Jed, our relationship is more permanent than an affair. We've been seeing each other for several months."

"In secret?"

"No!" She snickers, but it's fractured with unease. "Why would we?"

"For starters, because you're my doctor, which I'm pretty sure makes it unethical, no matter how you slice it."

Furrows appear on her forehead, and it's clear this situation is as uncomfortable for her as it is for me.

"Well?" I ask.

"I don't think love can ever be considered unethical," she says.

Her word choice raises my eyebrows. "So now you're saying we're in love?"

"Yes."

"That's ridiculous!"

"Why? Because you don't remember?"

"No, because I think I'd *feel* something."

If my outburst offends her, she doesn't show it. "Jed, let's look at the reality here. You can't even remember your middle name."

I stare at her from under a heavy brow, unable to admit she's right.

"You don't have one," she says at last. "A middle name. And that's my point. When you're in this state, nothing makes sense. Up is down, and down is up. You're like a fish out of water, breathing air for the first time. Everything is an assault on your senses."

"I think some part of me would remember if we were in love."

"Unfortunately, that's not how this works. Historical feelings attach themselves to memories. Until your recall crash subsides, you won't remember how you feel about me, or the fact you've declared undying love at least a dozen times."

I stare at her like a man learning for the first time that the Earth, which he thought was a globe, is actually flat.

"Look, Jed," she says, "I'm sorry to be so blunt. I know it's a lot to take in right now. To you, it's like you've woken up in a stranger's body, and understanding his life is a matter of survival. But you need to trust me that I'm telling you the truth. And I can't deny what we have. I wouldn't lie to you about something as important as that. We are in love. And for the record, I stopped being your doctor the day you discharged yourself from rehab."

Now I sit up straighter. "Wait a minute. Rewind. I thought you said I was part of some grand case study of yours."

"You are."

"And I know you prescribed my meds."

"Yes."

"But now you're claiming you're not my doctor."

"Not in so many words."

"So which is it, Sarah? You can't have it both ways."

"The truth is, it's complex."

"Well, it seems simple to me. It's a conflict of interest. That's what this is. I'm part of this case study you're conducting. And you write my scripts. Technically, that makes you my doctor. There is no way we should be romantically involved."

She sighs, and suddenly it's obvious to me that she has taken a ride on this runaway train each time my amnesia persisted long enough for us to end up at this spot.

"Jed, listen to me. Not everything here is black and white. The case study is real, but it's also unofficial. I'm conducting it in private, for a paper I'm writing. I guess you could make a case for inappropriate behavior right at the start of our relationship if you really wanted to. But it would be a pretty tenuous one. It's not even a case of poor judgment on my part. You were discharged weeks before you asked me out on a date. That was spring, and we've been seeing each other regularly since."

Every instinct in me tells me I should pick up what little there is left of my honor and run. Run the way I ran from Song. Swear an oath to eternal monogamy and spend the rest of my days making amends to Cassie. But I am rooted to the spot, suddenly uncertain about everything I think I know about my previous life.

"Yours are the clothes in the dresser," I say, realizing it as the sentence takes shape. "The makeup in the bathroom, the perfume. It's all yours."

"Yes."

"That's how you know about this apartment. That's why you have a key. You sleep over."

She nods. "Most weekends. Occasionally, you stay at my place. And as bizarre as it sounds to you right now, you've even asked me to move in."

All at once, something unholy is swirling around in my belly, and I feel like I should go to the bathroom and retch it up. All I can think about is that while Cassie is away on assignment, or believing I'm working late at the office, I fool around with my neuropsychologist, here in my Manhattan hideaway.

"I'm seeing someone else," I say, the words bursting out, too quick to stop. "Sarah, I have to be straight with you. I live with her. Somewhere other than here. As far as I know, we've been together all year. You and me, we're not real. I'm sorry."

I expect Dr. Merrick's taut expression to snap under the pressure of my declaration, but she just looks at me, seemingly unfazed.

"Jed, it's okay. I know about Cassie."

My heart judders, my thoughts sliding over each other, tumbling. "If you know about her, how could you do this?"

"Because Cassie isn't my competition, Jed. She's your crutch. Your mind's way of coping with trauma. Right now, it may not seem like it, but it's your relationship with *her* that isn't real. It's a figment of your imagination."

"What?" Now it's my turn to frown, as my uncertainty balloons into doubt.

It's a fact that my one-day-old belief system is built on scraps of information glued together with assumption, and it's easy to tear it down, but if what Dr. Merrick says is true, not only does it pull the rug out from under my feet where Cassie is concerned, it leaves me second-guessing everything I have learned so far.

And I don't think I'm comfortable with the idea of rebuilding my belief system all over again from the ground up so soon. Not without concrete proof.

I take a moment to assess, to get my cascading thoughts in line. I have to remind myself that it's Dr. Merrick's word against my own experience, and that I can't simply take her claim at face value, without corroboration. After all, I know Cassie is real. I've been at our home, smelled her sweet perfume on her clothes. I know the two of us are together in some sort of permanency. And I'm not sure what Dr. Merrick has to gain from trying to convince me otherwise.

I take out my wallet and hold up the picture of Cassie and me taken at the bar. "Cassie is real," I say. "This is us from last Christmas. Before you said I had my accident. Before you and I ever met. It proves I'm not making this up."

"I thought you'd thrown that away."

I flounder at her response. "You know about this? But you just said Cassie isn't real."

"No, Jed, I said your *relationship* with her is artificial." She sees the confusion wrinkling up my face, and adds, "Look, I know this is traumatic for you. I know it's a lot to process right now, to come to terms with. But I did say right at the start that you're not in full possession of the facts." She leans over, her fingers plucking the photo from my hand. "You're right. This was taken at Christmas. But it's the only one you have of her."

I'm about to tell her about the photographs of Cassie in my closet—the stalker's trophy wall, where each picture has been taken from a distance and probably without Cassie's knowledge, but I can't find the words that will exonerate such depravity.

I'm not ready to share something like that, even in confidence to my doctor.

Dr. Merrick places the photo on the table between us. "Go ahead, Jed. Check your phone, if you don't believe me. See what you find. These days, most happy couples take billions of selfies."

"I don't know the passcode."

"It's an uppercase 'S.' For 'Sarah.'"

Skeptical, I swipe the shape of the letter across the pattern of nine dots, but the screen remains locked.

"Turn the phone on its side," Dr. Merrick says. "And try it again."

I do, and the screen instantly brightens, allowing access.

"See, Jed. You can trust me."

There are at least fifty recent missed calls and text messages, the majority from Gary. I pass them by, navigating straight to the photo album, which seems to be bursting with images.

The last picture taken is of Song Chang, in profile, gazing impassively into her drink at Rafferty's, completely unaware that I am capturing her likeness. I don't know what it is about Song Chang—whether I am fascinated by the Far Eastern exotic or simply spellbound by her beauty. But there is a definite attraction.

Next is a group of shots of the party itself. Blurry images of body parts and fuzzy close-ups. Topless dancers and lines of coke. Several of Gary and Director Chang in focus, laughing like best buddies, their nostrils flared. Some of Chang snorting coke off the bare breast of a dancer, one hand high up her inner thigh.

Disgusted, I swipe them aside, skipping through random shots of buildings and bridges and other New York landmarks, before coming to the first of dozens of selfies, and it's difficult to prevent my jaw from dropping.

By and large, they depict Dr. Merrick and me, grinning manically at the camera and making clownish faces, arms wrapped around each other, looking for all intents and purposes like a happy couple.

I sense Dr. Merrick's gaze drilling into my head, and I keep skimming, faster and faster, hoping to find a picture of Cassie, to prove our relationship is real. But the only woman in any of the images is Dr. Merrick, taken at various touristy locations in the city, at Central Park in the summertime, cooking dinner in this apartment, riding a roller coaster at Coney Island, at the beach in the sunshine, the two of us eating ice-cream cones and looking deliriously happy.

There's not a single picture of Cassie anywhere, and once again I am faced with the depth of my infidelity.

"For the record," she says as I close my gaping mouth, "I have just as many photos of us on my phone."

"This only proves I'm leading two lives, and that I've kept them both apart."

"No, Jed, it proves there's something real between us. And that's why this is so difficult, for both of us."

I sense her internal struggle, her pain, but it fails to move me. Amnesia hasn't just severed my emotional connections, it seems; it's inhibiting my capacity to make new ones. Even if what she is saying is true, it will take time to process, to accept. I'm not sure my head is in the right place for either right now.

Would she revise her opinion if she saw the lake house with the personal possessions and the master bed? Or would it just expose the degree to which I have flitted between two loves, with no respect for either?

"This is crazy," I say. "*Ours* is the affair. I'm with Cassie. I *know* I'm with Cassie."

"You only know what your amnesia is allowing you to know." Dr. Merrick points at the photo on the table. "This time, when you were with Cassie, that was real. But it was over long before I came along. The recall crash is the problem here, Jed. It's interfering with your ability to separate fact from fiction. It's this mismatch that we've been working on. You're with me now, and what we have together is real."

Have I made a huge error in judgment by telling her I'm still with Cassie?

The look in her eyes tells me I ought to feel something for Dr. Merrick other than suspicion, but I don't. Feelings can't be manufactured on request. Still, it doesn't mean I felt nothing for her before yesterday.

"We've been using hypnotherapy techniques," she says, "to understand why you become fixated on Cassie each time you have a recall crash. We've made a bit of progress, but we're still a ways off from reaching our goal. I'd like to try it now, if you're up for it. See if we can revive your memories."

"By hypnotizing me?"

"Consider it a cognitive massage. It's designed to stimulate the synapses and get the neurons firing. It's worked before."

"I got my memories back?"

"Yes."

I look at her, chewing over her proposal. "Give me a moment."

Then I flop back in the chair, rubbing at my face and running my fingers through my hair, as though the friction will loosen the mask of denial fixed to my face.

I know my emotional reactions are all instinctive right now. I know I should be less resistant to those who know me and my history better than I do. I know I should be more open to accepting the person I am. But I can't help it. My mind is a mess, and logic is the luxury of a fully functioning brain. I know I don't hold all the answers. I know I can't trust my reactions. But in the vacuum of my mind, my instincts have rushed in and taken control, preventing me from behaving and thinking normally.

She must know this.

As it stands, the notion that I have been juggling two lives, two loves, is incredible. How have I managed to keep the two perfectly separated, one with Cassie in Eastchester and another here in Manhattan with Dr. Merrick? Do I have another phone somewhere, filled with pictures of Cassie?

Not such a perfect setup, I realize. Dr. Merrick is aware of Cassie. But without asking the question, I don't know how she came to know about her. To Dr. Merrick, it's possible Cassie is just a name, a past relationship, and a single photograph. Like she says, no threat. Maybe the other, less noble version of me convinced her that Cassie was in my past. Why he would do so, I don't know; I can play only with the hand I am dealt. The question that worries me now is, does Cassie know about Dr. Merrick?

Amnesia has me at a distinct disadvantage. Even though I am distancing myself from the other version of me with every step I take, I can't ignore the fact that his actions, his desires, have put me here. Perhaps I need to learn to walk before I run.

I let out a shaky breath. "Okay. So how does this work?"

"You close your eyes. Relax. Listen to my voice and let your mind wander."

"What happens if nothing happens?"

"Then we try something else. Or we sit it out. Sooner or later, your memory always comes back."

"Okay. I'm trusting you here, Sarah."

"You always do. Now close your eyes and relax."

I do, letting the armchair take the weight of my head. Dr. Merrick starts to speak, her voice soft, her tone lilting, and I let her words wash over me, convinced I am one of those people who can't be hypnotized. Instead, I think about the skeleton I have in my closet—the pictures of Cassie, each one probably taken without her consent—wondering how many of them were shot before we first met, and why.

One thing I know for certain is that amnesia is changing me, in the way that immovable obstacles alter a river's course. With each new turn I make, more silt is washed away, exposing the man I am, or was.

Dr. Merrick's voice grows distant, softer, like the roll of faraway waves breaking on a beach.

I picture myself sitting on warm sand with Cassie, the two of us wiggling our toes in the surf while the bloodshot sun bleeds into the ocean.

The sensory contrast of water and fire.

Sitting here with my eyes closed is conducive to sleep, and I'm happy to let my thoughts drift. As they do, I sense a fuzzy warmth pulling at the edges of my consciousness, and at first I put up a feeble resistance, but as the darkness descends, I let it sweep me up and carry me away.

It seems only a moment later that a blinding light breaks through the dark. And I open my eyes, blinking at the glare.

For a moment, I am disoriented, my surroundings tipping up and down, overlapping.

From somewhere within the brilliance, I hear a man's voice saying, "He's coming to. I think he's okay," and then a woman's voice saying, "Give him some room. Don't crowd him."

It takes a few seconds more for my eyes to adjust, for the searing light to diminish to a level where recognizable forms and colors take shape.

I am sprawled on the floor, on my back, with a half dozen concerned-looking strangers towering over me.

Exactly where I am, I have no idea.

This isn't my Manhattan hideaway, and Dr. Merrick is nowhere to be seen.

"Welcome back to the land of the living," says a man in a blue security guard's uniform. "You had us worried there for a second or two."

I try to get up. But everything tilts precariously, and nausea swells in my stomach.

"Take it easy," says a woman's voice, which I recognize as Cassie's.

She's behind me, out of my line of sight. I twist my neck, and she comes into view. "Hey."

She smiles, but there's an element of curiosity in it.

The security guard tells the onlookers that the show is over, that they should move on, and the crowd disperses. Then he hooks his big hands under my arms and hoists me up. "C'mon, buddy. Let's see if you can sit."

With his help, I am propped up against an aluminum bench seat. My eyesight is still a little blurry, like I'm wearing the wrong prescription glasses.

"You took a nasty fall there," he tells me. "I swear you hit the canvas like Mike Tyson against Buster Douglas."

Now that he points it out, the back of my head is a ball of pain. I touch it and wince, but thankfully my fingers don't come away with blood on them.

I turn my gaze to Cassie again.

She is crouched next to me, a worried look in her eyes and cute lines on her brow. "Sure you're okay?" she asks.

"I'll live. What happened?"

"As slapstick as it sounds, you fell backwards over this bench. I think you were trying to get the perfect perspective of one of my more challenging pieces."

I blink and look around us.

We are in a large white-painted space with big lamps suspended on chains from a vaulted ceiling. People are milling around; most are admiring the large black-framed photographs hanging on the walls, but one or two are looking our way.

"I call it *Full Tilt*," Cassie says.

I look back at her. "Excuse me?"

She points to a large black-and-white photograph on the wall behind us. "The picture that sent you tumbling."

It's the image of a great white shark bursting out of the water, its lips peeled back and its killer teeth gnashing. The canvas is square and at least eight feet along each edge, with the only splash of color being the terrible red of the shark's open mouth. But it's not the beastly composition that sends the senses askew. It's the fact that the picture has been rotated so that the shark appears to be falling out of a stormy sky, with that bloody maw coming straight for the observer.

"Must have been some fishing trip," I comment with genuine admiration. "I hope you got danger pay."

I put my elbows on the bench and try to lever myself up. The room has stopped swaying, but I haven't, and I drop back down to the floor with a thud.

"Give it a minute," the security guard says. "With a blow like that, you're probably concussed."

Again, I touch the back of my skull, this time feeling a soft lump, just above a harder ridge.

Cassie places a hand on my arm. "He's right. Stay still. There's no rush." She smiles. "You know, I aim to knock people out with my pictures, but this is the first time anyone has actually gone down for the count."

Her smile broadens, and I can't help myself from smiling along with her. Even on the gloomiest day, Cassie is a ray of sunshine.

"So how about I buy you a drink?" she says, squeezing my arm. "Of course, not right this second. Later. When the gallery closes and you're not in a daze. Consider it my way of saying sorry."

"You don't have to."

"I know, but I want to. I'm stuck in the city tonight—you'll be doing me a favor. Besides, it's the least I can do. You never know, I might talk you into buying one of my pictures."

With the security guard's assistance, I get to my feet.

"Feel okay?" he asks.

I start to speak, then clamp my mouth shut as the room falls into a crazy spin. It's like I'm on a carousel, everything blurring. My balance goes, and I close my eyes, feeling the floor drop from under my feet.

◆ ◆ ◆

"Jed? Jed, wake up."

I open my eyes and blink at Dr. Merrick. I am back in my apartment, slouched in a chair, with a cool sweat on my brow and pain thumping in my head.

"You fell asleep," she says.

"Figures. I'm tired."

"I'm guessing it didn't work?"

I shake my head, wincing.

"We can try again, after you take your medication."

"No." I push myself up. "What I need is some time to wrap my head around things. Like you say, it's a lot to process."

"You'd prefer I left you alone?" She looks disappointed, hurt.

I can't deny that Dr. Merrick and I have been seeing each other. The photos of us together are proof positive. But at the same time, I can't deny the fact that since finding her picture in my wallet, my untethered emotions have locked onto Cassie, overshadowing any feelings I might have for Dr. Merrick.

Without adding to her hurt, how do I tell Dr. Merrick that now, more than ever, I need to find Cassie, to prove to myself that I'm not imagining her?

My phone rings, saving me from making a decision.

"Thank God," Gary's voice says in my ear as I answer the call. "I've been trying to get ahold of you all day." His tone is still hushed, barely a few decibels above a whisper, but there's an unmistakable reediness of panic cutting through it. "It's the end of the world."

"What happened?"

"It's critical," he says. "Reset your doomsday clock, Jed. It's two minutes to midnight, and the world as you know it is about to go up in a puff of smoke."

I roll my eyes at Dr. Merrick. "Gary, just take a breath and tell me what's up, preferably in English."

"All hell's broken loose. You need to get over here before everything implodes."

"Where?"

"Saint Luke's."

"The church?"

"No, Jed. The hospital. Mount Sinai. I don't know how much longer I can contain things. I'm at the ER, basically holding a grenade with the pin pulled. You need to fix this ASAP."

I attempt to ask him what could possibly have happened to make him sound like he's been accused of murder, but he hangs up.

"Go fix whatever it is you need to fix," Dr. Merrick says. "I'll be right here when you're done. We'll finish this later."

Chapter Seventeen

The first thing I do when I leave the apartment is call Cassie, in the hope that her phone is now switched on, but all I hear is the same out-of-service tone.

It's late afternoon—a full day since being reborn—and I'm beginning to see my life before yesterday as a jigsaw puzzle. So far, I've been able to put part of it together. The darker edges. But not everything connects. The bigger picture has gaping holes in it. Crucial elements remain out of my reach. My gut tells me that Cassie holds the missing piece, and my desire to speak with her is now stronger than ever.

"Saint Luke's hospital," I tell the taxi driver outside the Majestic, and we edge into traffic.

Dr. Merrick's claim that ours is my primary relationship is understandable, given her perspective. As far as she is concerned, we're together, period, and Cassie has been demoted to a love interest from my past. A bit player in the movie of my life.

Somehow, devilish though it is, I have lived a dual existence since the accident, moving like a wraith between two worlds, to the extent that I have convinced Dr. Merrick that my relationship with Cassie ended before ours began. She has no idea that I'm spending time with

Cassie when I'm not with her, and that, because Cassie came first, it is Dr. Merrick and I who are having the affair.

Every way I look at it, my life is a mess.

It would be easy to lay this all at the door of the man I was before yesterday, to blame him for putting me in this fix, to wash my hands of all culpability. It would be easy to blame my intermittent amnesia for causing my present conflicts, to use it as a reason to excuse my bad behavior. But the truth is, I can't live with his lies, *my* lies. Even though I don't share his memories, I do share the consequences of his actions, and for as long as I remain this new version of me, I have to be honest with myself.

Other than confessing my sins to Cassie, I don't know where else to start.

I need to do everything in my power to put things right, now, while I still possess the capacity to be objective about my corrupted morals. Because once my memories return to swallow me up, the other version of me will take over, rubbing me out and erasing everything I have learned and changed.

For almost forty years, he's had the upper hand, been in control, called all the shots, as bad as they are. In comparison, my own reincarnated existence is a fleck of time, barely worth mentioning, a flea on the back of an elephant.

How do I go about making a permanent difference when I have no idea how long I will persist?

Can I prevent the other version of me from regaining his life and blotting me out?

The thought makes my stomach churn.

I take the pill bottle out of my pocket, wondering what would happen if I just stopped taking the meds.

The taxi brings me to the emergency room, and I find Gary pacing like an expectant father at the back of the waiting area. When he sees me approaching, he storms over, whispering fiercely:

"Damn it, Jed. This is absolutely the last thing we needed. You know what this means to us. It's the difference between basement and penthouse."

He stares at me with bloodshot eyes, as though I know exactly how to decipher his bad analogy. This close, it's clear he hasn't shaved, and there's a distinct odor that is more than everyday sweat. In fact, now that I think about it, he's still wearing the same clothes he partied in last night, and he looks disheveled, as though he slept in them.

"Where the hell have you been all day?" he demands before I can ask him what's going on.

"I've been busy. Something came up. Cassie's missing."

He frowns. "Cassie? What the—"

"Look, Gary, I've had a lot on my mind, okay? My memory still hasn't come back. I didn't know you were down here."

"Otherwise, what? You would've answered my fifty-nine calls sooner? Don't give me your juvenile excuses, buddy. You should've picked up. We're a partnership. You do remember that tiny little humongous detail, don't you?" He wags a finger between us. "This is something we don't do. We don't ignore each other in our hour of need. That's not how this thing works." The finger prods my chest, pushes. "This is all your fault. You need to get out in front of it before the whole thing burns down."

Even though Gary's voice isn't booming, heads have begun to turn our way.

We are two grown men locking antlers in a sensitive place, and we're beginning to attract the wrong kind of attention.

I smile shakily at a passing orderly, but it doesn't lift his frown or stop him from reaching for his walkie-talkie.

"Gary, listen to me. You need to calm down, or they'll throw us both out. Did something happen at the party after I left? Did one of our guests overdose? I'll try and fix whatever it is that needs fixing. But first you need to tell me why you've dragged me down here."

With a franticness that seems completely opposite to what I suspect is his usual collected self, Gary glances around with strained eyes, a visible tremor on his lips and beads of sweat popping out on his brow. He has every bit the look of a man who is facing a life sentence for a crime he didn't commit.

"Your great and wonderful master plan backfired," he says as his gaze rolls to mine.

"I have no idea what you're talking about."

"We're screwed. Totaled. All those months of planning. All the investment. The time, the money, the heartache. It's all been flushed down the toilet."

A vein throbs on his neck, and I'm worried he's going to have a full-blown panic attack, or something much worse.

Again, he looks around us, his nervous gaze jumping from one onlooker to the next. "It's bad, Jed. Worse than that, it's critical. Our deal, it's screwed. *We're* screwed. There's no coming back from this."

I take him by the shoulders, forcing him to look me in the eyes. "Gary, just take a breath and tell me, did something happen to Chang?"

"No," he says, his shoulders trembling under my hands. "It's the daughter."

"Song?" Dread blossoms in my chest.

"She's in a coma."

"What?"

"I know. It's the worst thing imaginable. Chang's going to pull out. Our deal's dead in the water. And it's all because of you." He throws off my grip, his stance switching from frightened to angry. Then he backs away a little, shaking an accusing finger at me. "That's right, buddy. She's at death's door, and she probably isn't going to make it. And you're to blame. You killed her."

I am horrified, and it burns yet another hole in my gut.

All around us, the busy waiting area has come to a standstill, and there's a marked drop in the volume of chatter. All eyes are on us, all ears tuned our way.

"You're making a scene." I try to take Gary by the elbow, to lead him aside before somebody raises the alarm, but he pulls out of my reach.

"Get your hands off me. You've ruined everything."

"I don't understand."

"Do I have to spell it out?"

He unbuttons his blazer and holds it wide open for all the world to see.

I hear someone gasp.

Gary's formerly white shirt is caked in dried blood. It's like he's wearing a red bib.

"This isn't mine," he says. "It's hers. She was attacked. If you'd answered even one of my calls, you would've known this by now. Instead, you left me here all day, on my own, with my finger in the dike and my thumb up my ass."

"Song was attacked?" All at once, my throat is tight with anguish, my heart banging wildly behind my ribs. "That's crazy. How? Who by?"

"The police think it was the Central Park Slasher."

"The . . . what?"

"The Central Park Slasher."

"Yes, I heard what you said, and so did everybody else in here. I just don't understand."

"That's because you're still stuck in that blank spell of yours. Snap out of it, will you? The Central Park Slasher has been terrorizing the city for ages. You knew this already."

"And you're saying he attacked Song?"

"Not me. *Eyewitness News.*" He nods over his shoulder to a man and woman standing outside the doorway to the ER. She is on her cell and animated, while her colleague is adjusting a professional video camera. "Chang's a respected foreign businessman, and the press are milking it."

My mind is whirling, trying to make sense of what I'm hearing. "But the last time I saw her, she was at the club."

"She left after you did."

"What?"

"She left, shortly after you stormed out of there without even saying good-bye. We all saw you leave, buddy. Chang's daughter followed you about a minute later. It was intense. What happened in the bathroom?"

"The bathroom?"

"Between the two of you. I saw your face when you came out. You looked mad about something, furious. Then she followed you, clearly upset. Chang tried comforting her, but she wouldn't listen. She picked up her stuff and left."

"Song was attacked?" I'm still struggling to process the information and hitting a brick wall. "Where? It was like a circus on the streets last night."

"Where do you think? Central Park. That's where he hunts. She was in the bushes, covered in knife wounds and bleeding out."

I can't stop staring at his bloodied shirt, and now it's his turn to take me by the shoulders, redirecting my gaze back to his.

"Listen to me, Jed. I'm your best friend in the whole wide world. You're like a brother to me. With that expression on your face, last night when you abandoned the party, I was worried about you. I had to go after you. I've never seen that look in your eyes before. You scared me, buddy."

"*You* found Song?"

"Chang was concerned. We all were. I told him I'd find out what the hell was going on. The last thing any of us needed was a lovers' spat jeopardizing our deal. It was a miracle I came across her when I did or she'd be dead by now."

Again, I glance at our audience, knowing that at least a dozen strangers are listening in on what should be a private conversation.

"I'm telling you, Jed. It was awful. I've never seen anything like it. There was blood everywhere. I tried to stop the bleeding, but there was just too much of it. I did my best. The paramedics say I saved her life."

I feel his hands shake, and he removes them from my shoulders. My heart is thudding, my breath fiery. "Where is she?"

"In the ICU. Chang's in there with her. They've had her in and out of surgery all day. But forget it. They won't let you see her."

"I have to try." I turn in the direction of the reception counter.

"There's something else," Gary says, halting me. "The police want to speak with everybody involved."

"I'm not surprised."

"Not just about the attack." He moves into my personal space so that his face is only a few inches from mine. "The doctors ran routine tests. Par for the course. They checked her blood. Which means the police know about the drugs."

"So? It's that kind of town."

"So they know you supplied them, buddy. And the police want to speak with you about it."

More heat plumes in my chest. "You've got to be kidding me? Who told them?"

"I don't know. Probably one of Chang's aides. Your guess is as good as mine. The point is, they know, and they're not happy."

"Okay. I'll speak with Chang."

"Good luck with that. As you can see, I've been here all night, and I still haven't been granted an audience. I haven't been standing here covered in her blood and missing out on my beauty sleep for no reason, Jed. Anytime, I could've gone home. Got myself cleaned up, got some shut-eye. But I stuck it out, for the sake of the firm, for us."

"You haven't spoken with Chang?"

"His sidekicks blocked every one of my attempts. I'm not sure if they used jujitsu or Jedi mind tricks. But if you do succeed where I failed, please check if our deal is anywhere close to being salvageable."

"What do you mean?"

"One of his aides said the deal was on hold."

"It's understandable, Gary. Look where we are and think why we're here."

"All the same, I have this sinking feeling that if she dies, they'll renege. And we can't afford to let that happen. You need to do whatever it takes to keep this deal alive. I'm counting on you."

I give Gary a startled look, but it's lost on him. Song Chang has one foot in the grave, and Gary's top priority is our precious design deal. Surely, even we aren't this cutthroat?

"Leave it to me."

"Thanks, buddy."

Bit by bit, I'm beginning to understand the nature of the man I am, or at least the man I was before yesterday. The cheater, the liar, the philanderer, the man who will do whatever it takes to secure a deal, his whole lifestyle shaped by selfishness and recklessness.

But I'm in charge now, and I know that knowing your enemy is the first step to defeating him. Inside me, I have the power to change who I was, to remodel myself into a better human being, and it's becoming ever more apparent that it would be a blessing if I never got my memories back.

The thought is like a lightning bolt in my brain.

I leave Gary to his hand-wringing and head into the emergency room, drumming up the courage to face the music as I go.

I don't need to be a psychic to predict the kind of greeting I'm in for. Chang's daughter has been attacked viciously. She's a heartbeat from death, in a foreign country. Like any father, he will be at his wits' end with worry, fraught with fear for her welfare. Our precious deal will be the last thing on his mind.

In such circumstances, people feel the need to attach blame. I was the one who supplied the drugs. I was the one Song chased after, late at night, in an unfamiliar city. If it wasn't for me, she wouldn't be here in the hospital. And Chang knows this.

In a roundabout way, this is all my fault.

An attendant directs me to a private room in the ICU, where I find two of Chang's aides guarding the closed door, both of them deep in separate and heated conversations on their cell phones. When they see my advance, they put aside their conversations and intercept, ranting in Chinese and gesturing at me to back off.

I don't need to understand their native tongue to know what they're saying; their body language is at full volume.

"I need to speak with Director Chang."

I try to sidestep them, but they block me, hissing and snarling.

"I'm serious. Don't try and stop me."

I attempt to push my way between them. The bigger of the pair grabs me by the wrist, wrenching my arm up my back and pressing me face-first against the wall. The position is more embarrassing than painful.

"Your presence is not welcome." His words are a fierce hiss in my ear. "Go home."

"Tell your boss I'm here, and that I need to speak with him right away. Tell him it's of the upmost importance. Let him decide."

The aide leans in, forcing my arm higher up my back and grinding my cheekbone against the plaster. I hear a door open and the sound of a verbal exchange in Mandarin, then the aide swings me around and pushes me through the doorway.

The room is quiet, the lighting turned respectfully low.

Eyes shut, Song Chang is lying on her back in a hospital bed, a crisp white sheet covering the wounds that bled all over Gary. Her skin is bloodless, almost translucent, as though she is fading.

A heartbeat—the difference between this world and the next.

A plastic tube connects her mouth to a ventilator. Monitors softly bleep as colorful fluctuations flow by. Everything seems calm and peaceful, with no indication that she has endured a traumatic knife attack.

Director Chang is stooped at his daughter's bedside, cupping her limp hand in his, a sense of funereal stillness settled over him. Like

Gary, he is wearing last night's party clothes. But that's where the similarity ends. Unlike Gary, Chang doesn't look disheveled in any way. No crumpled shirt, no messy hair, no sweat-lacquered skin, and no terrible bloodstains. His composure is altogether immaculate, admirable, and yet somehow robotic and cold.

A controlled explosion, detonating on the inside.

In his dark-blue suit and with his head bowed, he could be a mourner at a graveside, or the incarnation of Death reaping Song's soul.

Without looking up from his comatose daughter, Chang asks, "Why?"

It's a small word of an incomparable magnitude.

And I have no starting point from which to address it.

Unsurprisingly, there is no mention of our deal, and I have no right expecting there to be. Unlike Gary, Chang's entire focus is on Song. She is his top priority, always was. Right now, the reason they came to New York means less than nothing to him. All that matters is the life of his child. This is what happens when a loved one is gravely ill: for those who care, everything else pales into insignificance.

For a moment, there is an uncomfortable silence between us, a bottomless gulf that neither of us wants to cross, and I feel like an intruder. For long seconds, we stand like statues, while the soft bleeps of the monitors mark the passage of time.

The sight of Chang staring inanimately at his stricken daughter stirs hot guilt in my gut. And I am struck suddenly and harshly with the emotional blow that I know absolutely nothing about my own parents, whether they are alive or dead, or even if I have any siblings.

When it comes to relationships, it's not enough to drift from one to the other. Every boat needs an anchor.

If my amnesia sticks around, learning about my family is something I need to put time into.

I take a hesitant step forward. "Director, please forgive me. If I'd known, I would have been here sooner."

He holds up a hand, an instruction for me to keep my distance.

I look at Song, at her porcelain face, feeling my stomach knot.

Right or wrong, it bothers me that I am unable to recall my interactions with Song in Shanghai. However immoral they might have been at the time, I can't deny there must have been something between us during my trip overseas. Something not all bad. Something that caused her to think that we would continue where we'd left off, here in the States.

And that's why she chased after me.

"Why did she follow you?" Chang says, as if reading my thoughts.

"I don't know." Another lie. "I didn't even know she had until Gary told me about it a couple of minutes ago. I thought she stayed at the club."

"You were arguing, in the bathroom."

"No."

"This is not my impression."

"Director, let me assure you, we weren't arguing. I respect Song. It was a misunderstanding, that's all. Something and nothing."

"And yet, enough for this to happen." He lays out a hand, palm up, mimicking Song's motionless position.

In a circuitous way, he's right, and I can't defend it.

I played my part in putting her here. She probably knew nothing about my personal situation back home, of my relationship with Cassie, and even though I had good reason to flee the nightclub, it doesn't make me any less of a scoundrel.

Every way I look at it, Song is here because of me.

In spite of his wish, I take another hesitant step closer. "Director, please believe me when I say this: I had no idea Song would be in danger. I'm as shocked as you. If I knew this would happen, I would never have left the club."

"Why did you?"

I almost tell him the truth. "I was having a bad day, and it was all too much. I felt sick. I needed some fresh air. I didn't intend any disrespect by leaving early."

"And yet you are here, at my child's deathbed, to remind me of our deal."

He swings his heavy gaze on me, and the weight of it presses down.

Chang makes it sound cut-and-dried, and perhaps it is. If Gary had his way, he'd have me sell my soul to save our deal. And that's probably what would have gone down here if this had happened before yesterday, when I was my other self. Even so, I'm not sure how much of a soul I have left to barter with, or if it's even worth saving.

"I won't lie to you," I say. "Of course, we're worried Xian Airlines will pull out. This is a big deal for both sides. But that doesn't mean it's more important than Song's life. I want to be clear about that. Song is the number one priority here. The deal can wait. All I need is your assurance—"

"My assurance?" The pain in his eyes is luminous. "Mr. Allen, I will say one thing. He who stands on a pedestal has nowhere to step but off."

Now I gape, incapable of interpreting the meaning of his words.

Instead, I bite down on my guilt. "Gary said they ran tests. What did her doctors say?"

"They speak of hope, but their words are empty promises."

"She's in the best place. They know what they're doing here."

Chang emits a snorting sound, and I realize he's in the worst place imaginable for this kind of family crisis to occur. The medical attention here at Saint Luke's might be world-class, but it doesn't change the fact that he is in a foreign country, with his daughter's life in the hands of a foreign health-care system. It's like pouring salt on his wounds. In times of emergency, there is no place like home and being with family. For as long as he's here, he'll need support, guidance. He'll need friends. As far as I know, Gary and I are the only two people he knows in New York, which means he'll need us. Our deal might not have been struck as of yet, but I am beholden to him all the same, and I will need to do everything I can to alleviate the pressure, for Song's sake.

"People come back from comas all the time," I say.

It's a throwaway comment, the kind that people make without thinking. Something based less in fact and more in faith.

Chang doesn't respond, not directly. He places a hand on his daughter's shoulder. "Her joyful spirit is already journeying to the Pure Land."

He states it like it's fact, despite the breathing apparatus keeping Song alive and her weak but steady pulse feeding blood to her brain.

He's already accepted that her condition is fatal.

"Director, I can't begin to imagine what you're going through right now. But you can't give up on her. Where there's life, there's hope, right? It's okay to be . . . I don't know . . . scared."

My statement is borderline trite, and Chang stares at me with soul-sucking eyes.

"You will excuse me," he says, coming around the bed toward me. "I must attend to the matter of repatriation."

I block the doorway. "Please, let me help."

"No. You have done enough for one lifetime."

"But you can't just leave her. You're all she has."

"Mr. Allen, what counts is the life that one leads. My daughter has led an exquisite life, accomplishing much greatness without cost to her family. She will not be delayed on her journey."

And suddenly it clicks. It would be a mistake to think that Chang is defeated. That's not the case. His customs are different than ours, his beliefs founded in a culture that is essentially alien to me. Although he talks of death, his tone is upbeat, and possibly even anticipatory of better things to come.

Chang claps his hands, the door opens, and his aides rush in. Without speaking, they take me by the arms and manhandle me out of the room. Once in the hallway, I am thrown out like the trash, and it's an effort not to go sprawling flat on my belly.

◆ ◆ ◆

"Keep walking," Gary tells me through the corner of his mouth as I meet up with him in the waiting area. I start to ask, but he puts a finger to his lips. "I'll explain once we're outside," he says, hooking an arm over my shoulders and steering me toward the exit. "Dare I ask how it went?"

"With Chang? Terrible."

"You couldn't make him listen to reason?"

"His daughter was dying in front of him. Our deal with Xian Airlines wasn't the main talking point."

"But you said—"

"Yeah, well, maybe I was being overly confident."

Gary withdraws his arm. "Honestly, Jed, I don't believe you. You know this is a matter of life and death for us."

"What about Chang? For that matter, what about Song?"

"The least you could've done was remind him about our gentleman's agreement, if nothing else. The Chinese are big on keeping face. You should have stressed that. We had one shot, and you blew it."

We head through the sliding doors and out onto the street. It's the weekend, and Manhattan is abuzz.

"So why are you rushing me outside?" I ask.

"To save you from being arrested."

"What?"

"Chang's doctor called the police. Two detectives turned up while you were inside. You walked right past them. We need to get you as far from here as possible, get you a good lawyer."

I dig my heels in. "Hold on. What are you talking about?"

"For starters, felony homicide. It's called 'death by dealer.' They can put you away for twenty-five years."

"And you know this how?"

"I watch the news."

"But Song isn't dead."

"In their eyes, a technicality."

"Except the drugs aren't the issue here."

"Jed, you don't need to persuade me. It's the boys in blue you need to convince. Or, on second thought, maybe that wouldn't be such a great idea. Now, come on. Let's walk and talk."

I glance over my shoulder once or twice as we make our way to the intersection of Amsterdam and West 113th. It's impossible to tell if we're being followed.

"Between you and me," Gary says as we arrive at the corner, "I had a quiet word with one of her doctors."

"They spoke to you?"

"Let's just say he made an exception." He sees my frown and adds, "Extenuating circumstances. I'm the one covered in her blood, remember? So, anyway, it turns out that some of those ecstasy pills of yours contained GHB, otherwise known as—"

"The date-rape drug. Holy crap."

"Added to the fact she was attacked, and you can see why they're so hot on having a conversation with you."

"But I didn't do anything."

"That's not necessarily true. You supplied her with the drugs. Drugs that probably reduced her ability to fend off her attacker. Plus, you were the last person to see her in one piece."

I come to a stop. "Wait a minute. They think I did that to her?" The thought is unimaginable, and my stomach turns.

Gary shrugs. "Who knows what they're thinking? We all took those drugs. Including Chang. If he's after pressing charges . . . well, suffice it to say, we'll be talking about the pot calling the kettle black."

"But I was the one who brought those pills to the party."

"And that's why we need to work out what to do next. Because if she dies . . ."

Gary doesn't finish his sentence, because the seriousness of the situation is unspeakable.

"I need to go back," I say, starting to retrace our steps.

But Gary jumps ahead of me. "Major mistake." He holds up his hands. "Please, Jed, just stop and think about this for one second before you go and do something we'll both regret. She seems like a nice girl, and I know you've got a soft spot for her. And God knows, it's terrible what's happened. But this"—he flaps a hand at me, apparently signifying his disapproval—"all this being virtuous and honorable crap, it's just not you, buddy."

"Step aside, Gary."

He stays put, barring my attempts to pass. "Listen to me. She's the daughter of a high-profile foreign businessman. If she dies, this escalates at the speed of light, going way beyond death by dealer. Don't be fooled by mild-mannered Chang. He has real clout. He's a major-league hitter. He's played golf with the president, for heaven's sake. We're talking federal charges, Jed. *Federal.* They'll want to make an example. They'll hang you out to dry. That kind of publicity will ruin us."

Gary's true colors are off the visible spectrum. All at once it's clear what his primary concern is, and it isn't Song. In fact, it's not even me, and I'm the one who stands to lose the most. It's him. Gary is all about Gary. The crux of it is, if I go under, he doesn't want me taking him down with me.

He stabs a finger into my chest. "I'm warning you, Jed. Quit being so damn selfish. It's not just your future on the line here."

"Get out of my way." I push him aside.

Gary grabs my arm and swings me around on the spot. "You do this and you're as good as throwing our whole lives away."

This is the first time I have heard his voice raised louder than a fierce whisper and seen his muscle tension so tight.

I stare him down, and after a second to think about it, he releases my arm.

It's early evening and getting dark. Plenty of pedestrians on the Upper West Side. And once again we are attracting the wrong kind of attention.

Gary waits until there's a gap in the crowd before saying, "You owe me, Jed. You might not recall it right now, but I was the one who got you to refocus after your parents died. I was the one who picked you up out of that god-awful rut you'd gotten yourself in. I was the one who set you back on your feet, who saved your life. I was the one who helped you realize your dreams. If it wasn't for me . . ." His voice chokes up, and he looks to the darkening sky, as if for inspiration.

Meanwhile, I stand stock-still, the news that my parents are dead reverberating in my brain.

Minutes ago, I had big hopes to seek them out, to reintroduce myself to my family, to moor my boat in a safe harbor. But Gary's revelation has scuttled my plans.

When his gaze comes back to mine, his eyes are rimmed with tears. "I won't beg you, buddy. All I'm asking is you give me the courtesy of delaying whatever madness it is you're intending, at least until we've talked it over. Not here, though. This isn't the right place to decide our fates." He slaps me on the arm. "Come on. I need a drink. Maybe two or three. Tall, strong, and quick. You look like you could do with one, too."

"I don't want to talk this through."

"Okay. Just drink with me, then. It'll give you time to reevaluate. You never know—you might come up with a plan B."

"What about your shirt?"

He looks down at the dried blood. "It's New York. They'll think it's designer."

We find a place nearby. A red-fronted bar with mirrored windows. It's almost empty inside, the Saturday night revelers still to gather. Even so, there is a knot of male patrons seated in a round booth—all in casual clothes but with their faces daubed in heavy theatrical makeup.

A poster on the wall advertises tonight's big drag event.

Gary summons the bartender by name—a thin guy with a white rockabilly hairdo and lips that look inflated—and I get the impression this isn't Gary's first time frequenting this place.

He tells the bartender, "The biggest badass daiquiri you can lay your hands on. And for my best buddy here . . ."

"Water," I say. "Water's fine."

I have seen what happens when I drink on my meds; adding alcohol is like throwing gasoline on a naked flame.

Gary shakes his head. "And an Evian on the rocks for my fearless partner."

We lean against the bar while our drinks are prepared.

One of the men seated at the booth waves at us. He isn't yet clad in his drag outfit, but at a glance he could pass as a catwalk model.

"Hey, gorgeous," he calls, and I hope it's to Gary. "You staying for the show later?"

Gary lets out a sigh. "I'm afraid not. Working this weekend. A sinking ship to bail out. Maybe next time."

"Oh, bummer." The drag queen makes an exaggerated sad face and forms a heart shape with his fingers. "I'll miss you, honey. You have the voice of an angel."

Gary sees my questioning expression and explains that tonight is karaoke night, everybody welcome, and that I shouldn't stand in judgment of his choice of Saturday night entertainment. I ask him if he comes here often, and he gives me a look that tells me he spends too much time here.

Other than the knowledge that we're friends and business partners, I realize I know nothing about Gary Quartucci, including his sexual preferences.

Our drinks arrive. Gary instructs the bartender to repeat the order and to bring them over to our table.

"I won't change my mind," I say as we sit down in a quiet corner. "No matter what the outcome, I need to do the right thing."

"We'll see."

"I mean it, Gary. This is as bad as it gets. This is on me. I need to come forward. Tell the truth."

"Other than to ease your conscience, what good will your confession do?"

"It's not about what's good for me, or you. It's about doing the right thing."

"With devastating consequences for all concerned. Drop that bomb, Jed, and the ripples will be far-reaching. You won't be the only one burned by the fallout. It's not your fault she was attacked."

"Indirectly, it is. If I hadn't left the club—"

"If you hadn't been born . . ."

I frown at him over the top of my Evian. "That's not quite the same thing, Gary, and you know it."

"What I know is you can't go through life taking on other people's bad choices. Chasing after you was *her* mistake. You didn't ask for that. She exercised free will, buddy. You didn't force her at gunpoint into the park."

"But what happened to her—"

"Isn't your cross to bear."

"Easy for you to say. It's unthinkable. She took the drugs I brought. Everybody knows GHB suppresses inhibitions. It made her vulnerable. I'm culpable."

"You had no way of knowing about the GHB."

"All the same . . ."

"You can't hold yourself accountable for the actions of others."

I shake my head at him, unable to relate to his detachment. "I wish I lived in your black-and-white world, Gary. The air must be sweet-smelling on top of that ivory tower of yours."

"Until yesterday, we shared the same view. Normally, when you're not absent upstairs, you and I think very much alike. Something like this, you would've dismissed it in a heartbeat. Forgot about it. Moved on. What's happened to you?"

"I woke up." I take a swig of the water, its coolness barely touching the fire in my throat.

Gary's character assessment of me confirms the opinion I've been forming about the man I was, and more than ever it reaffirms my desire never to wear his shoes again.

Gary tips his daiquiri at me. "No one knows you better than I do, Jed. I've seen this android version of you before, remember? You have the luxury of forgetting each time this happens. I don't. And I know it's only a matter of time before this watered-down you vanishes. Once that happens, you'll realign your priorities."

"Waiting for my memories to come back won't change what happened."

"No, but it will change the way you deal with it."

It's a thorn in my side, but Gary is right. Everything I have learned about the man I was tells me that once the old me returns, so too will his diabolical ways.

Amnesia has replaced my corruption with a conscience.

"Gary, I can't sit this one out and say nothing, just in case my memories come back and I do a U-turn. It doesn't matter how you dress this up and try to disguise it: Song is lying in that hospital bed because of me."

"So that's it. You're ready to go to jail?"

"I don't think it will come to that."

"But what if it does? The firm will collapse into bankruptcy, and we'll fall into financial ruin."

"I'm just trying to be realistic. Some things are worth more than money, Gary."

"You're talking about truth."

"I'm talking about being a decent human being."

"Perhaps if you'd had the decency to pick up even one of the calls I made today, this whole misunderstanding could've been avoided."

Now my frown deepens. "I wouldn't call attempted murder a misunderstanding."

"You know what I mean."

"No, Gary, I don't. And even if I had been down here first thing this morning, it wouldn't have changed anything."

"It might have taken some of the pressure off me. Where were you, anyway?"

"I had my own crisis to deal with."

"So you said." He stares at me like nothing in my life compares to what he's been through today, regardless of the Chang family's suffering.

I spread my hands. "Look, I'm sorry you feel I'm letting you down."

"Betraying me."

"That's a little strong, don't you think?"

"Not one bit."

"Okay. If it makes you feel any better, I'm sorry you think I'm betraying you, Gary. But not everything is about you."

He takes a noisy slurp of his cocktail. "You're right. There was a time when it was all about Jed. And I didn't complain. Not once. With unwavering support, I stood by your side. Through thick and thin, I was your rock while you were going to pieces. I helped put you back together, set you on the path to success. No exaggeration, buddy, but if it wasn't for me, you'd be a deadbeat by now. And this is how you repay me, by abandoning me in my hour of need? You might as well knife me in the back."

I don't say it, but all I can think about is that Gary is such a drama queen. Instead, I ask him to clarify his point, and he spends the next five minutes stating a case for exactly why I should be steadfast in my loyalty.

It's not all sunshine and roses, and I am left feeling worse than before he started.

Not only have we been best friends since kindergarten, he tells me, our families lived on the same street, and our parents were the best of friends. Mine owned a prosperous construction business that employed his parents and a couple of dozen other people in the community.

Neither of us had siblings. We were still in elementary school when Gary's father left and never came back, and it wasn't until Gary was a few years older that he grew to understand why.

His mother was a raging alcoholic, prone to mood swings and tantrums, and Gary became one of those children forced to take care of a dysfunctional parent. Worse still, she abused Gary both verbally and mentally, in ways that no mother should ever treat a child.

Gary was twelve years old when he came home from school to find his mother dead in a pool of her own vomit.

Something like that leaves a lasting impression.

With no family to take him in, ours had, and Gary and I had lived as brothers ever since.

Then tragedy struck again when Gary and I were at college. Only this time it was my parents who had met with an untimely death.

It's old news, of course—they died almost twenty years ago—but it hits me as though it happened yesterday.

"And that's when you went to pieces," Gary says. "Their death was a shock to the system for both of us. But it cut you deepest, and for a while you completely lost it. And I mean totally freaked out, for months. Your grades took a slide. You started doing drugs and drinking yourself into oblivion. It was a miracle I managed to turn you around." He reaches across the table and squeezes my arm. "Jed, I know you don't remember any of this. But it doesn't change the fact that it happened. I'm not saying you owe me your life. I'm just saying I think I deserve a little consideration before you destroy everything we've worked hard to achieve. Don't lose all you've gained over a principle. Don't fall on your sword for her."

I release a tremulous breath. "You'll survive without me. So will the company."

"That's where you're wrong. And the other you knows it. This deal is make-or-break, buddy. We've invested everything we had in it. As things stand, we're up to our eyeballs in debt. We're not talking pocket change here either. If this deal with Xian Airlines falls flat on its face, the banks will foreclose on our loans and we'll go bust."

"So we refinance."

"I wish it were that simple. Short of doing a deal with the devil, we've maxed out all available revenue streams. We're at the point where the banks won't touch us. For months, we've been meeting the payroll out of our own pockets."

"It explains the final notices I found."

He nods. "Our personal credit is in the gutter. We're down on our hands and knees, scrabbling for pennies."

The bartender brings our second round of drinks, and Gary nearly drains his daiquiri in one gulp. In his expensive, albeit bloodstained, clothes, with his gold watch glinting, Gary looks anything but broke. And I get the impression that his idea of financial hardship is akin to trading in the company jet for a lifetime of business class.

Even so, I am not surprised to learn how reckless we have been. To reach the top in any line of business, a certain element of ruthlessness is sometimes necessary. But that kind of aggressive behavior comes with its drawbacks. Risks often go understated or are miscalculated, while rewards are overinflated and dressed in their Sunday best.

All it takes is one loose screw, and the whole structure comes crashing down.

Near the bar, the drag queens erupt in a bout of deep-throated laughter, highlighting our melancholy.

"I'll speak with Chang again," I say. "Convince him that sticking with the deal is the best option for both parties."

In the fallout from Dr. Merrick's revelation and Song's hospitalization, begging Chang to stay true to our agreement is not my top priority. But I have to accept that I am in this to the end—not just invested, but also obligated.

Gary raises his glass. "Good luck with the rematch." He pours the last of the daiquiri down his throat and smacks his lips. "Be right back," he says, getting to his feet and heading in the direction of the restrooms.

My phone rings. I don't recognize the number, which comes as no real surprise.

"Hello?"

"Mr. Allen, this is Detective Westfall at the Eastchester PD."

"Detective?" I glance around the bar, as though expecting to see him waving from a nearby booth. "How'd you get my number?"

"It's not rocket science."

Westfall sounds pissed, and in no mood for chitchat.

I can't help wondering if being a police detective is his dream job or a calling he endures.

"I've run a few checks," he says.

"On the dress?"

"No, Mr. Allen. On you."

"Me?" I sit a little straighter. As it is, my nerves are frayed already, and the thought that Westfall may have uncovered more of my dark secrets is unsettling.

"What game are you playing?" he asks.

"Excuse me?"

"You heard me, Mr. Allen. Ordinarily, I'm a patient man. I know people make mistakes, and so I make allowances. But you're beginning to test me."

"I have no idea what you're talking about."

"Okay, then let me say it in words you do understand. Like I said, I ran some checks. On you. They didn't come back the way I was expecting."

"I'm still none the wiser."

"You don't own property on Lakeshore Drive."

I feel my forehead scrunch itself up. My memories—of being at the lake house, of going through the boxed possessions, of sleeping in the master bed, of rifling through Cassie's dresser—make Westfall's statement nonsensical. "That's crazy. *I've been there.* Today, as a matter of fact, right before I came down to the station to see you."

"You have amnesia."

"Except, it doesn't affect my short-term memory. Check your facts, Detective. I'm not imagining a whole house. I'm headed up there later. If you want me to get back to you with the exact house number . . ."

"Please, Mr. Allen, don't put yourself out. One of the things I've learned in my time on the force is that facts are immutable. You can bet your life on them. Facts are the same today as they will be in a million years. You get my drift?"

"No."

"I checked your facts, thoroughly. One of which is you don't own any property in Eastchester. No one by the name of Jed or Jedidiah or any other permutation for that matter."

"Maybe your source is wrong."

"Not according to the land records."

I chew my lip, trying to think of a reason why my name wouldn't pop up on Westfall's search. This is a conversation I can live without right now. "Maybe the house is in my firm's name?"

"You mean you don't know?"

"I have amnesia, remember?"

"The well-thumbed excuse in the book of lies."

"I'm sorry?"

"I cover all my bases, Mr. Allen. No mention of Q and A Architects owning property in Eastchester. And then there's your girlfriend's name."

"Cassie."

"Right. Cassie. The girl with no last name. I checked everyone listed on Lakeshore Drive. Guess what? No one by the name of Cassie or even Cassidy. Now do you get it?"

For the first time, it occurs to me that Cassie and I haven't lived together at the lake house for very long, maybe not long enough for the records to be updated, and that's why all our possessions are still boxed up. Not only that, but I have no idea where Cassie lived before she moved in with me.

"Could the deeds be under another name?" I ask.

Westfall lets out a sigh. "Such as?"

"I don't know. I'm grasping at straws here. Maybe the house was an inheritance of some kind."

"Only, you grew up in Pleasantville."

My mouth opens, but no words come out.

"It's no secret," he says into my silence. "It's in your bio on your company's website. Both you and your partner grew up in Pleasantville, New York. And absolutely no mention of you living anywhere in Eastchester."

"I don't know what to say."

"Well, for my own peace of mind, I ran a tenancy search, thinking that maybe you rented the property. Everything came back nada. Mr. Allen, you don't live up at the lake. For that matter, as far as I can see, you don't live anywhere in Westchester County. So I'll say it again, and you should think carefully before you answer this time. What's your endgame here?"

"I haven't got one."

"Mr. Allen . . ."

"No, Detective, I'm serious. And I don't appreciate you implying I have an ulterior motive. I'm not trying to dupe you here. It's been twenty-four hours and my girlfriend is still missing. I'm not lying or deliberately sending you on a wild-goose chase. I can't explain about the house. Not right now. But I know my girlfriend hasn't come home, and I'm worried for her safety."

"You think it's *her* blood on the dress?"

"The truth is, I don't know. I'm hoping you're going to tell me it's not."

"Well, it could be some time before we rule it out. I've sent the dress over to the lab. But it's the weekend and they're understaffed. So why don't you help yourself in the meantime and buy yourself a little more credibility. Give me your real address."

I tell Westfall about the apartment on Central Park West, adding that I didn't know of its existence when we spoke earlier.

"There you go," he says. "That wasn't too difficult, was it? And your girlfriend, I take it she lives there with you?"

"No."

"Mr. Allen . . ."

"Let me explain. The apartment is a convenience. I use it through the week. It's mine, and it's in my name. You can check the records. I have mortgage statements to prove it. You'll see I'm telling the truth."

"So, what about your girlfriend?"

My silence is deafening.

"Mr. Allen, you can see how this doesn't add up. I'm trying to be of assistance here, but you're being selective with the truth. You do understand it's a crime to file a frivolous police report, and that falsely reporting an incident can be a Class A misdemeanor?"

Every nerve ending in my body is tingling, and the ache in the back of my head feels like a fist squeezing my brain. Without doubt, recent events have gotten me stressed and jumpy. The last thing I need is Westfall misinterpreting that stress as guilt.

I sigh, loud enough for him to pick it up. "Look, Detective, I'm sorry I'm coming across the way I do. I don't mean to be argumentative or obtrusive. You've got to understand—my head is all over the place. I'm turned upside down with this amnesia of mine. All I know is that my girlfriend is missing and I found a dress with what could be her blood on it. That's it. You know as much as I do. I'm not deliberately concealing anything."

Except for the skeleton in my closet.

There is silence on the other end of the call for a few seconds while Westfall, I imagine, is trying to balance my flimsy words against the weight of evidence against me.

Without concrete proof, and in his position, I'm not sure I'd believe my story either.

"Look, Mr. Allen," he says at last, "I'm not blind to your situation. I know you've got difficulties to contend with. For now, I'm willing to stay open-minded. Let's see what the tests turn up. Then you and I will have another conversation."

"Thank you, Detective. You'll let me know what they find?"

"You bet. But don't hold your breath. Unless it's a priority, these things can take weeks to turn around. In the meantime, you be sure to let me know when your girlfriend comes home safe and sound. But if I do find you're playing a game here . . ."

"You can arrest me, Detective."

"Oh, you can be sure of that." Westfall hangs up, leaving my ears burning.

I release a shaky breath to settle my nerves.

"You're talking with the police?"

I look up to see that Gary has returned. "I told you, back at the emergency room: Cassie's missing."

"So you did. Forgive me for forgetting in all the excitement." He waves at the bartender to fetch him another drink, and then he drops onto his seat, like the weight of the world is on his shoulders. "So, tell me again, in the grand scheme of things, who the hell is Cassie?"

I stare at him, at first unable to make sense of his words, but then I realize the answer: I have kept my life with Cassie a secret even from him, the same way I seem to have kept to myself the fling with Song. Exactly why I have done so, I have no idea. Gary is supposed to be my best friend; why would I keep things like this from him? The other version of me, the person I was before Friday, knows the truth. But his memories are inaccessible, and I can only guess.

Of course, there is another explanation. And that is that Dr. Merrick is right: I have everything turned around in my head, and Gary knows nothing of Cassie because she's the one I'm having the affair with. But how does an affair explain the lake house and our life there?

"My girlfriend," I say, dipping in a tentative toe to see what bites.

"You mean Sarah? Okay. What about her?"

"The two of you, you've met already?"

"Not quite. We're like ships passing in the night. We haven't been formally introduced. And it's not through lack of interest on my part. You've been keeping her all to yourself. Then again, you've always kept your girls locked away from me."

"My girls?"

A knowing smile makes a brief appearance. "Don't act so innocent, buddy. You're a player. A predator. We both are. It's in our genes. We're free spirits. Which is why I'm surprised you and the good doctor are still together."

"What have I said about her?"

"By all accounts, that she's the real deal and you're head over heels. That you've all but moved in together. It's so sweet I could cheerfully puke. I swear, for the last few months, when you and I aren't talking shop, she's your hot topic of conversation. I'm guessing it's only a matter of time before you two do the decent thing and get hitched." Gary sees the astonishment on my face and adds, "You can't pull the wool over my eyes, Jed. I've seen the photos on your phone. You're a pair of lovebirds. Say good-bye to bachelorhood. You look dreadful, by the way."

"Headache."

"Another?"

"Same one. I can't seem to kick it."

The bartender brings Gary's third daiquiri, and Gary dives in.

I sit back and chew on the cud of my bad choices.

As far as Gary is aware, I am in a happy and monogamous relationship with my former shrink. He has no clue about Cassie, or that I have been with her since before Dr. Merrick.

It's likely he knows nothing of the lake house either.

Gary's phone rings. He takes it out and puts it to his ear. I see him nod, once, twice, and then the color drains from his face. For a second, I think he's going to faint, but he clings on, his breathing shallow, eyes unblinking.

Then he ends the call and hangs his head.

"Gary, what is it?"

"Things just went from dire to cataclysmic," he says, looking up at me. "She's dead, Jed. Chang's daughter. And we're officially screwed."

Chapter Eighteen

Out on the sidewalk, I breathe in deeply the cool evening air, quenching the flames burning through my lungs. In my present incarnation, I have no real emotional ties with Song Chang. My affair with her in Shanghai is nothing but a shameful act. My encounter with her at the nightclub is only an awkward moment. On a personal basis, she means nothing to me. Even so, I am human, and amnesia can't prevent me from forming new feelings, most of which are bad and seated in regret.

Although I didn't wield the blade that killed Song, I was instrumental in her death.

Vomit stings at my esophagus, and I swallow it down.

I thumb through the contacts on my phone, finding a number for Xian Airlines and then calling it.

"I need to speak with the director," I tell an aide.

"Director Chang is not available," the aide informs me in a curt tone. "He has returned to the hotel in order to prepare for his departure. You will be wise not to telephone this number again."

The connection terminates, and I stare at the screen for a moment before making my way to the nearest intersection, weaving around people as I go.

At street level, the city is a rainbow of light. But the hulks of darkened buildings loom over everything.

I wave down a taxi and jump in.

Emotional gravity wants to pull me back to the lake house, to the place where I feel the strongest connection to Cassie. Even though I've looked, it's possible I have missed something to lead me to where she is, alive and well. More than anything, I want to find Cassie, but I have other obligations to consider, other forces acting upon me, pressures that can't be ignored.

As the taxi heads south on Columbus Avenue, I dial Dr. Merrick's cell, telling her I won't be returning to the apartment anytime soon, and that she should leave.

"It's Saturday," she says. "I'm sleeping over."

"No."

"It's what we planned."

"No," I say more firmly.

"Jed, I don't think it's a good idea for you to be on your own right now."

"Is that my doctor or my girlfriend speaking?"

"Can't it be both? I'm worried about you. Let me help."

"Sarah, I'll be fine." I don't say that I'm in no mood for being psychoanalyzed or experimented on. Nor do I need a babysitter. "There's something I need to take care of."

"Does it concern what happened at the hospital?"

"Yes."

"Do you want to talk about it?"

"No."

"Please," she says quietly, "don't shut me out. I'm here for you."

"And I appreciate the offer, but there's nothing you can do. It's a work thing, and it's only me that can fix it. Besides, I need space to think about everything—especially about us. You've given me a lot to wrap my head around. I'll call you, tomorrow."

And then I hang up, denying her the opportunity to protest.

I still don't know what to make of my relationship with Dr. Sarah Merrick, professional, romantic, or otherwise.

The taxi drops me off outside the Mandarin Oriental at Columbus Circle, and I practically run inside the hotel, gambling on taking Chang by surprise.

On request, the clerk at the front desk places a call to Chang's suite, speaking quietly into the phone as the call is answered. Then he covers the handset, informing me that Chang isn't accepting visitors. I reach over the counter, seize the phone, and tell Chang's aide that I have pictures of his boss snorting cocaine, and that if he doesn't grant me an audience, I will go to the press with them.

A minute later, I am striding toward the presidential suite on the fifty-third floor.

Chang is dressed in a black suit over a black shirt, with no trace of the pain I saw previously in his eyes. "You play a dangerous game," he says as I am escorted into the opulent suite.

On the tip of my tongue are the words *It's what desperate people do.* But I don't say them. Instead, I dip my head and tell him how deeply sorry I am to hear of his daughter's passing.

"And yet here you are," he says, dismissing my sincerities. "Like an ill wind."

"I'm here for the good of both parties."

"With an offer of blackmail. Is this how Americans prefer to conduct business?"

"Unfortunately, I think one side having leverage is how a lot of business is done these days."

It's no excuse, I know, and it doesn't sit easy with me.

"It is without honor."

"You're right." I follow him to what appears to be a study, with wood-paneled walls and a stunning view over the evening New York skyline. "Look, I know my timing sucks. Song is gone, and there's nothing I can do to bring her back. For everyone involved, this is a disaster. But my coming here isn't personal. It's business."

"It is completely personal. Presenting your threat. Not only is it personal, it is distasteful."

"And, believe me, it's the last thing I wanted. With respect, Director, we had a deal. We *have* a deal. It's a good one. I didn't know Song all that well, but I think she wouldn't want your business to suffer because of her."

"Because of you." He goes over to the window and stares out.

I draw a deep breath, feeling every bit responsible for his concealed heartache. "No one could have seen that coming. Certainly, none of us intended her any harm. She took those pills of her own free will. We all did. No one forced her. She wanted to. We were all consenting adults last night. What happened after was unpredictable and unthinkable. As horrible as it was, you shouldn't let it dictate your business strategy. Is this how you want to mark Song's death, with the demise of your company?"

Of course, I have no idea how financially sound Xian Airlines is. But I do know that ditching our deal will set them back years, and possibly make their investors wary. I know Q & A Architects will be doomed.

Chang stares out at the nighttime view, his cool solemnity forming an invisible and yet tangible barrier. "I will not be blackmailed."

"I know." I take out my phone, bringing up the multiple incriminating images of Chang snorting cocaine. "And that's why I want *you* to delete these photos."

Now he turns from the window, the city lights glittering in his eyes.

I show him the picture of him enjoying the attention of a topless dancer perched on his lap. "I'm not your enemy, Director. We both have more at stake here than losing face. I know you're married. I know Song's mother would be devastated to learn that while her daughter was being brutally murdered, her husband was doing this." I hold out the phone. "It's your trust I need. Without it, our deal's worthless anyway. Our firms can prosper together. Let them. That's what Song wanted, and that's why I won't be e-mailing these to the press or to your wife back in Shanghai." I place the phone in his hand. "So go ahead. As far as I know, these are the only copies. Erase all the evidence. And after, even if you still want to call this whole thing off, I promise I'll walk away and you'll never hear from me again."

Chapter Nineteen

Whenever Seltzer came home to Soundview, he heard people saying that the old neighborhood was still the same. It wasn't true.

The old neighborhood hardly existed anymore—at least not in the shape it had when he was a boy. A wave of urban renewal beginning in the eighties had given the South Bronx a long-overdue facelift, and much of it was now unrecognizable. Slums were being replaced by upscale stores, and hard memories softened over time.

Not everything had been bulldozed to make way for the big-name chain stores and renovated housing, though. Many family businesses had survived the purge and prospered because of it. Hardy leftovers that had risen to become landmarks and even tourist attractions. Much like the diner where Seltzer now sat.

Sandwiched between a fried-chicken shack and a check-cashing outlet, the diner had stood in the shadow of the elevated railway for as long as he could remember. Aside from the rare lick of paint, the décor never appeared to change. It still had the same checkerboard floor tiles and mirrored walls he'd grown up with. But, like him, it was beginning to show its age; the original white foam ceiling tiles were now nicotine yellow, and decades of impatient silverware users had carved their history into the Formica tabletops.

"Meatloaf," Seltzer told the waitress, and then waited until she had walked away before partly opening the briefcase lying on the tabletop.

Inside was an inch-thick collection of papers, final bills, bank statements, and insurance documents, plus a few personal certificates and memento photographs—on top of which was a cell phone and the revolver he'd gotten at Mama Butterfly's.

At the sight of the gun, Seltzer glanced up, his furtive gaze scanning the diner. It was early evening, and the place was packed with locals. A few young couples here and there, but mostly old guys reminiscing, and groups of loudmouthed youths who used the eatery as a hangout when the weather was cold. No one was paying him any attention. Even the local beat cop, who was seated at the window near the door, was drinking coffee and watching activity out on the street.

A year ago, Seltzer could never have imagined sitting here, thinking dark thoughts and contemplating taking a life. Back then, he might not have been blissfully happy, but at least he'd had the stability of a family, a home, a well-paying job, and the promise of better years ahead.

His wife's death had taken all that from him, and in the blink of an eye.

Seltzer leaned back in the booth and closed his eyes, suddenly drained after his conversation with Dr. Vargas.

He hadn't slept properly since his wife's death. His rest periods had been reduced to fitful naps, and usually at inopportune moments. Embarrassingly, he'd taken to catnapping on public transportation, often missing his stop and waking up miles from his intended destination. And when he wasn't snoozing on the subway or curled up at a bus stop, he'd find himself skulking around twenty-four-hour supermarkets, plodding up and down the aisles like a zombie, or sitting in parks and staring at the stars.

Ironically, the home they had shared together was the last place he wanted to be.

After his wife's funeral, when the insomnia had set in, Seltzer's primary-care physician had offered him sleeping aids, saying that Seltzer was going through "one of those phases" in which his mind was out of sync with his body.

"You've got to face it, Arnold," the physician had told him as Seltzer perched on the end of the examination table, feeling wired and sleepy both at the same time. "Right now, you're still emotionally traumatized. At some point, your cycle will reset on its own, but it won't hurt to give it a nudge in the right direction." The physician had written up a script for diazepam and handed it over. "Also, I'm giving you the number for a therapist. She's good, and her techniques are effective. Either way, Arnold, you will get through this."

Seltzer wasn't won over by the physician's optimism, and once he'd left the office, he ripped up the prescription. He needed sleep all right, but not at the cost of becoming comatose.

And so he'd gotten used to power napping, and that was why he missed the young man sliding into the seat facing him, registering his presence only when the youth said, "Got to be the best meatloaf in the city."

Seltzer opened his eyes a crack, then fully, realizing he'd dropped off for a few minutes and that while he was snoozing, the waitress had brought his dinner and the youth had started eating it.

The youth wore an old New York Yankees jacket and a knit beanie and looked like he'd been sleeping rough for quite some time.

"Who's Sandra?" he asked Seltzer as he ate the meatloaf.

Annoyance lifted Seltzer out of his slouch. "Excuse me?"

The youth pointed with the fork. "You were calling out her name. Attracting all kinds of weird looks. Trust me, that takes some doing in these parts."

Seltzer glanced around the diner. It seemed fuller than it had been before he'd dropped off, with all the tables taken. If anyone had noticed the youth joining him in the booth and helping himself to Seltzer's dinner, no one had intervened.

"That's mine," Seltzer said, reaching for the plate.

The youth hunched over it, obstructing. "Hey. Don't even go there, man. This is my first hot meal all week."

"That's not the point. You can't help yourself to someone's dinner just because they fell asleep."

The youth kept digging in, and Seltzer sat back, trying to put a lid on his rising irritation. Even for New York, the youth's barefaced audacity was an eye-opener, and not something that would have happened in the old days.

"I thought they didn't let homeless people in here," he said.

"They let you in, didn't they?"

"What's that supposed to mean?"

"It's self-explanatory, bro. Do the math."

"I could get you thrown out."

"Sure you could. You could make a scene. Rant and rave, and make everybody in here think I stole your dinner."

"You did."

"But you won't."

"You have no idea what I'm capable of."

The youth stabbed the fork into a chunk of meatloaf, then buried it in his mouth. "Oh, I have your number all right, Arnie. Can I call you Arnie? You're the kind of guy who thinks the world owes him a favor." The youth nodded at Seltzer's briefcase. It was no longer on the table. The youth had moved it to his seat. "While you were sleeping, I did the

Arnie Seltzer crash course. Got familiar with the whole woe-is-me sob story of yours. I wish I could say it makes for interesting reading, but honestly, in my humble opinion, it's kinda pitiful."

"You went through my stuff?"

A mixture of fear and anger ballooned inside Seltzer, lifting him up in his seat. He leaned over the table, making a grab for the briefcase, but the youth seized Seltzer's wrist halfway there, preventing him from reaching it. Then he pulled Seltzer back down to the table.

"Why you acting so dead-ass, bro? Relax. You don't want to be upsetting the clientele."

"Just give me back what's mine." It came out as a growl. The blood had begun to course through Seltzer's veins, much faster than normal, and there was a hint of a tremor stirring in his chest.

The youth just snickered at Seltzer's demand. "Or else what, Arnie? You'll call the deadbeat cop over? Yeah, you go right ahead and do that. I'm sure he'll be real understanding about the concealed weapon you got here in your briefcase. Don't even take it there, bro."

For a second or two, Seltzer stopped breathing, as though a noose had tightened around his neck. The blood continued to pump into his head, though, burning his cheeks and making his eyes feel like they were bulging.

"I'm not interested in stealing the gun," the youth whispered, an inch from Seltzer's heated face. "I'm a pacifist. I abhor confrontation. So why don't you sit back down and be sociable? Get yourself a fork. I'm willing to share."

He released Seltzer, and Seltzer dropped back onto the seat with a thud, rubbing at his wrist. "What do you want?"

"Other than to enjoy my dinner in peace?" The youth scooped up another forkful and crammed it into his mouth. "I'm kinda interested to know why somebody like you feels he needs to carry a gun around in his briefcase."

"It's none of your business."

"What you got planned, Arnie?"

"Planned?" Seltzer's voice was a tight whisper. He glanced around at the other diners again, suddenly feeling like everyone was watching. "What do you mean, what I've got planned?"

The youth motioned with the fork. "Come on now, Arnie. You feel me. I'm not talking retirement, babies, or where your next vacation's gonna be. I'm wondering who's the unlucky dude you're gonna pop with the .38 Special."

Now Seltzer's heart was drumming, his blood pressure swelling, his paranoia escalating. It felt like a hot spotlight was beaming down on him. "I have no idea what you mean."

"Sure you do. You're gonna break the sixth commandment. It's written all over your face."

For a moment, Seltzer said nothing, did nothing, his insides squirming and every nerve jangling. His options here were limited, he knew. He didn't need some stranger getting under his skin and exposing his truth, but he also didn't want to snag the cop's attention and be found in possession of an illegal street gun. Even so, he couldn't just sit here and let this kid dictate his actions, or worse still, talk him out of what he did have planned.

Dry-mouthed, Seltzer watched the youth devour the meatloaf. Then, as the youth savored a particularly huge mouthful, Seltzer reached over the table, grabbed the briefcase, and slid out of the booth, all in one smooth motion.

Taken by surprise, the youth made no attempt to stop him. Instead, he looked up at Seltzer and grinned with food in his teeth. "No hard feelings," he said. "Hope it works out for you, Arnie."

Seltzer couldn't resist. He reached down and flipped the plate of meatloaf onto the youth's lap. "Hope you can pay for the dinner." Then he turned, clutching his briefcase to his chest and hurrying for the exit.

He was almost there when the waitress intercepted him.

"Leaving without your meatloaf?" she asked, holding out a plate of steaming food.

Seltzer glanced back at the youth, his annoyance suddenly falling away. The kid was on his feet, scraping bits of meatloaf off his jacket but in no way looking aggravated by Seltzer's childish actions.

"I can box it up for you, if you like," she said.

"No, thanks." He handed her twenty dollars. "Give it to the kid over there. The one in the knit beanie. And please tell him I'm sorry."

Chapter Twenty

The night watchman checks my ID against the information popping up on his screen. "Mr. Jed Allen. Q and A Architects. Looks like you're all closed up for the weekend."

"Believe me, it's not my idea of fun." I offer him a thin smile as I take back my ID. "You know how it is. Those last-minute files that can't wait until Monday."

Disinterested, like he's heard it a hundred times before, the security officer points to a log book. "Sign here. And make sure you sign out before you leave."

Our offices are in darkness, with just the city glow picking out those features nearest to the windows. Everything is cocooned in an absolute hush that comes from being this high up. The creak of my shoes is the only sound as I walk across the carpeting. No longer lit from within, the design replicas stand around like druid stones in the open-plan work space, and I'm not sure if it's a trick of the poor light or my imagination working overtime that makes them appear more imposing than before.

The computer in my office comes out of hibernation with a shake of the mouse, and I sit down at the screen, one eyebrow raised as the desktop wallpaper takes shape.

It's an airbrushed photo of a suntanned seminude model sprawled across the hood of a bright-orange muscle car parked on a sunlit beach. Her long blonde hair is spilled across the shiny metallic paintwork, her bronzed skin gleaming, her lips pursed suggestively.

The girl looks nothing like Cassie or Dr. Merrick.

"Jesus, am I this superficial?"

I refocus on a column of folder icons at the right-hand side of the screen, clicking on the one labeled XA.

The Shanghai Tusk design contract is at the top of a long list of Xian Airlines documents whose time-stamped dates span the last two years.

I open up the contract and look it over, realizing as I do that the legal jargon might as well be in Mandarin.

I do, however, recognize the words Electronic Signature at the head of the document, pointing to a URL. And clicking it leads to a website, which displays a copy of the legally binding contract, this time with highlighted sections for signatures. Gary's, Chaz's, and my signatures are already in place, but the sections corresponding to our Xian Airlines counterparts are blank.

A flashing link at the bottom of the page says Send, and without hesitation, I click on it.

The document folds itself up and is sucked into a finite point, then it's gone.

I sit back in the chair and let out a breath. "That was easy."

Now it's up to Chang to uphold his end of our gentleman's agreement. Given the option to erase the incriminating images of him on my phone, Chang had declined, saying that trust was everything, and that without it there could be no business between our firms. I hadn't deleted them either, and I didn't know why. Maybe as a kind of insurance policy if everything went south? He'd left his fate in my hands. Either the documents will come back unsigned, signifying the termination of our business relations, or they will be signed, and I can stop Gary's blood pressure from spiking.

While I wait, I use the computer to search for Cassie, more to satisfy my own curiosity than to prove Dr. Merrick wrong.

To my surprise, there are a lot of women named Cassie living in New York, with most of them seemingly eager to share every private facet of their lives. But none of their purse-lipped self-portraits match my Cassie.

Other than my interaction with Cassie in my dreams, what do I know about her?

I twiddle my thumbs, thinking and coming up blank.

Without my memories, I have no idea where she grew up or what school she attended. No way of knowing if she has brothers and sisters, or even where her parents live, if they're still alive.

I don't even know her last name.

"Focus on what you do know."

Cassie looks younger than me, in her early thirties. She's white, with dark hair and blue eyes. In my dreams, she doesn't have a noticeable accent, which means she could be a New Yorker, like me.

Could I know her from my youth?

Gary mentioned that he and I grew up in Pleasantville. I narrow the Internet search—looking for people named Cassie born in my hometown—sifting through dozens of random images before it occurs to me that if Cassie was part of my childhood, then Gary would remember her. And he doesn't.

I think about the dream I had of her at the photography exhibition, and I add the words *photography*, *New York*, *exhibitions*, and *art galleries* to the search criteria. There are more than two million hits. I start to scan the results, at first hopeful, but it's a mammoth task, and my hope soon crumbles to dismay when I see there are more than one hundred art galleries and exhibition centers in Manhattan alone. And yet more girls named Cassie who take an insane number of selfies, especially at public exhibits.

"Maybe you're going about this the wrong way?"

If Cassie is a successful photographer, it's likely she has a website, promoting and showcasing her freelance business.

I type more keywords into the search. "Come on, Cassie. Show me the way."

The results come back revealing that there are several other New York photographers who share her first name, but none that are her. And a couple of dozen pages in, it's obvious I'm not making any progress.

I push back in the chair and deflate my lungs, amazed that I can't find any mention of Cassie online. In a world where our lives have been digitized and made accessible everywhere, it's as though Cassie never existed.

And yet, I know she does; I have the photos to prove it.

I think about my sordid discovery, hidden away in my closet at the apartment. Rightly so, the existence of the secret stash creeps me out a little. I am at a loss to fully explain why I have pictures of Cassie hidden away.

"Devotion or depravity?"

Either way, it's weird, and yet another idiosyncrasy of my former self that I have to live with.

I try to visualize the mosaic of photos to see if anything pops out, such as landmarks in the background or, ideally, an image of her at the mysterious art gallery, but it's all just a colorful blur.

My recent memory is good, but it's not eidetic.

For a while I close my eyes, imagining my memory is a vault, and that if I concentrate hard enough I will crack it open. I focus on what I know about Cassie and what I don't. I focus on my conversation with Dr. Merrick, her pictures on my phone, and the photo of Cassie in my wallet. I focus on my parallel lives, the lake house and my pad in the city. I focus on the kamikaze cuckoo and the garbage bag floating in the dark water. Then something occurs to me, and I run a new search.

After my soaking in the lake, Officer Davis mentioned he'd met me once before, back in January. He said I was waiting for my girlfriend at a Wells Fargo bank near an urgent-care clinic on White Plains Road.

The search produces several hits, but only one with a Wells Fargo across the street in Eastchester.

I call the number listed, and after several rings, a recorded message comes on, informing callers that the clinic is now closed until the morning.

Despondent, I hang up.

My gaze wanders to the window, and then out to the nighttime cityscape.

The geometric landscape of dark mountains and valleys of light should make me feel connected to something bigger than me, but it only emphasizes my isolation.

There is no lonelier place in the world than being alone in a city of more than eight million strangers.

The computer chimes, announcing new messages, and I open the inbox to find a bunch of e-mails, with those that have arrived since my awakening on Friday afternoon in bold and unread.

Several spam messages promise to boost my productivity, both at the office and in bed.

The most recent is a message from the digital signature company, confirming that my document has been delivered to the other party.

I am about to switch from the mail app to the search window, my finger poised over the mouse, when I stop short.

A word is jumping out at me from the e-mail list:

Cassie.

My heart warms at the sight of her name. I move the pointer over it, then hesitate before opening the message, the heat in my chest suddenly giving way to a crushing chill.

The subject line reads:
PLEASE LEAVE ME ALONE.

Couples break up and go their separate ways for all sorts of reasons. Sometimes the cause is understandable. The couple grows apart and falls out of love. Sometimes the cause is a lack of communication, and the couple reunites after working it out. Sometimes the cause is destructive, and there's no going back.

I think about the photo I found in Cassie's underwear drawer, taken at the Ambient Lounge and dated last December. The same time of year that Cassie and I were photographed together at a bar.

The time stamp on the e-mail is early January.

Did Cassie and I go through a temporary breakup, and that's why she sent this message?

With nerves in my belly, I open the e-mail, worried about what I may find, but the message area is blank.

"What happened last December?"

I find the Ambient Lounge online and pore through its gallery of photos. The club is located in one of the city's premier hotels and is a venue for all kinds of events, from weddings to fund-raisers. I take out my phone and call the listed number.

A man answers—possibly the same man who took my call earlier—and I ask him about the events held there last December.

"We held a total of twenty-six events that month," he tells me after interrogating his computer records and complaining about processor speed.

I ask him to e-mail me a list, and he tells me it's not going to happen, because of client privacy.

"Come on. Give me a break," I say. "At least, can you say if there were any photography-related events? Maybe for one of the big magazines, like *National Geographic* or *Rolling Stone*?"

He murmurs a comment I can't quite make out, and then tells me that all but three of the December events were Christmas office parties hosted by companies, with the three exceptions being two weddings and a highbrow birthday bash.

"Can you please check again? It was a black-tie event. To celebrate the opening night of an exhibit, I think. If I e-mail you a photo of a woman, can you tell me if—"

"No," he says, cutting me off. "If you're looking for someone in particular, I suggest you call the police."

"What if I come down there, show you her picture in person? I'll make it worth your while."

"We're not a dating service, and I don't accept bribes. But I can't stop you from coming over. Just do me a favor and leave it till after eleven?"

"Who should I ask for?"

"Murphy."

"Thanks."

He says good-bye and hangs up.

The dull ache in the back of my head returns with a vengeance, and I take the pill bottle out of my pocket, tipping it onto my palm.

But no pills roll out.

At first, I am slightly alarmed at the sight of the empty container. The medication is designed to reduce stress, a known trigger of my intermittent amnesia. I should be freaked out and on the phone to Dr. Merrick, imploring her to write another script. But as I stare at the empty container, I come to an enlightening conclusion. It's the stress that has given me a new lease on life, and the reality is, if I continue to go down the medicated route, it will only pave the way for a comeback of the old me.

I can't let that happen.

I have to change.

Easier said than done.

As it stands, my world is constructed on lies. A series of exploits, selfish decisions, fabrications. It will take some serious excavating to lay a new foundation, to build a better life.

Except . . . it's not my life.

It's *his* life.

I can sense him in the darkness, a mute presence but still capable of influence, waiting to resume his life, waiting for his moment to banish me to obscurity.

This body, this mind, this soul—it belongs to the other me. The corrupted version. The risk-taker, the womanizer, the drug user. The immoral Jed Allen, who existed before I came into being.

Although I am the present tenant, I am an illegal squatter. He is the rightful owner. Sooner or later, I will outlive my stay and he will oversee my eviction.

I can't let that happen.

"And that means no more meds."

I drop the empty pill bottle in the trash.

From the computer, the incoming mail chime sounds again.

It's a new entry from the digital signature company, confirming that all parties have now signed the document. A link redirects back to the online contract, and now at the bottom of it, in the Xian Airlines section, are three e-signatures, including Director Chang's.

I ought to feel celebratory, uplifted, but the gloom of being unable to find Cassie has cast a shadow over me that I am unable to shake, and all at once I'm exhausted.

It's almost nine o'clock. Two hours to kill before I can ask around at the Ambient Lounge and hopefully find someone who can positively identify Cassie.

Resigned to waiting, I heap the cushions on one end of the couch and then lie down, letting sleep rush in.

A second later, the office door flies open, almost banging off its hinges, and I look up to see Cassie storming in. She's wearing a white raincoat and matching heels, her dark hair scooped up in a bun.

I know I am dreaming, because the office is filled with a cool winter sunshine, and a daytime tabloid talk show is playing on the TV in the corner of the ceiling. Even so, I get to my feet, a passenger in my own body.

I hear my voice say, "Hey, Cassie. This is an unexpected pleasure."

In her hand is a bouquet of red roses, which she discards on the desk, scattering papers and petals.

"Enough," she says with a snap.

"What's up?" My hand reaches out for her. "Cassie?"

"Do you want me to make a scene? Because I will, if you keep pushing me."

I glance at the people sitting at their workstations on the other side of the glass partition. Already, several are staring, whispering to their colleagues.

"Stop sending me flowers," Cassie says, drawing my gaze back to her. "Stop calling me day and night. Stop treating me like I'm your property. Whatever this is"—she stirs a finger in the air between us—"it ends here, right now, or I swear I'll call the police."

She turns to leave, but I move to intercept.

"Cassie. Wait. I don't understand. What's going on here? I thought we were solid? I don't get it."

"And that's the problem. Now please move out of my way."

I put myself between her and the door. "Just talk to me. Whatever misunderstanding there is, we can work it out."

"We talked already. None of it made any difference. I'm through talking."

I hear my voice say, "I'll change. I promise. You can't leave it like this. I love you." My lips form an encouraging smile. "I'm committed to this."

Her doubting expression turns to one of horror. "What did you just say?"

"I'm committed to this."

"No, before that."

"I love you?"

Cassie shrinks from the words, like I just spit out something vile and toxic.

"Listen to me, Jed. I won't say this again. Leave me alone."

Then she pushes past me, and she's through the door before I can do anything about it.

Every eye in the office is focused on our fight.

"What the hell is happening here?" I call after her. "Just tell me."

"Hopefully, the end of *this*," she calls back. "You need help, Jed. I hope you get it."

My hand reaches for the door and slams it.

And I wake up with a jolt to find myself still curled up on the office couch in the semidarkness, a cool sweat varnishing my skin and my heart racing.

I push myself into a seated position and run my shaking hands through my hair, telling myself, *It's just another bad dream.*

Or a returning memory, one steeped in emotion and strong enough to break through the amnesia barrier.

On unsteady legs, I make my way over to the window. Beyond the glass, the city lights hold back the night. Down below, the red-and-white garlands of traffic crisscross Manhattan. According to the clock on my phone, I have been asleep for over an hour. It doesn't feel like it.

As I'm looking at it, the phone rings, shrill in the silence. I recognize the number. Detective Westfall.

"We need to stop doing this," I say as I answer. "People are going to start talking."

"That's the least of your worries," Westfall says in my ear. "I'll cut to the chase, Mr. Allen. I need for you to come down to the station right away."

"Why?"

"News from the lab. The FBI put a rush on the results."

My breath catches. "Is it hers, the blood on the dress?"

"Now, that I don't know. Not yet anyway. I'm hoping those results will be back pretty soon, given what they found."

I lean against the cool glass. "Found?"

"We'll discuss it when you get here."

"Why do I get the impression this isn't a polite request?"

"Because it's not."

"And if I'm busy? I need to be somewhere else in less than an hour."

"Then I suggest you reschedule, or you'll leave me with no choice but to send a car to bring you in. Where are you at, Mr. Allen? You at your apartment in the Majestic? Me and my boys can be there in thirty minutes."

I push away from the glass. "What's going on here, Detective? Am I in some kind of trouble? Because right now really isn't a good time, and I'm not sure I like where this is headed."

"No need to get antsy, Mr. Allen. Aside from the latest development, which I promise I'll discuss with you when you're here, I need for you to come down to the station and make a statement."

"I did that already."

"I need another one. Not about your missing girlfriend this time. You need to make a new statement concerning the dress you found in the trunk of your car. Answer a few pertinent questions, for the record. Just to get all our ducks in a row."

My heart is thudding, and warning bells are ringing in my head. "Whatever it is that's really going on here, it'll have to wait. I have things I need to take care of."

"Mr. Allen, don't fight me on this. You were the one who introduced the fox to the henhouse. You can't turn a blind eye when feathers start flying. So let me be blunt. If you're not here within the next hour, you will be arrested."

My throat is tightening. "For what? I haven't done anything."

Of course, this isn't true. I have no doubt I've done plenty of illegal things in my time, including supplying recreational drugs.

Is that it? Does Westfall know about my part in Song's death?

Westfall is silent for a few seconds, and when he speaks again, his tone is calm but serious. "Mr. Allen, you need to tell me exactly where you are and then stay there."

Panicked, I end the call.

Chapter Twenty-One

Westfall's words are echoing in my head as I arrive slightly breathless at the Majestic. A cool breeze is whipping up, rustling those leaves still resisting their fall, and there's a feeling of a change in pressure.

I may be amnesic, but I'm not stupid.

If a police detective threatens you with the word *arrest*, then it's a safe bet that he has good grounds to suspect you're guilty of something he needs to take action on, and quickly. Why else would Westfall be willing to make a personal appearance at this late hour on a weekend night? The chilling conclusion is that the bloodied dress I found in my car must point to someone being either savagely injured or even murdered. That that someone could well be Cassie.

And Westfall thinks I am responsible.

The sudden realization that Cassie could be seriously hurt or even dead hits me like a wrecking ball, and I clutch a streetlight for support.

A doorman rushes over, holding on to his hat. "Here, Mr. Allen, let me help you." He takes my weight, walking me into the entranceway.

"Thanks. I'm okay."

But I am far from it, and he sees the dread filling up my face. Even so, he could have no idea about the dark thoughts swirling in my head.

Since coming off the phone with Westfall, I have been slave to a compulsion, an urgency, a *need*, to get to my apartment before Westfall and his boys turn up. The detective's words implied more than simply throwing on the handcuffs and marching me to the nearest cell. They suggested the issuing of a search warrant for my apartment, in which case I need to remove every last trace of the stalker wall squirreled away in the closet before it corroborates Westfall's suspicions.

A protection of my interests that officers of the law call *destroying evidence*.

But what choice do I have?

I don't want to believe that I have harmed Cassie, but it's not important what I believe. It's what Westfall believes that matters. And without a memory to prove otherwise, I'm not in any position to defend myself, or even to come up with an alibi.

As I cross the lobby on hurrying feet, I hear someone calling my name, and I look around to see the building's superintendent waving at me from the desk. Standing with him are a pair of police officers.

Flames scorch my lungs.

My first instinct is to pretend I haven't heard, continue to the elevator, lock myself in the apartment, and burn all the photos. My second impulse is to run—anywhere, far from here. But before I can get my brain in gear, the police officers come over, flanking me, effectively barring my escape.

"Officers Frantz and Malone with the NYPD," one of the officers announces. "Mr. Allen, we'd like for you to accompany us down to the station."

"Can I ask what this is about, Officers?"

Of course, I'm confident I know the answer, but I don't want to appear like I'm expecting it, or provide the superintendent with more cause for suspicion.

Even from the little I've seen of the Majestic, the setup here is first-class. News that one of its tenants is involved in a heinous crime won't go down well with the residents' association.

As though picking up on my thoughts, the officer glances at the super, then back to me. "It's a sensitive matter. You need to come with us. Discuss it in private."

"Really? Because right now I need to be someplace else. So if this can wait until morning—"

"It can't." He gives me a grave expression to back it up.

I turn my back on the super. "Look, could you cut me a little slack here?" I say to the officers. "This is embarrassing. Can you at least give me five minutes while I run up to my apartment to grab a few things?"

"I'm sorry, Mr. Allen."

I release a flustered breath, but I don't argue the point, and five minutes later I am escorted into a small beige-and-black interview room at a nearby police station.

No one has said much about anything on the short ride over, other than to assure me that it is in my best interests to cooperate fully and without reservation.

"I thought we were going to Eastchester," I say as I am seated at a table.

"Just sit tight, Mr. Allen. Someone will be with you shortly."

Then I am left to my own devices, wondering how many murderers have sat in this same chair, and worse still, if I am one of them.

Unlike in the movies, there is no one-way mirror on the wall. Instead, a small closed-circuit TV camera is mounted in the corner, its little red light shining.

Fifteen minutes pass, with every elapsing second giving Westfall more time to acquire his search warrant. One by one, I go through the scenarios of him and his men poring through my apartment, and each time it ends with the same devastating discovery: that I am a stalker.

The heat is off in the room, but soon I am drenched in sweat.

Eventually, the door opens and two people enter. Neither is wearing a police uniform, and neither of them is Detective Westfall.

The first is a gray-haired woman with one of those faces that looks like it would melt if it saw direct sunlight. She is heavy in the hip area, and her suit pants seem to be a few inches too short. Hanging on a red lanyard around her neck is a photo ID with SNP on it. Tight on her heels is a tall man with salt-and-pepper hair and the aura of someone who has just had a dressing-down. The permanent creases in his suit imply he spends too much time behind a desk or on the road.

I sit up, all thoughts of Westfall tearing up my apartment gone.

I have seen both of these people before. At the hospital, talking with Song Chang's doctors, right before Gary whisked me away.

The realization that my being here has nothing to do with Westfall should come as a relief, but it doesn't.

This is just as bad.

The woman pulls out a chair and sits down. "Mr. Allen. My name's Karin Sorenson, and I'm an assistant DA, currently assigned to the Office of the Special Narcotics Prosecutor."

I stretch my neck, feeling completely out of my depth.

"And this is Special Agent Dooley with the DEA."

Dooley nods, then perches himself on the end of the table, folding his arms and looking down at me with an expression that swings between irritation and impatience.

Sorenson says, "Has anyone spoken to you about the reason you're here?"

"No. But I think I can hazard a good guess."

"Then I expect you're wondering why you're not being interviewed by detectives from the homicide division?"

"Honestly? It hadn't occurred to me."

"Well, the answer is simple, and I won't beat around the bush. The daughter of a high-profile foreign national has died unlawfully on US soil. When something like this happens, it's all hands on deck. And since this particular death is drug-related, it falls under our jurisdiction. Hence, Agent Dooley and I have been tasked with this part of the overall homicide investigation. You, Mr. Allen, are what we call a person of interest."

"Shouldn't you be out there looking for the actual murderer?"

"That's not our department." She takes a file folder from her bag and places it on the table. "A short while ago, the Chinese ambassador met with Mayor Rubenstein. You may or may not be aware of this, but Sino-US relations are tense at best, and a high-profile death like this could tip the balance. The Chinese want answers. But, more importantly, they want to see justice served."

"Don't tell me—it needs to be swift and decisive, and it's my head on the block."

She doesn't say so either way. But we both know the facts, the implications of what happened last night. My part involves providing illegal drugs to Song, who ended up dead. The assistant DA's part involves making sure someone pays with their liberty.

"Is this the point where I ask for a lawyer?"

"That's your prerogative, Mr. Allen. But as of right now, you are not under arrest. As far as we're concerned, you're helping us gather information."

I offer her a fake smile. "That's a relief to know. For a second there, you had me quaking in my boots."

My nervous sarcasm goes unappreciated, and right away I regret making light of a dark situation.

"Where this goes from here on out," she says, "is dependent on your full cooperation. Should this change, you will be informed as such, read your rights, and then processed accordingly. At that point, you will be advised to seek legal representation, as is your right. My hope is it doesn't come to that. I know I speak also for Agent Dooley when I say I'd prefer not to go down the prosecutorial route. My guess is that you don't want to either."

"Now that I think about it, given the choice—"

"Why should you pay for someone else's crime, right?"

I say nothing—not because I have nothing to say, but because I have too many words that don't need to be said.

Although I didn't slice Song's skin to ribbons and then leave her to bleed out in those bushes, the drugs I brought to the party would have had a negative influence on her ability to make rational and safe judgments. Without saying it, we both know my actions facilitated what happened in the park.

Sorenson taps a finger against the file folder in front of her. "You should know that earlier today, your business partner provided a sworn statement, indicating that you supplied the narcotics found in Miss Chang's system."

My belly curls into a ball. "Wait a minute. *Gary* told you that? You've got to be kidding me. Gary's my best friend. That doesn't make any sense."

"When their backs are to the wall . . ." She pushes the file an inch toward me. "Please, take a look. It's all there in black and white."

With trembling hands, I open it up. The statement is short and simple and condemning, and is signed *Gary Quartucci*, time-stamped this afternoon.

I look up at her, knowing that my internal struggles are emblazoned on my face for all the world to see. "I can't believe he betrayed me like this." My words are just the surface of my disbelief; my sense of treachery runs deep to my core, shaking me within.

"We all have our breaking points, Mr. Allen. Don't blame Mr. Quartucci for your mistakes. He did the right thing. His civic duty, no less. This is your one and only chance to be equally upstanding."

I push the file back to her, knowing that my choices are extremely limited. "Okay. What do you need from me?"

"A name." She sees my indecision, and she spreads her hands preacherlike, as though she's about to absolve me of my sins. "I have no idea what relationship you have with this person. I'm hoping for your sake it's purely business. If so, it'll make this a whole lot easier for you."

"You're asking me to betray a trust."

"I'm asking you to think about Miss Chang lying in the morgue, and then you can decide if this dealer of yours is the one who's going to prison, or you."

I rub the back of a hand across my brow. It comes away damp.

Dooley clears his throat and speaks for the first time. "We're offering immunity in exchange for helping us get a conviction. It's a one-time deal, partner. You have exactly ten seconds to make up your mind, after which time we're taking you down to booking." He looks at his watch. "Ten . . . nine . . . eight . . ."

Chapter Twenty-Two

The prodigal son returns," Maurice announces as he opens the door leading into Tess's apartment. He's wearing a black satin bathrobe and matching slippers.

I don't wait for an invite, or even consider exchanging pleasantries. I push past him, striding through the shadowy hall, shouting out Tess's name as I go.

The living room is dimly lit, with most of the illumination coming from concealed mood lighting and a number of candles dotted around the room. There's a distinct aroma of incense, and atmospheric music tinkles from hidden speakers.

Tess isn't anywhere in sight.

"Tess!"

Maurice comes scrambling around in front of me. "Hold your horses. You can't just barge in here. What do you think you're doing?"

"Where is she?"

He blocks my path, trying to make himself big. "Tess is meditating. And she doesn't need a wanker like you disturbing her after business hours. Get me?" He makes a stern face.

I sidestep him, headed for the master bedroom.

"You're not allowed in there!" he shouts after me.

The master bedroom resembles what I imagine the insides of a Bedouin tent might have looked like during the time of *The Arabian Nights*. Heavy silks and tasseled fabrics hang against the walls and are garlanded around the room. Mounds of colorful cushions soften the contours, and the gentle flicker of candle flames adds to the sense of the exotic.

Sitting in a lotus position on a round bed is Tess, fully nude and looking skeletal, her long black hair hanging like a mink stole against her bloodless skin.

"Put some clothes on," I say. "We need to talk."

Maurice rushes in behind me. "Tess, I tried stopping him."

"It's okay," she says, opening her eyes. "We're all friends here. Be a gentleman, Jed, and pass me my robe."

I hand her a black silk kimono from the back of a chair.

"Did it work?" she asks as she puts it on.

"What?"

"The care package. Did it jump-start your memory?"

"No. And to be honest, as things stand, I don't think I want my memory back. Something else happened, and I have a bigger problem to deal with right now."

"And you need my help to fix it?"

"You can't."

Tess looks at me with questioning eyes. "Then why are you here?"

"As a courtesy, I guess. Because I needed to tell someone, and I can't just tell anyone. This is as bad as it gets."

"You're not making much sense."

"Remember those little yellow pills you gave me?"

"The ecstasy."

"Indirectly, it killed someone."

Maurice makes a sound of ridicule, but Tess's expression shows she's genuinely aghast.

"And not just anyone," I say. "The daughter of the head honcho we've been dealing with. She's dead, Tess. And those pills played their part."

"Jed, I'm so sorry." She takes a cigarette pack from the pocket of her kimono and lights one up, sucking deeply. "This has never happened to us before. You must be in shock. Are you okay?"

"Put it this way—I've been better."

"How can I help?"

"You can't. Unless you can perform miracles, it's too late to do anything about it. She was attacked in the park, after the party. The police say if she hadn't taken the drugs, she might have thought twice about being there."

"That's a big stretch. I can see why you said 'indirectly.'"

"Even so . . ."

"Was she drinking?"

"We all were."

"But they aren't raking the club owners over hot coals, are they?" She blows out smoke. "As terrible as this is, Jed, it's a fact that alcohol is more effective at diminishing inhibitions than anything in that care package of yours."

I shake my head at her attempt to pass the buck. "Tess, there's no getting around it. Those drugs contributed to her death. You sold them to me. I gave them to her. That makes both of us accountable."

"Indirectly."

"It doesn't change what happened."

For a moment, there are no words spoken between us; my news has enough gravity to suck them back down into our throats, where they threaten to asphyxiate us.

Finally, Tess exhales smoke, saying, "What were you doing in the park last night?"

"Excuse me?"

"Don't deny it. I saw you through the telescope. You were in the park late last night. And you said this woman was assaulted there, right?"

"Yes, but . . ." I flick my gaze from Tess to Maurice, and then back to her. "You can't seriously think I attacked her?"

"To be perfectly honest, Jed, I'm wondering what to believe. You show up here at this late hour, looking like the devil is snapping at your heels, expecting me to share the blame in a death that, only in a very circuitous way, I could be associated with. You speak about the police asking awkward questions about the drugs in her system, when we both know that the connection to me is flimsy and wouldn't hold up in a court of law. And, I don't know . . . it all feels a little calculated to me. Something doesn't quite add up."

I wipe sweat from my brow. "There's no big conspiracy here. I just thought I should give you a heads-up, that's all. It's the decent thing to do. I don't remember how long we've had this arrangement of ours, but I'm guessing that, as my dealer, you've taken care of my needs at the drop of a hat. I owe you. This is my way of paying back."

Tess takes a long pull on her cigarette before blowing it out the side of her mouth. "I love you, Jed. We've had a good run. And I wish only the best for you. But it's over. Maurice will see you out."

Then she retreats to the bathroom, leaving a trail of smoke behind her.

Round-shouldered, I follow Maurice to the apartment door.

"You can shove your insincerities where the sun doesn't shine," he says as he waves me out. "Now piss off and don't come back until you can pay us everything you owe."

Chapter Twenty-Three

S eltzer was walking home when his phone rang.

"Your name Seltzer?" came a man's voice as he answered.

"Who's asking?"

"We spoke a few weeks back, about this guy you're looking for."

Seltzer slowed his pace. "I've been speaking to a lot of people."

In fact, he'd talked to dozens of possible eyewitnesses recently, in various locations across the city, insinuating that he was working with the police on the hunt for a wanted criminal and that any assistance they could give might lead to an arrest. He'd found this exaggeration of the truth to be the easiest way to unzip lips without raising suspicion.

"I work at the Roosevelt, on Madison Avenue," said the caller. "That picture you left—I asked around. It took some time, but I got a name."

Now Seltzer came to a stop, glancing up and down the quiet street at the big houses barely visible in the dark. "I'm listening."

"So, turns out he used to be a regular."

"In what way?"

"He'd stay overnight, maybe two weekends out of every month."

"For what reason?"

"I don't have that information. I do know he used our fitness-and-health center when he was here. It was a personal trainer who recognized him."

"Did he say anything at all about this guy?"

"Only that he remembers he said he worked on Wall Street, but it wasn't in finance."

"And he no longer stays at the hotel?"

"Not for a while."

Seltzer nibbled at the inside of his cheek. "This is probably a long shot," he said, "but do you have his home address?"

"No. And, anyway, even if we did, we value guest privacy."

Seltzer almost said, *Except here you are, breaking your own rule.* Instead, he told the caller he appreciated his help and then asked for the guest's name.

When he had it, Seltzer hung up, a strange kind of calm settling over him.

It felt weird, this sudden, complete cessation in his angst. For so long, his torment had remained a constant din in the back of his head. Even the momentary elation he'd felt when buying the gun hadn't quelled the background noise. Words failed him. It was as if the second he'd heard the man's name, the demon raging inside him had packed up and shipped out, leaving a vacancy filled only with silence.

Seltzer stared at the wedding band on his ring finger, remaining motionless for at least a minute while his thoughts raced in his head. Then he opened up a browser on his phone and ran a search on the man's name. He found who he was looking for almost right away, on a business website complete with directions to a Wall Street address, along with a thumbnail image and a bio of the man responsible for ruining his life.

When he'd read as much as he could stomach, Seltzer crossed the street, headed for the house that he hadn't been able to call home since the day his wife died.

Chapter Twenty-Four

Dazed, I leave Tess's apartment. Deep in the back of my mind, I can recall someone once saying, "We are where we are because we put ourselves there."

A group of people are congregated by the elevator, each one watching me silently and expectantly as I approach.

"Please tell me you got what you needed," I say to Sorenson as she separates herself from the somber-faced men and women in DEA windbreakers.

"It's a start," she says. "Enough, at least, to get you off the hook, for now anyway."

I unbutton my shirt and pull the tiny microphone off my chest, plucking out hairs as the surgical tape rips away.

The pain is nothing compared with the shame of duplicity.

Dooley takes the gadget from my hand, then nods at his colleagues to execute their task, and they stream around us, striding toward the black door at the end of the hall.

"You did the right thing," Sorenson says.

"Yeah, well, it doesn't feel like it."

Dooley prods a finger against my bare chest. "This can still go tits up, Allen. In which case, we'll be talking again. So hang in there, partner. Don't speak about this to anyone. And don't leave town."

Seconds later, I am in the stairwell, trudging down the steps to the fifth floor, each footfall sending shock waves up my spine.

As I descend, I think about how my life spiraled out of control in the course of twenty-four hours, and all the questionable decisions I must have made that brought me to this point.

Something inside me feels trapped, and I'm not sure if it's guilt clawing away at my gut, or the other version of me struggling to reach the surface and take back what was his.

Every decision I made tonight was made without his consent.

My vision spins, and I grab the metal handrail, holding on as the stairwell carousels around me. The vertical shaft seems to lengthen, up and down, stretching into opposite infinities. I slam my eyes closed, clinging, barely breathing, until the dizziness subsides.

"You need to toughen up," I say as my vision steadies.

But I have a feeling it won't happen overnight.

After everything that's gone on, even with the police breathing down my neck, my overriding instinct is to find Cassie. I am convinced she holds the answers to explain my upturned life. And I have to believe that the blood on the dress is not hers.

Will my stalker photos lead me to her?

I don't get the chance to find out.

As I come out of the stairwell at the fifth floor, I see a police officer standing outside my apartment door, and I come to a dead stop. The apartment door is wide open, and I get a glimpse of movement inside.

With fear squeezing my heart, I retreat back into the stairwell, where I lean against the wall, sucking in air and fighting back my body's desire to collapse in a quivering heap.

My phone rings, harsh and echoing. At first, I don't answer it, thinking it's Westfall trying to pinpoint my location. Then I see Dr. Merrick's name on the screen and I take the call.

"Jed, the police are at the apartment."

"You're still there?"

"Yes."

"I thought I said—"

"I know what you suggested. But Doctor knows best, remember? Anyway, it's a good thing I'm still here. Otherwise they would have beat down your door."

"Is it Detective Westfall?"

"Him and a bunch of FBI agents."

"The FBI?"

"Plus, officers from the NYPD. They arrived a couple of minutes ago with a search warrant. They're going over the place with a fine-tooth comb. Jed, what's going on?"

"Nothing. I mean, obviously, *something*. Just nothing to do with me."

I sound panicked, like I'm making excuses, and I'm sure it shows.

"You need to be here," she says.

"Well, that won't be happening anytime soon. The crux of it is, Westfall thinks I did something I didn't do. It's a long story. The second I turn up there, he'll march me off in cuffs."

"They're tearing the place apart."

I visualize Westfall chancing on the false door at the back of the walk-in closet, his eyes growing to the size of eggs as he realizes the depth of my sleaziness.

"Is this about what happened at the hospital?" she asks.

"No. That's another enormous mess entirely. Chang's daughter was attacked. They think it was this Central Park Slasher person."

"Oh my."

I hear her breathing quicken, and I imagine the speed of her thoughts accelerating toward a deadly conclusion.

"And I had nothing to do with that either," I say before she comes up with the wrong answer.

"I didn't think for a second you did."

"Has Westfall said anything?"

"Only to ask if I know where you are and if I'm expecting you home anytime soon."

"What did you tell him?"

"Nothing. Because I don't know anything. And that's the truth. Jed, I'm worried. If this is all a huge mistake on their part, you need to come home and clear your name."

"You mean prove my innocence? One big disadvantage, Doc—I can't remember anything before yesterday, including alibis."

"Jed, where are you?"

I take a deep breath. "In the stairwell."

"Here?"

"Yes."

"Stay right there. I'm on my way."

The call disconnects, and as it does, the phone vibrates in my hand, notifying me of an incoming text from an undisclosed number.

I tap it open, and then stare wide-eyed at the message:

JED, I'M AT HOME. COME TO ME?

I am still reeling from the realization that Cassie is alive and well and waiting for me to come home, when the stairwell door swings open and Dr. Merrick appears, framed in the hallway light. She sees me loitering on the next landing below and hurries down the steps, and before I can say anything, her arms are around my neck, her lips pressed against my ear.

"You've got me shaking like a leaf," she whispers as she clings. "And I don't scare easily."

I let the embrace linger, at first reciprocating out of politeness, but stiff to her touch, my mind figuring out the fastest way to the lake house.

On a conscious level, I have no recollection of being intimate with Dr. Merrick. My subconscious, however, recognizes her: the shape of her face, the curves of her body, the warmth of her touch. And as her body heat penetrates, as the smell of her hair, her skin, pervades my senses, muscle memory takes over, and I soften to the hug, molding my body to hers.

"You have to believe me," I say. "I didn't do it."

"I do believe you, Jed. Heck, I know you better than you know yourself." She releases me, and I let her go, but not too quickly. "Exactly what do they think you've done?"

"I'm not sure. But you can bet it's something terrible." I glance down the deserted stairwell, then back up to the door leading to the fifth floor. "This morning, I found a dress in the trunk of my car."

"Not one of mine, I'm guessing."

"That's just it—I don't know. Are you missing one?"

"Not that I'm aware of. Then again, I haven't checked."

"Anyway, this afternoon, I took it to the police. That's when I met Westfall."

She frowns. "And now the FBI are ransacking your apartment? I don't get it, Jed. What aren't you telling me?"

"The dress was covered in blood."

Her frown takes on a suspicious bent. "Um, okay. You never mentioned any of this earlier."

"It's not something you share with just anybody."

Now she looks hurt.

I take her by the arms. "Sarah, listen to me. I'm sorry. I didn't mean that to sound the way it did. It's just . . . you gave me so much to think about when we spoke earlier, about you and me, about what we have together. I guess I got sidetracked."

"Understandably."

"And the topic never came up. Plus, I wasn't exactly dwelling on it, anyway. I assumed there'd be a logical explanation."

"Just not one that turned you into a wanted man."

Now it's my turn to frown. "Trust me. This thing with Westfall, it's just a big misunderstanding. I didn't do anything."

"Jed, you don't have to work so hard to convince me. I'm on your side. My only concern is, it still doesn't explain how the dress ended up in your car."

In her eyes, I see the need to tie up loose ends, to get to the root of the problem, and I let her go. "You're right. It doesn't. I'm guessing the other me—"

"The *other* you?"

"The man I was before yesterday, before the amnesia took hold. That's the other me." I start to pace the small landing, trying to burn off nervous energy. "Look, I know it sounds weird, and no doubt you'll tell me it's not good for my long-term psyche, but separating the before and the after is the easiest way for me to get a handle on what's happening. At first, I thought I was losing my mind, but I'm not."

"But you are teetering."

"Maybe. Possibly. Is it any wonder? Look where I am."

Dr. Merrick watches me pace, the worry in her face as bright as a beacon.

"Jed, you do realize that refusing to deal with this crisis will ultimately work against you."

"No other way around it."

"Plus, if you don't face your accusers right now, it will only make you look guilty further down the line."

"It's my word against theirs. And my memory can't exactly be counted on. I won't have a leg to stand on."

"You've got *me*." She grabs my hand as I pass, putting an end to my pacing. "Jed. I'm serious. You need to come home with me, right now. Clear this up. I'm sure Detective Westfall is a reasonable man. It's not in his interest to arrest someone without probable cause."

"I can't."

"Why?"

I hold back, unable to tell her about the text, and my urge to rush to the lake house, to Cassie's side.

I pull out of her grasp. "He thinks I killed somebody."

"What?"

"Just look at the facts, Doc. First off, I reported Cassie as missing . . ."

"You did what?"

I stare at her, realizing my error. "I was confused, okay? Memory issues. And secondly, I handed Westfall a dress covered in blood."

"Cassie's blood?"

"That's just it—I don't know. Maybe." In truth, out of cowardice, I have avoided speculating. "I mean, what other reason is there for him trashing my apartment?"

"A bloodied dress in itself isn't proof of anything."

"Try telling that to Westfall. I spoke with him on the phone a little while ago. He told me he sent the dress over to the forensics lab and that he needed to speak with me in person, urgently, about what they found."

"Which was . . . ?"

"He wouldn't tell me. He was too busy insisting I drop everything and come running to the police station. Whatever information they came back with, that's his motivation. The dress was torn up, like someone had hacked at it. I left my car parked at the police station, too. For all I know, he probably found the knife in the glove compartment already."

With a start, I realize I hadn't mentioned the hunting knife to her before, and her silence is intense, her stare drilling into mine.

"I have to go," I say, backing away.

"Jed . . ."

She reaches out, but I keep going.

Above us, the door leading to the fifth floor opens, revealing a familiar figure framed in the hallway light.

"Mr. Allen," Westfall calls as he sees us on the lower landing, "stay right where you are."

But I do the exact opposite. The nervous energy in my legs catches fire, and I run, leaping down the steps, five at a time.

I hear Dr. Merrick shout, "Wait! Jed! Please! Stop! You're making a mistake!"

But I keep going, hurtling down one switchback after another, the air in my lungs igniting.

Behind me, Westfall gives chase, calling for me to desist.

I don't. I keep going, fueled by fear, superheated blood thundering in my head.

I hear Westfall take a tumble, cursing as he hits the floor.

At ground level, I break out onto the street through one of the building's side entrances, snatching a panicked look left and right. In one direction, Central Park lies less than a hundred yards away, shrouded in darkness, and my first instinct is to flee toward it, lured by the promise of dark hiding places. But I go right instead, sprinting at full speed down the sidewalk toward the bright taillights of a yellow taxi dropping off a passenger.

"Take the West Side Highway to Eastchester," I say as I fall inside. "Fast."

Everything is pounding: my heart, my brain, my eyeballs. Sweat pricking out all over my skin.

I flatten myself on the back seat, breathing hard and repeating my request to the taxi driver, who is peering at me over his shoulder.

"You on the lam," he says, "fare's doubled."

"Okay, Jesse James. Whatever. Just go."

As the taxi pulls away, I risk a peep through the rear window, just in time to see Detective Westfall come bursting out onto the street. For a heart-stopping second, he looks my way and I think he's spied me, but then he takes off in the direction of the park.

And I give in to my nerves, shaking uncontrollably.

Chapter Twenty-Five

The desire to distance myself from the Majestic is almost as strong as my need to shorten the gap between Cassie and me. Her text is a ray of sunshine breaking through a stormy sky, and the thought of being reunited with her is all-consuming. Even so, I spend most of the thirty-minute taxi ride to Eastchester fighting off the distractions of my adopted life.

Despite having no memory of my past, the last day and a half has opened up a window on it, giving me an insight into the corrupted world I created for myself, a system designed with me at the center.

It seems, since the death of my parents, I organized my life to suit only me. I used up my inheritance on bright lights and tinsel, trading values for victory. I greased the gears of the Jed Allen machine with self-indulgence and powered it with avarice, indulging in my day job and my nightlife with equal passion. Every way I look at it, it's clear I put myself first, and it's served me well for decades.

But at what price, and to whom?

You can't build a house without hammering in nails.

In the world that existed before yesterday, the other Jed Allen was a successful architect. He worked hard and he played hard. And yet, other than on a physical level, I feel no bond with him. Nor do I feel his creative urge, or any inclination to chase the beast again, the way I did at Rafferty's. Now that I think about it, being an architect means nothing to me. Nothing.

Is this normal?

I started out thinking of my condition as a disability, that my empty brain was in some way an impediment. But I was being short-sighted. The amnesia is a blessing. It has opened my eyes and brought an unprecedented clarity, given me a unique retrospection.

It's as though I have been reborn.

My phone rings. It's Gary. I deny the call.

Gary claims we are like brothers, but it's a lie. No best friend would stab the other in the back the way he has.

How many other times has he laid me out as a sacrifice?

Other than our shared stewardship of the architecture firm, I have no further responsibility toward him. Now that the China deal is secure, cash will start to flow again, in instead of out. The firm will rise from the quagmire of its financial liability, and we will be debt-free.

If I want it, I can take my share and go, start over, with Cassie.

The taxi pulls up outside the lake house and leaves me standing on the curbside, my breath steaming in the cool night air.

Beneath a moonless sky, Lakeshore Drive is deathly still, a mourner's veil drawn over the charcoal trees.

It's after midnight, and every part of me is excited to see Cassie. And yet I linger.

For the new me, this will be our first meeting, and suddenly I am struck with a palpable apprehension. My whole impression of Cassie is constructed on snippets of discoveries, and dreams that didn't end well. Other than the little I have pieced together, figured out, assumed, I know nothing about her, as a person or as a lover, and I have no idea what I am walking into, or even if she will live up to the image I have of her.

What if I fail to live up to hers?

After all, she's in a relationship not with me, but with him, the other version, and it occurs to me for the first time that Cassie has fallen for the old me, with his debased ways and his winner-takes-all mind-set.

What if she doesn't approve of the change?

My phone rings, a siren threatening to disturb the neighborhood, and I expect to see Gary's name in lights, but it's Dr. Merrick's on the screen.

"Jed," she says as I take her call, "where are you?"

"In Eastchester."

"How did you—?"

"Taxi."

"What are you doing in Eastchester?"

"There's this house on the lake that . . . listen, it's a long story, and I expect you won't understand when I tell you about it later. I know I wouldn't. Either way, right now I need to be here. I can't escape it."

"It's late. When will you be back?" She sounds disappointed, and something else. Tense?

I look at the house, noticing a faint glow in one of the upper windows, and a flame of hope ignites in my chest. "Honestly, I don't know."

"Jed, you need to come home."

"Did the police leave already?"

There's a pause, in which I hear a muffled exchange, and then a man's voice comes on the phone:

"Mr. Allen, this is Detective Westfall. Listen to me, you need to—"

I end the call, putting the phone on silent.

"I haven't got time for your conspiracy theories," I say as I stuff the phone back in my pocket.

Then I take a deep breath and make my way up the front walk, feeling loose in my own skin, as though nothing fits.

Even before I reach the door, I see that it has been left slightly open, inviting entrance, and I go inside, hardly breathing, closing the door behind me.

The note I left for Cassie, pinned to the newel post, is gone.

Coming from the upper landing, a wedge of light is illuminating the stairs, splitting the dark. And like a moth, I am drawn to it. Adrenaline propels me up the steps three at a time.

"Cassie?"

The light is on in the master bedroom.

I rush inside, and then come to a full stop, every shiny bit of excitement crumbling to dust and blowing away.

A man is sitting on the end of the bed. There's a revolver in his hand, pointing at me.

"Hello, Jed," he says. "I see you got my message."

It takes a second for my mind to catch up, and when it does, it starts to spin. "Wait. *You* sent the text? How'd you get my number?"

"From your online profile." He sees my mystified expression and adds, "Your firm's website."

I stare at him through narrowed eyes. "Who the hell are you?"

"The name's Seltzer," he says, getting to his feet. "Arnold Seltzer."

◆ ◆ ◆

"Seltzer?" I stretch the word out, as if by doing so it will take shape and make more sense. It doesn't. "You mean like the antacid?"

"Right down to the bubbly character."

He motions with the gun, and I put my hands up, sucking myself into a narrower profile. But it's a pointless exercise; I am only a few feet from the muzzle, and even a bad shot couldn't miss at this range.

"You look familiar," I say. "Do we know each other?"

"In a roundabout kind of way. We've never been formally introduced. But I know all about you, and maybe at some point you've checked me out, too. It's surprising how much personal information you can find online these days. I know you're a hotshot architect with million-dollar offices on Wall Street. I know you're a playboy and a homewrecker. And I know I could kill you right where you stand for trespassing, and I'd get away with it." He smiles a hollow smile.

"Look, if I owe you, and it's money you're after . . . let's just start by you putting down that gun, and we can talk this through, like gentlemen. Because I really have no idea what's going on here."

"Don't play games. You're *here*. You know what this is about."

"Well, maybe that's true, and I did, before Friday. But right now, I'm in the middle of something called intermittent amnesia, which means if you and I have crossed paths in the past, I have no recollection of it." I see him start to frown, and I add, "I'm not making it up. It's a real medical condition. So you're going to have to fill me in. First off, you can explain why you're in my house."

"*Your* house?" His frown deepens. "This is *my* house."

"What?" At first, I'm shocked, but then I remember Westfall stating he couldn't find any properties in my name on Lakeshore Drive. Have I been mistaken from the start?

"Or," Seltzer says, "at least it's still my house for the next three days. After that it'll belong to the bank." He motions with the gun again, forcing my hands higher. "For the record, I bought this house five years ago, with my wife. Our dream home—or so we thought. Things didn't quite work out as planned. Either way, it's my name on the deed. My bet is you live in the city. I don't know where exactly, but I'm guessing it's pretentious. An apartment near the park with décor that is mediocre at best." He gestures at our surroundings. "I mean, come on. Will you look at this, and then look at you? This house oozes taste. And you don't. If you don't believe it's not yours, check the address on your driver's license."

Keeping my movements slow and obvious, I take out my wallet and then my license. In all of the confusion of coming to at the office, I hadn't noticed the address printed on the card, and I hadn't thought of it since. It corresponds to the apartment at the Majestic, supporting Seltzer's claim over the lake house.

Seltzer shakes his head. "Wow, you really are messed up. You should pay my therapist a visit. She'd love you."

"I have amnesia."

"So let me jog your memory."

He takes out his phone and brings up a photo on the screen. Then he turns the phone so that I can see the image, and my world flips on its head.

It's the same photo I found in Cassie's dresser, and I realize with a jolt why Seltzer's face seemed so familiar; he's the man in the picture, with Cassie.

Something like anger swells inside me, but before I can confront him about their affair, Seltzer says:

"Recognize her? You should. She's my wife, and you slept with her."

"Your wife?" The words leap from my lips, but not before leaving a bad taste behind. "I don't understand. That's Cassie. She's my girlfriend."

Seltzer glances at the phone, sticking out his lower lip. "Cassandra hasn't gone by that name since we were kids. When we married, she switched to using Sandra. She said that Sandra Seltzer, photographer, had more gravitas, for commercial reasons."

"You're married?"

My spinning mind comes to a sudden stop, hurling my thoughts to the farthest reaches, and it takes a moment for the chaos in my head to settle. When it does, I sift through the debris, searching for something to counter Seltzer's claim, but I find nothing. It's as though my whole belief system has been torn down and trampled underfoot.

And all I can say is, "She's playing both of us."

It's a serious allegation, but Seltzer laughs it off.

"Don't flatter yourself," he says. "You've got this all turned around. I think that convenient amnesia of yours is playing mind tricks on you.

Sandra was never your girlfriend. I don't know what kind of fantasy world you live in, up there in your ivory tower, but you were never anything more than a mindless fling to her. She was even considering getting a restraining order against you."

I want to say *That's a downright lie,* but I have no proof.

It's just one more so-called fact that I can't refute, and it leaves me breathless and dazed, the ache in the back of my head returning in full glory.

Seltzer retreats to the bed, where he opens up a briefcase on the comforter. With the gun still aimed at me, he takes a plain white square card from inside and then holds it out. "Go ahead. Take it."

I do, turning it over, realizing that it's a photograph taken by an instant camera.

"It's your Polaroid moment," Seltzer says.

The photo is identical to the one I have in my wallet, only this version hasn't been trimmed down to the size of a credit card.

A wider angle of the bar area is visible, with Cassie and me in the middle of the composition, snuggled up, multicolored lights garlanded around us. In this shot, more patrons are visible at the sides and standing behind us, drinks in hand. And farther still is part of the nighttime Manhattan skyline, lit up like a Christmas tree. The photo was taken outside, I realize, at a rooftop bar.

I look up, heart pounding. "Where did you get this?"

"I found it in one of her purses. I don't think she even knew it was there. The night it was taken, that was your one and only time together. Sandra told me everything. She told me how you met at the gallery, how you got her drunk that night, how you laced her drinks with drugs, how you forced yourself on her." He comes up to me, prodding the muzzle against my ribs. "Men like you, men with no moral backbone, you're the worst kind of spineless vermin. You think you can take whatever you want, with no consequences. Like you own it already. You take advantage of vulnerable women, sweet-talking them with your wealth and your status. You make me sick."

I can taste his revulsion.

"In fact," he says, his eyes narrowing into spiteful slits, "Sandra despised you. She begged you to leave her alone. But you were obsessive. You couldn't accept it was a mistake. You wanted her, at any cost. You ruined our lives. And now she's dead because of you."

My belly is a cauldron of molten lead, burning through flesh and bone.

I am speechless, my thoughts in disarray, unable to process Seltzer's words. Cassie is . . . *dead?*

Is that why I haven't been able to find her? Because . . .

I. Killed. Her. Each word comes wrapped in razor wire, slicing up my brain on the way out.

The idea is unthinkable, and yet, one after the other, death scenes strobe through my mind like the blood-spattered pages of some macabre flip-book. Gruesome images of my stranger's hands strangling the life out of Cassie, of beating her head to a pulp with a frying pan, of holding her head under the surface of the lake until every last bubble of air is squeezed from her lungs.

Seltzer returns to the briefcase, where he removes a document and holds it up. "Her death certificate," he says. "Just in case you don't believe me."

All at once, I can't breathe, and the edges of my vision seem frayed. What have I done?

Seltzer resumes his push with the gun against my sternum. "Sandra insisted it was a one-night stand. At first, I didn't believe her. I couldn't imagine her doing something like that, even just once, and especially not with someone like you. We were going through a rough patch. But the idea of her cheating on me was inconceivable. Even so, she stuck to her story, swore by it, right to the day she died. As far as I know, she'd never lied to me about anything before you came along. She was adamant it was a mistake. A momentary lapse of judgment brought on by the drugs you gave her. God knows, I wanted to believe her. I wanted to forgive her. But then she died because of you, and I never got the chance to say *anything*, and she died thinking I despised her."

The murder scenarios in my mind have stopped flickering, and I'm fixed on a scene of me stabbing Cassie repeatedly with the hunting knife, making shreds of her dress, until we are both drowning in a bloodbath.

Resulting in a bloodied dress that I hid in my car, and later handed over to the police.

My fate sealed.

It's as though someone is playing racquetball in my head.

Seltzer taps the revolver against my cheek, refocusing me.

"I've been looking for you for months," he says. "Ever since the funeral. Under every rock and down every sewer. Do you have any idea how hard it is to find someone with just a photograph to go on? Literally, it only came together in the last hour or so. Just enough time to look you up and confirm what a sleazebag you are." He pulls a piece of crumpled paper from his pocket and slams it against my chest. "I was going to confront you at your office on Monday. Shame you in public. But I found your little love note when I got home, and at first it puzzled me. What the hell were you doing in my house? And why leave a note? Then it occurred to me that I could make you come *here*, to me, with just one text. And look what happened."

My whole face is agape. As incredible as this is, I can't defend myself. Without the support of my memories or a credible witness to say otherwise, it's Seltzer's word against mine, and right now my word is *amnesia*.

Cassie is dead because of me?

I don't feel like a killer. Then again, I don't feel like my old self either. Is it possible that the other version of me was capable of taking a life? Did *he* kill Cassie? As hard as it is to accept, just because I don't remember performing the heinous act doesn't mean it never happened.

"Why?" I ask, my voice a tight creak.

"Probably because you're a rich kid with a personality disorder. You've been bred to believe you're untouchable."

"No, I mean why would I kill Cassie? I don't get it. Even if what you're saying is true, why would I kill her? Just think about it. I adored her."

Seltzer must have seen the blood drain from my face, because he says, "Well, I'll be. You didn't know she was dead, did you? That's why you're so cut up about it, nine months down the line. You didn't know she's dead. Jeez. Did you even know she was pregnant?"

Now, an emotional blowtorch burns a hole in my heart. "What?"

"Apparently, with your bastard child. That's right, Jed. You got her pregnant during that one-night stand of yours. Sandra and I hadn't had sex in months, so I knew it wasn't mine. And she'd already insisted you were her only mistake." He says it like there's poison on his tongue. "But don't worry. Your debauched bachelor lifestyle isn't in jeopardy. The government won't be chasing you down for child support. The fetus died with her, in the car crash."

As bombshells go, this one has the power to blast away every bit of me not nailed down. "Cassie died in a crash? But I thought you said I killed her?"

For a second, Seltzer just stares at me as tears blur his eyes, a tremor twitching at his lips. Then he starts to speak, and it's as though he's in a confessional, his words pouring out.

"It was January, right in the middle of a snowstorm. Sandra asked me to pick her up at the urgent-care clinic. She'd been sick all week. We both thought she had a virus. She got in the car, and I knew something was wrong. She couldn't keep it in. Turned out she was pregnant, and it didn't take a genius to figure out who the father was. We started driving, arguing. I was mad. I was so mad. Right then and there, I hated her for what she'd done. Not only had she betrayed me, but she was pregnant with your child. Understandably, I was distracted. I wasn't paying attention. The road was icy. A car clipped us from behind. And then . . ." He swallows, breathes, closes his eyes for a second. "I don't know what happened. The police say my car hit black ice and skidded out of control. The next thing I knew, we were headed into oncoming traffic and . . ." Now his voice cracks, and he drops to a seated position on the end of the bed, tears beginning to stream down his cheeks.

I am immobilized by shock, my pulse thumping in my throat.

Seltzer blows out a long, undulating breath and sniffs back his tears. "So . . . the inevitable happened. There was this terrible bang. It was so loud, like the sky had fallen. And the car just crumpled around us. I mean, it just folded, like paper. Glass everywhere. Metal screaming like you've never heard. It all happened so fast. There was nothing I could do. At some point, the car rolled. And the last thing I saw . . ." He swallows back a sob, a tremor running through him. "And the last thing I saw was Sandra's terrified face as the roof caved in, crushing her."

My heart is ablaze, stoked by the fire in my lungs. I can't believe what I am hearing.

Cassie . . . dead . . . since January.

Did the other version of me know this already? Did his stalker wall become a shrine to her memory? Is that why he took up with Dr. Merrick? If so, I can think only that some selfish part of him chose not to leave a note informing his amnesic self that Cassie is deceased.

Trembling, I reach out to Seltzer. "I'm . . . sorry."

He knocks my hand aside with the gun. "No, no, no. Don't say that. You don't have the right to be sorry. To *feel* sorrow. That's mine. Don't take it away from me. This is my loss, not yours. If it wasn't for you, Sandra would still be alive."

All at once, Seltzer looks beaten. He slumps in on himself, as though the anger that was keeping him inflated has leaked out.

There is no doubt I have played a part in hurting this man, deeply and irreversibly. Plunged him into a personal hell from which he has found no escape. I don't remember the exact moment my selfish actions changed his life forever. I can't leaf through the file cabinet of my mind and pull up the memory. It's all there, but I don't have the key. Still, it doesn't change the fact that my old ways have wreaked widespread damage.

I want to tell him that I am a changed man, that I'm not the Jed Allen who ruined his life. But given what he knows about the other version of me, why would he believe anything I say?

"Killing you is all I've thought about," Seltzer says as he wipes away his tears. "For months, it's eaten up every minute of time and every bit of me. Hunting you down, thinking about all the ways I could make you suffer, make you pay for my loss, as painfully as possible. And now, here we are."

I can feel the blood pulsing through my head. "So, what now? How's all this going to pan out? You're going to kill me, here, in Cassie's bedroom?"

Seltzer dismisses my comment with a shake of his head. "That was my intention all right, or some version of it. But then something changed, and I had a better idea. You see, it occurred to me that killing you wouldn't end my suffering. Maybe it would dilute it for a while, bring a momentary satisfaction. But there'd be no permanency in it, at least not for me anyway. Sandra would still be gone. And I'd have your death on my conscience, on top of everything else." His gaze lifts up to mine, his eyes rimmed red, his cheeks gray and hollow, sweat beading on his high brow. "I tried moving on. I really did. I went to grief counseling. I fooled myself into believing I'd be okay, someday. That I could pick up the pieces and move on, a brave smile plastered on my face. But nothing changed the fact that Sandra's gone and she's never coming back. As time passed, the thought of spending the rest of my life without her became intolerable. And the truth is, I don't think I can live another day without her. Simple as that. And that's why I decided that this was my only option. Killing two birds with one stone. The only way to make you feel my suffering, and end mine. This is all your fault."

Seltzer puts the muzzle under his chin, and a horrifying second passes before instinct launches me away from the dresser, to reach out with both hands, my voice yelling, *"No!"*

But I am too late.

The loud crack of the gun stops me in my tracks, and I blink, incredulous, as hot blood sprays across my face.

All I can do is stand there, my thoughts fleeing to the darker reaches of my mind as Seltzer's lifeless body flops back on the bed. His fingers uncurl from the revolver, and it drops to the floor.

Chapter Twenty-Six

Immortality is the stuff of films and fantasy. In reality, no one lives forever. Sooner or later, we all die. Sometimes, death chases us, inflicting terrible diseases that prolong the inevitable, killing us slowly, until it finally catches up. Sometimes, it comes rushing at us like an express bus, head-on, and, unable to step aside, we are gone in the blink of an eye. And sometimes, for either selfish or selfless reasons, we invite it.

Half a minute passes before I remember to breathe, and then it's like cymbals crashing in my ears, my heart drumming, every blood vessel in my brain twanging like it's been plucked.

An uprush of vomit hits the back of my throat, and I twist to the side, puking with enough force to make my legs quake. I grab at the dresser to stop the floor from rising up and striking me in the face, every sense screaming at me to turn and run.

The notion that Seltzer has taken his own life as an ultimate act of revenge isn't just incredible; it's momentous, and I can't shoulder the enormity of it. Instead, I focus on Cassie, and what has brought me here. Even after seeing irrefutable proof, I want to believe that she is still alive and waiting for me to find her. But her image is now tainted in blood, and there's no escaping the fact that she's dead.

More vomit sprays the dresser, and I struggle to breathe, spitting out globs of acidic phlegm and blinking away vinegar tears.

Seltzer's in-my-face suicide should overshadow the discovery that Cassie is gone. But it doesn't. Nothing can come close to that soul-destroying fact. Since my awakening at the office on Friday, I had begun to build my brave new world on the basis that it is cohabited by Cassie. Now that world is crashing down around me, and the weight threatens to crush me out of existence.

When at last I find the courage to look at Seltzer again, I see a growing patch of blood on the white sheets, seeping from the ruptured hole in the top of his skull. Crimson stars are spattered across the ceiling. And there's a strange sense of stillness in the room that is counter to the chaos churning away inside me.

But it's not the sight of Seltzer committing suicide that has gutted me. It's knowing that I caused it.

Self-recrimination is unavoidable.

Every way I look at it, there must be something wired wrong in my brain, in the other Jed Allen's brain, something that made me think it was normal to be so narcissistic. Has it always been this way? Was I off-center even before the accident? As a child, or perhaps traumatized by the death of my parents? Is that where this began? A life in the fast lane, a lunatic in the driver's seat, with my amnesia being the only thing stopping him from retaking the wheel.

Regardless of what I would prefer to think, I am responsible for Seltzer's death. And not just him. Indirectly, Cassie's blood is on my hands.

The realization sends superheated blood coursing through my legs, and I flee the bedroom, clattering down the stairs and out into the cold night air.

I have no idea where I am headed. I can't run away from the diabolical things my alter ego has done. I am stuck in his body. And I can't escape the consequences of his actions. The evidence shows that I stalked Cassie, that I harassed her. How many other women were there before her, their photos pinned to my secret wall? Did I progress from stalking to something even more contemptible? Is that the explanation behind the bloodied dress I found in my car? Have I committed crimes that I know nothing about?

I am halfway across the front lawn when the world around me bursts into blinding light, and I come to a full stop, squinting against the glare.

"This is the FBI!" a voice booms from behind the brilliance. "Get on the ground! Do it now!"

Chapter Twenty-Seven

An hour later, I am back in Manhattan asking for my lawyer, for what seems like the hundredth time. And my request produces the same response it has each time I've asked it: "Sit tight, Mr. Allen. He's on his way."

It's almost dawn on Sunday morning, and we have been at this verbal dance for some time, going around and around until it has left me dizzy and off-balance.

The interrogation room in the FBI building at Federal Plaza is a concrete box, no bigger than a prison cell, with a metal table bolted to the floor and a solitary fluorescent light behind a grille. Three metal chairs, a braced door, and no windows. Gray walls to match the pallor of my skin. Unlike in the NYPD interview room, the top half of the facing wall is a mirror I assume is one-way, polished to perfection.

While I have been sitting here with my wrists cuffed to the table, my sweat oxidizing the metal, I have caught my stranger's face glaring at me from the mirror-wall more than once; each time his eyes are tormented and eager to look away.

Although I have been Mirandized, no one has delved into any specifics regarding my detention. It's impossible to have a conversation when one half of it refuses to speak.

My interrogators are both men, both middle-aged, both unable to hide the disdain on their faces: O'Donnell, with his sandy hair and ginger mustache, and the kind of sharp dress sense that pairs a red necktie with a green shirt; and Escobar, with his shaven scalp and boxer's nose, and an annoying habit of continually cracking his knuckles, even when there is nothing left to crack.

Other than requesting legal representation, I haven't spoken another word, and their frustration is palpable.

The aftershocks of the night's revelations are still working their way through me, keeping me on edge, and it's an effort to stop my whole body from trembling. To make matters worse, a frigid breeze is blowing from the air-conditioning vent, which is strategically aimed in my direction. Even so, my clothes are soaked with sweat.

I can't believe Cassie is dead.

"We need for you to explain how you know Paulina Gonzalez," Escobar is saying as he cracks his knuckles.

It must be the tenth time he's asked the question, and I let him see my frown, the same frown that has been in place since I was bundled into the FBI van outside the lake house and then driven into the city. Not once have they asked me about Seltzer or even about Song. They seem obsessed with Paulina Gonzalez, and I have no clue who she is. I could guess, but guesses often involve assumptions, and I am learning that when it comes to my life before Friday, it's best to assume nothing.

Escobar shakes his head, his gaze fixed on me. "We're not calculating orbital trajectories here or figuring out escape velocities," he says. "This is kindergarten simple."

My frown grows into a scowl.

O'Donnell licks at his mustache and then leans back in his chair. "In a less verbose fashion, what my partner means to say is, this isn't rocket science. You're an intelligent guy. We've explained how this works. Right now, we're in a unique mutually beneficial position to help each other out. Soon as your lawyer shows up, any deal we're working toward will be off the table."

In an effort to pile on the pressure, they both stare at me, hoping I will crack.

I put my manacled fists under the table, hiding my trembling hands, and refusing to let the fear swarming through my veins break the surface. Although already in tatters, my new life is still in its infancy. If I hope to make it through this craziness intact, I owe it to myself not to crumble.

Several seconds of stalemate pass before an observer on the other side of the one-way mirror knocks on the glass.

O'Donnell pushes to his feet, his metal chair screeching across the polished cement, and he leaves the room.

"Last chance," Escobar says.

I close my eyes, telling myself that everything—no matter how irreparable it seems—is fixable one way or the other. It's an idealistic silver-lined way of looking at the world, involving compromises and negotiated settlements. But it's all I have.

The door opens again, and I look up to see O'Donnell loping back into the room.

"Is your lawyer really named Chaz?" he asks as he flops into his chair.

I sit up. "Is he here?"

"Nope. He bailed."

"What?"

"He bailed, Allen. Vamoosed. Took one look at the dung heap you're standing in, and he hightailed it to the hills."

I blink at O'Donnell, openmouthed.

"He did ask me to pass this message on, though. He said he's no trial lawyer, and you should seriously consider hiring yourself a good one, ASAP." The tip of O'Donnell's tongue strokes his bushy mustache again. "So before we proceed, have you got anyone in mind you want us to call?"

I don't need to think about it. "Detective Westfall," I say. "I'll only speak with Westfall."

◆ ◆ ◆

The first thing Detective Westfall says to me as he enters the interrogation room, a thick file folder jammed under his arm, is, "Thanks to you, I sprained an ankle."

Almost a full hour has passed since my request to bring him here, in which time I have been abandoned to my own company, left to ride the carousel of my own misgivings, with my incendiary thoughts burning holes in my brain.

I can only guess at how many protocols my request has bent or broken. It can't be every day that a detective from an outlying region gets to sit in on an FBI interrogation, let alone conduct it. The fact that the FBI has acquiesced to my request at all speaks of their urgency to get me talking, and the importance of what I might say.

For them, it's paid off. Solitude has left me itching to unload. If this was my interrogators' intention, then it has worked. The only problem is that they will be expecting a full confession, yet how can I give one when I don't know what crime it is they think I've committed?

"Why'd you run?" Westfall asks as he sits down.

I shrug. "Any number of reasons. Embarrassment, I guess. Instinct. Fear, maybe? Why does anyone run from the police?"

"In my experience, usually because they're guilty."

"Except I didn't do anything."

"You're sure?"

"Absolutely."

Westfall nods in the way that someone does when they've heard every excuse under the sun, even if the person saying it is being sincere.

"And now we're here," he says. "Kind of pointless, your running, don't you think?"

"That's just it. I wasn't thinking. I was reacting. I've been reacting since I came to at the office on Friday. It hasn't been easy, coming to grips with being thrown into someone else's life. My head's been all over the place. I haven't been thinking clearly. I shouldn't have run. I see that now."

"Things might have turned out differently."

I look at Westfall, knowing that he's referring to the lake house and what happened there. Of course, he's right. If I had surrendered to Westfall at the Majestic, Seltzer might still be alive, and I would still believe the lies my mind had manufactured.

I swallow against the ache forming in my throat.

Seltzer's death is something I will have to deal with, I know. But right now, it's wrapped up in shock and stowed away in the darkest recesses of my brain, saved for the day when my mind is not so bruised and battered. Right now, every bit of my mental energy is being consumed by other things, like trying to accept that the life I know is a lie. It's enough to eat me up from the inside out. At some point, I know I will need to come to terms with my part in Seltzer's suicide. But now is not that time.

The rule of survival is a selfish one.

"I'm ready to cooperate," I say. "Let's just get on with it."

"Okay." He puts the file on the table between us. The stack of documents inside is two inches thick. "As you can see, there's a bunch of stuff we need to get through. Agents Escobar and O'Donnell are the lead investigators on this case. They've been working it for months. They know it intimately. I don't. So you'll have to bear with me. First off, I want you to be aware that this interview is being recorded, which means anything you say can be used against you in a court of law."

"They read me my rights."

"Which is comforting to know. I hear you waived your right to a lawyer?"

"He bailed."

"I'm sorry to hear that. Do you want us to provide you with counsel?"

"No."

"You're sure?"

"Yes." I lean forward a little, irritated by Westfall's continual double redundancy. "I just want to get this over and done with, with the least hassle possible. I'll tell you everything I know."

Westfall laces his fingers together, tapping the tips of his forefingers against his chin and giving me the same look he gave me when he listened to my tale of woe back at the Eastchester police station. "Mr. Allen, there are no exceptions. We all have secrets. I keep stuff from my wife all the time. Things she doesn't need to know about, because if she did it would give her nightmares. And, believe me, my life is much quieter when my wife gets a good night's sleep. I talked with your fiancée, by the way. She seems like a good woman. Heart in the right place." He sees my frown deepen and adds, "Sarah Merrick. She was at your apartment."

"She's not my fiancée. She's my doctor."

"She's concerned about you is what she is. And she has every right to be. I know if I were the one sitting where you are, my wife would be ripping her hair out with worry."

"Did she also tell you I'm crazy?"

"No. She told me all about your condition, though, and how it's impacted your mental health, and that I shouldn't be too hard on you. She's a credit to you, Mr. Allen. You have a respected neuropsychologist in your corner who understands what makes you tick. Me, on the other hand, I won't pretend to know anything about how the brain works—or doesn't work, as the case may be. But I am now convinced your amnesia is for real, which I guess puts us all in a difficult situation moving forward."

I snicker without any mirth in it. "Welcome to my world. Can we just get on with it?"

"Okay. But before we get down to the nitty-gritty, first things first. You were picked up this evening at the home of Arnold Seltzer. The same residence you purported to own when you filed the missing persons report."

I spread my hands as far as the cuffs will allow. "I knew this was coming, and I know how it looks. I made a mistake, okay? In retrospect, I got it wrong. The Eastchester address was on the navigation system in my car. Friday afternoon, after the amnesia kicked in, I assumed it was where I lived, and that's why I was up there. It was a genuine mistake. And I didn't kill Seltzer." I say it before Westfall can accuse me outright.

I have to remember how this looks from the outside. The FBI caught me running from a crime scene, spattered in blood. They found Seltzer bleeding out on his bed, his brain pulped. Although I know otherwise, to everyone else, I had no right being there at that late hour. It wasn't my house. I thought it was, but I was wrong. The same way I thought Cassie was my girlfriend, but she wasn't.

Cassie . . .

The shocking realization that she is dead swamps me again, bringing with it a wave of nausea, and it rocks me in my seat.

"You okay?" Westfall asks.

"It's been a strange thirty-six hours."

"Let's get you some water." He raises his hand and gestures at the one-way mirror.

An FBI agent enters the room, placing a plastic bottle on the table in front of me. I pick it up in both hands and guzzle. The water is tepid, but it acts like a salve on my scratchy throat.

It's too soon to fully process everything that I've learned or experienced since Friday. My intermittent amnesia, the car crash, my stalking of Cassie, my relationship with Sarah Merrick, Seltzer's suicide, the assumptions I made about the life I had and the man I was—they are all a jumble of facts, like the shards of a shattered mirror that will take time and patience to piece back together, with no guarantee that any coherent image will ever take shape.

"I didn't kill Seltzer," I repeat after draining the bottle. "If there's one thing I do know, it's that. I didn't even know he was there. You can imagine my surprise when I found him with a gun in his hands. He shot himself right there in front of me. It was awful. And that's when I ran from the house."

"We didn't find a suicide note."

I shrug.

Westfall opens the file and pulls out an 8 × 10 photograph. "Can you explain this?"

It's a picture of the hidden space at the rear of my closet, with its array of Cassie-themed photos taken covertly.

My stomach closes into a hard ball. "I guess it's exactly what it looks like."

"This is Mr. Seltzer's wife. You were stalking her. And that's why their address was logged so many times in your car's navigation system."

"I don't remember any of it. But I guess I was." I wipe at a trickle of sweat running down my cheek, hating the other version of me. "Look, I'm not proud of it. I was as surprised as you were when I found those photos."

The interview is barely under way, and already I want the ground to open up and swallow me whole.

"Let me get this straight," Westfall is saying. "You stalked the wife of the man who took his own life tonight while you watched. Doesn't that sound more than a little far-fetched to you? What am I missing?"

I shrug. "I can't speak for Seltzer's behavior. He seemed stressed. Freaked-out. He mentioned he'd been in counseling. Maybe you need to speak with his therapist."

"We will."

His stare is piercing, and more sweat pricks out on my skin.

"What do you want from me, Westfall?"

"The truth."

"Everything I did before Friday is a complete blank. All I can tell you is what I know since then."

"Feel free."

I take a deep breath. "Okay, so I got this text I thought was from Cassie. I went out there thinking she'd come home. I didn't know Seltzer would be there, and that *he'd* sent the text."

"Why?"

"To lure me there. He seemed unhinged, burdened. Unable to live with his loss."

"Sandra Seltzer, the woman you stalked, was killed in a car crash back in January. You knew that, didn't you?"

Westfall's words cut deep through my gut, and another bead of sweat rolls from my hairline. "No."

"How about when you reported her missing?"

"Of course not. I didn't even know she went by that name. Otherwise, I would have told you. To me, she was Cassie. The first I knew about her death was when Seltzer told me at the house, right before he . . ." My heart is knocking against my ribs, my skin aflame.

Westfall's demeanor is calm and cool in comparison. "Mr. Allen, you need to know, if there's one thing I'm good at, it's digging for information. And I did some more digging into you. And guess what? It turns out the car crash you were involved in was on the same section of road as the Seltzers', at the same time. How's that for a coincidence?"

"I . . . what?"

"The conditions were bad. Multiple vehicles crashed that day, including yours and the SUV belonging to Mr. Seltzer. I believe it's how you came to get that head injury of yours. So I'm curious. Why did Mr. Seltzer choose to kill himself in front of the man who stalked his wife? It's a puzzle. What's your theory, Mr. Allen?"

I open my mouth, then close it again, aware that anything I say will come out wrong. Although I can't recall my own accident, I do remember Seltzer mentioning his car being struck by another from behind, and the obvious comes to mind. Was I stalking Cassie that night? Did I get too close and cause the crash that took her life?

My skin is an inferno, and more sweat has begun to gather at the edge of my hairline, ready to race down my brow. My reflection in the one-way mirror is deathly, broadcasting my fears to the observers on the other side. And as I catch my stranger's eyes staring back, someone raps their knuckles on the glass. Westfall holds up a hand in acknowledgment.

"I guess I'll leave that thought with you," he says. "If we have time, we'll come back to it later. For now, let's move on to why you're here."

He replaces the picture of my stalker wall with another color 8 × 10 from the file. This time it's the blowup of a DMV photo, showing a young woman's head and shoulders against a sky-blue backdrop. She appears to be in her early twenties; she's pretty, with olive skin and dark wavy hair and eyes the color of varnished walnuts.

"This is Paulina Gonzalez," he says.

"Agent Escobar mentioned her name."

"This is how she looked before she went missing a few days ago. And this is how she looked when she was found on Thursday." He slides another photo next to the first, watching my reaction as I peer closer.

The second picture shows the same composition of head and shoulders, but in this one, Paulina's eyes are closed, her facial muscles loose, and the background is brushed steel. Her lips are blue, and the dark cavities of her eye sockets are visible through her waxy skin. At the bottom of the photograph, several wounds are evident in her neck and shoulder area, some crisscrossing, each a ragged slash an inch or so in length.

My stomach clenches, and I shake my head at Westfall. "I don't understand. I've never met this woman. Why is everyone fixated on her?"

Without answering, Westfall adds a third photograph. This one shows a torn and bloodied dress laid out on a white surface, the blood-stains and the rips labeled with little yellow plastic markers.

"Do you recognize this?" he says.

"It looks like . . ." I stop, midsentence, tongue-tied as my thoughts unravel.

"It's the dress you found in the trunk of your car." Westfall slides the photo across the table toward me. "The one you handed me earlier."

My throat now feels like it has ice in it.

Westfall sees my confused expression and says, "It's our understanding that Paulina was last seen wearing this dress on Wednesday evening, right before she disappeared. The blood is hers. We checked the DNA."

The clamp around my stomach squeezes.

"Mr. Allen, has anything come back to you at all since we last spoke? Anything about how the dress happened to be in your car?"

I shake my head, too dumbfounded to offer any lucid reply. I can see where this conversation is headed. We both can. It's a runaway train, and there's not a thing I can do to stop it from careening over a cliff.

Westfall places yet another photo in front of me. It shows a jagged hunting knife next to a ruler, to give dimension to the brutal blade. "Have you seen this knife before?"

I want to say no, but my voice says "Yes."

"When the lab returned the positive DNA match for the blood on the dress, we searched your car. Conveniently for us, you left it in our parking lot. We found this knife in the glove compartment. When my FBI colleagues processed your arrest, you were fingerprinted. In the last few minutes, your prints were compared with the ones we found on the knife handle. And, lo and behold, they're an exact match."

My mind flashes back to the moment I found the knife in the car. I'd picked it up and examined it in my office building's parking garage.

But before I can offer up my account, Westfall puts another picture next to the last one. It's a close-up of the part of the knife where the steel blade meets the handle. He taps a finger against the image. "See what looks like rust around the guard? It's blood. In fact, I am told it's several types of blood. As we speak, the lab is running DNA tests to determine what belongs to whom." His finger points at the image again. "See the trace of blood here on the plunge line? Forensics has already been able to match it to Paulina Gonzalez. They're confident they can do the same with several more of these victims."

One after the other, Westfall adds more photos to the growing montage. Before-and-after pictures. DMV blowups of healthy-looking young women, followed by images of unholy violence. Corpses and decayed remains. Bones and skulls caked in dark earth. Black patches of dried blood on shredded clothing.

I look up at him, the imaginary ice in my throat thickening, suffocating. I can't believe what I am seeing, or the implications.

"Wait," I gasp. "You think I'm the Central Park Slasher, don't you? That's what this is all about. I saw it on TV, the mass grave they found out in the woods near Kensico Reservoir. The maniac who's been abducting women from Central Park and slicing them to ribbons. Oh my God. You think it's me."

The word *disbelief* doesn't come close to describing the tornado of emotions that rage suddenly through me, knocking me sideways, pulse clattering, blood pounding. It rips through my heart and mind, devastating all it touches, leaving me a wasteland littered with debris.

It can't be true. I can't be a mass murderer. Every feeling, every sensation, tells me I couldn't carry out such atrocities. It's not me. And yet . . . before Friday, I wasn't me. I was someone else. A stranger. The other Jed Allen. A man who stalked women, and whose moral code was written to serve only himself.

How can I vouch for someone I don't know?

Westfall sees the look of sheer terror on my face and shrugs. "Mr. Allen, it doesn't make a jot of difference what I think. It's what the evidence says that matters. So let's see how this stacks up." He counts points off on his fingers. "There's Paulina's bloodstained dress you found in your trunk. There's the murder weapon we recovered from your vehicle. There's the fact that Paulina was found at a dump site together with multiple other human remains. And then there's the fact that the dump site is a stone's throw from where you grew up, in Pleasantville."

"What?"

"Kensico Reservoir is less than five miles from your hometown. You must know the area."

"I . . . I . . ." I can't say that I do or that I don't. "This is insane. I didn't hurt any of those girls."

"You're sure about that?"

"Yes, damn it, Westfall. I'm sure." A trickle of sweat runs down my chin.

"And yet you have no recollection of what you did before Friday, which kind of makes anything you say moot."

"It doesn't mean I'm a killer." I push back in my chair, the chain on my wrists snapping taut.

Westfall doesn't flinch. "When we spoke at the station, you told me your amnesia is triggered by stress. The same kind of stress you would have experienced on Friday morning when you learned your dump site was discovered."

I stare at him, knowing I can't disprove anything he's saying. Not because it's true, necessarily, but because I can't offer up an alternative explanation. I know the previous version of me left a lot to be desired. I know he stalked Cassie and maybe others, too. I know he wasn't a model citizen, and that if I met him now in real life, I'd avoid him like the plague. But being selfish and even a stalker doesn't mean he was capable of multiple murders. Does it?

"And so it's my theory," Westfall says, refocusing me, "that on Friday morning when the news came out, you panicked, and that heightened state of panic triggered your amnesia. The murder weapon was in your car. Clothing belonging to your last victim was in your car. You were stuck at the office, and yet you knew you had to dispose of both items. But then your amnesia kicked in, and you never got around to covering your tracks."

My stare is intense, scalding tears forming in my eyes. "You've got to believe me. I didn't . . ." Then I fumble for the words to describe the horror spanning the table, but I can't find them. I'm not sure there are any. How do you begin to describe unmitigated evil in one sentence?

Westfall places another photo on top of the rest, and the sight of it sends my stomach into a spasm.

It's a sterile picture of Song Chang lying on a slab in the hospital morgue, her porcelain face grayed with death, her skin like marble. There are stitched knife wounds on her chest and neck, smaller than those on the previous photograph of Paulina, as though they were made with a pocketknife but with equal force.

"We left you sitting here for as long as we did," Westfall is saying as my ears start to ring, "because we were interviewing an eyewitness, who claims to have seen you attacking Miss Chang in Central Park."

"No." My voice is a rasp, my heart banging, my pulse crashing. "That's not true. It's impossible. I wasn't even with her."

"We know you were at a business dinner at Rafferty's on Friday evening and that Miss Chang was also at that dinner. Eyewitnesses there saw you leave, and her follow. Where did you go immediately after?"

I glance again at the horrific image of Song Chang, at the stark profile of her bones pushing up her slack skin. My recollection of failing to find a ride home, of seeking sanctuary in the darkened park, of sitting on the bench to think, of finally catching a cab and leaving for the lake house, is vivid and fully intact. There is no memory of encountering Song in the park, let alone . . . *this*.

"It's Tess, isn't it?" I say at the same time I realize it. "Your star eyewitness. She said she saw me through that damned telescope of hers. She's lying about me and Song. I swear. It's her way of getting back at me. She's only saying it because I helped the DEA make their case against her."

Westfall doesn't corroborate my outburst with so much as a nod. Instead, he says, "I spoke with Officer Davis. Do you remember him? He was the first responder to your nine-one-one call in the early hours of Saturday morning. A little crucial fact you neglected to mention when you came to see me at the station. It's only since the house on Lakeshore Drive became a crime scene that his report came to my attention. Anyway, the long and the short of it is, he told me you seemed intoxicated, and that there was what he thought looked like blood on your shirt."

"It was wine." A droplet of sweat drips off the end of my nose.

"That's what he said you said."

"That's because it's true! Song threw her glass of merlot . . ." I stop, realizing I'm digging my hole even deeper. "Look, this is ridiculous. I didn't kill Song. Why would I? I was in the middle of brokering the firm's biggest-ever deal. Harming her in any way would have been like committing financial suicide. Why would I jeopardize the future of my company by attacking her?"

"Because both of you were under the influence of mind-altering drugs, and maybe what started out as a bit of fun ended in tragedy."

"You mean the killer in me took over and I couldn't help myself? Come on, Westfall. That doesn't make any sense."

Of course, it's a flimsy argument. I have known *me* for only two days. I have no idea what I am capable of.

"You'd be surprised what can make a man snap," Westfall says. "I come across people with masochistic tendencies all the time. Ordinary people who, for one reason or another, suddenly self-destruct."

"I didn't kill Song."

I want to believe it, *have* to believe it. It's less about facing the possibility that I did it and don't remember, and more about clinging to a hope that the new me isn't turning into a carbon copy of the old me.

"You were alone in the park together."

"No."

"Maybe you came on to her a little too strongly and she rejected you."

"No. It wasn't like that."

"And the narcissist in you lashed out. And before you knew it, you were attacking her."

I bang my fists against the table. "No!"

Westfall eyes me for a moment, and I'm not sure if it's to let my temper settle or to allow the magnitude of his words to penetrate.

"Mr. Allen," he says at last, spreading his hands, "as you can see, we have enough evidence here not just to hold you, but to charge you with at least two counts of homicide. You need to know that my FBI colleagues are right now speaking with your coworkers and looking into your schedule. It's only a matter of time before they put you in each of the locations where these young women disappeared. As things stand, the evidence points to you having murdered Paulina Gonzalez and Song Chang. Tomorrow, and in the days that follow, possibly dozens of other homicides will be added." He fans the photos out on the table until the surface is a macabre mosaic. "It's over, Mr. Allen. You don't need to hide behind your amnesia anymore. With or without your memory, you need to face up to what you've done here. You can't ignore these facts. The evidence against you is insurmountable. You need to work with us. Because this isn't going away. If anything, it's only going to get much worse as things develop."

A crushing pain presses at my chest. It feels like I am being squeezed from all sides, pressurized. Like there's molten lava in my veins, about to erupt in a volcanic rush of emotion. All at once, the walls of the interrogation room seem a few feet closer in, like one of those ancient traps where the walls come together to crush those trespassing. I have no idea if I suffer from claustrophobia, but my panic is real, and it's rising inside me, scorching everything it touches. I want to shout the words *I'm innocent,* but my jaw is locked. Sweat stings at my eyes. My pulse thwacks in my throat. Every adrenalized cell in my body urges me to run.

I think this could be more fear than I have ever felt before. Truly, I am terrified—not just with the severity of the accusations leveled at me, but with the thought that my accusers might be right.

All I know is that the life I led before Friday is hidden to me, and if my amnesia holds, then it will be forever absent. If this is it, if this is as good as my memory gets, how will I ever know firsthand what possible atrocities were undertaken by the other version of me?

Already, I know his morals were in the gutter. I know he never thought twice about taking recreational drugs. I know he acted recklessly, selfishly, and with a total disregard toward other people or for consequences. After all I have been through, after choosing to lead a better life as the new and improved version of me, what if it turns out that the police are right? Will I be forced to learn all the terrible facts about what I am from the mouths of my accusers as they delve into my past, uncovering more sordid secrets as they go, until I am stripped bare and exposed for the psychopathic murderer that I am?

Is that it—am I a killer?

From far away, I hear my stranger's voice saying, "I did it. I must have. I killed them all. I'm sorry."

Then, freed by the emotional release of my confession, my tears start to flow, and I hold my face in trembling hands, weeping without restraint.

Chapter Twenty-Eight

Although Sarah Merrick had long since mastered the ability to pigeonhole her cognitive processes, she let her thoughts drift and intermingle as she drove north on Mount Kisco Road, an upbeat song on the radio reminding her of less trying times.

The events of the past couple of weeks had been a drain, for sure, taxing her emotionally and psychologically, and each day had brought new challenges to her heart and mind. Not only had she been forced to cope with the external pressure of having her life thrust under a microscope, she'd had to deal with her own internal pressures, too. The hows and whys common to every relationship, followed by the self-doubt, the self-recrimination, the numbing self-awareness, and the unending introspection that accompany such personal trials.

Sleep had become a luxury, and some of her clothes had begun to hang a little too loose. What's more, her hair had lost its shine, becoming lank and lackluster, and no matter how many times she reapplied her makeup, she couldn't escape the harrowed look of someone on the edge.

Worse still, when it came to Jed and the crimes he was being accused of, she was no closer to an understanding now than she was the day her world imploded. Though it had been two weeks since she'd learned of

Jed's arrest and subsequent arraignment, she still couldn't fully believe what had happened, and how quickly events had run away from her. As was her nature, she'd tried to stem the bleeding as fast as she could. She'd pleaded with the FBI's public affairs specialist to hold back on making a press release before all the facts were on the table. She'd sought legal advice in an attempt to keep Jed's name out of the papers. She'd even called a friend at the mayor's office to do *something*.

All for nothing.

Within hours of his confession, Jed's face had been splashed all over the media, every news channel running with the same story of CENTRAL PARK SLASHER SUSPECT IN CUSTODY, or words to that effect. Overnight, Jed had become an infamous serial killer, as reviled as the likes of Ted Bundy, with all the attention that came with it.

Within twenty-four hours, Jed's life became the hot topic of talk shows and analytical debates across the nation.

From their glass houses, pundits profiled Jed, comparing him to every mass killer known to man. Remotely, they sliced open his brain and poked around, determining which wires were crossed and which ones had never been connected in the first place.

According to these self-proclaimed psychologists, Jed possessed an antisocial personality disorder, displaying characteristics common with high-functioning psychopaths. His life, they said, was a textbook example of good kid gone bad, demonstrating that with the death of his parents, he'd suffered a tremendous loss at an impressionable age, and one that birthed a killer mind. Rather than dealing with it, he'd bottled up his hurt, compressing it inside until the pressure had transmuted it into rage. Being narcissistic was an inevitable trade-off. Plus, they said, his inherited wealth had been an enabler, cheapening relationships and the value of those less fortunate than him. Where Jed was concerned, other human beings were, at best, playthings, and, at worst, inconveniences. In a world where money could buy anything, even lives, Jed had existed on a permanent power trip, knowing that he could buy himself out of any fix.

Of course, Sarah knew in her heart that they were wrong. She knew Jed, probably better than anyone, including Gary. She hadn't intended to, but she had fallen in love with him, and when Jed's recall crashes weren't throwing up barriers, he and Sarah were as close as any loving couple.

In the beginning, her psychology training had made her more aware than most of his imperfections, of his character flaws. She knew Jed was far from perfect, and early in their relationship she'd recognized both his obsessive nature and his narcissistic traits. But instead of rejecting him, she'd embraced his imperfections, seeing them as a challenge and not an abomination. And in the weeks that had followed, she'd learned how to live with and how to mitigate them.

Sometimes, a person simply couldn't help who they fell in love with.

Yet nothing she had experienced had given her any impression that his faults made him a murderer.

She could understand his infatuation with Cassie and, to some extent, how that infatuation had led to him stalking her. But he wasn't a killer, and his confession didn't make any sense.

Even so, within forty-eight hours, a judgmental nation had made up its collective mind, and the people on the streets were baying for blood. Never slow on the uptake, the self-appointed experts had been quick to surf the rolling swell of unrest, calling for a one-time special-circumstance reinstatement of the death penalty, just for Jed, to appease the growing public outcry and the grieving families of his victims.

In a judicial system built on the premise of innocent until proven guilty, the media had hung Jed out to dry.

In those first few days, and in spite of the public backlash, Sarah had been strong—not for herself, but for Jed.

With no family to speak on his behalf, Sarah had stepped up.

She'd been supportive, available, and she'd petitioned the authorities to let her see him, both as his neuropsychologist and his girlfriend. But as the first week had come to an end and the initial shock had worn off, her fried emotions had gotten the better of her, and she'd spent the entire weekend cocooned in the womblike safety of her bed, exhausted and crying.

She told herself that the truth would come to light and Jed would be exonerated.

But no such truth had come to light, and she'd had to face the fact that no matter how innocent she believed Jed was, the overwhelming majority didn't agree with her.

It didn't prevent her from doing everything she could to help him. And it didn't change what she felt for him.

The hubbub had died down a little now—Jed was no longer the top story in every newscast—but with each new reported development in the FBI's case, his trial by media seemed far from over. As far as Sarah was concerned, it seemed the press had no intention of letting anyone forget anytime soon about the monster locked up at the Metropolitan Correctional Center just blocks from the office where he had been a successful architect, or the fact that she was his lover.

No one would have criticized her if she'd given up or exploded into a million pieces. The media spotlight was brutal. Her family and her friends had pleaded with her to distance herself from Jed, to limit the damage caused through association. But that wasn't who she was. She could no sooner turn her back on Jed than she could believe he was guilty. Her life had changed in a heartbeat, for sure, but making the decision to ride out the storm instead of running for cover hadn't even been a choice.

If she ever wanted to be with Jed again, she knew she'd have to take matters into her own hands.

Sarah realized she was gripping the steering wheel hard enough to turn her knuckles white, and she flexed her fingers, telling herself to relax. Up ahead, she could see a shimmer of gray water beneath a steel-wool sky, and the road reaching over the water on stilts. The semiskeletal trees, which had been hemming in the highway for the last couple of miles, thinned and then disappeared altogether, giving way to a flat expanse of water. As her car thundered across a concrete bridge, she glanced to her left, at the long limb of treed land jutting out across the water, and her belly knotted up with nerves. Then the water was gone from view as the bridge gave way to land again.

A mile later, the road curved west, and half a mile after that, the steel guardrails ended.

Sarah spotted a white pickup truck parked in a long dirt crescent across the road, and she waited for a gap in the traffic before pulling next to it.

"I'm sorry I'm a few minutes late," she said as she climbed out of her car.

A man was walking toward her from the pickup. He had on jogging pants with work boots, a padded jacket, and a black wool beanie pulled tight on his head. Although she'd seen him only in photos, and usually wearing designer suits, she had no difficulty recognizing him as Gary Quartucci, Jed's best friend and business partner.

"I was beginning to think you'd stood me up," he said, half smiling as he approached.

"It's been one of those days." They shook hands. "Thanks for agreeing to meet with me."

"My pleasure. Although I have to say I'm a little freaked-out by the location and what you might have planned for me."

She smiled. "Bear with me. There's a method to the madness." She nodded toward the pickup. "I never pegged you as a truck driver."

"Oh, that monstrosity? It's a rental. I'm helping a friend dejunk his garage."

"Nearby?"

"In Pleasantville. So please don't tell anyone you saw me driving this thing. If I weren't doing my neighborly good deed, I wouldn't be caught dead in it."

"Your secret's safe with me."

"I appreciate that, Sarah."

"And I promise I'll try and not keep you in suspense any longer than I need to." She motioned to the woods. "Shall we?"

She headed toward the trees, but Gary hung back.

"You want to go in there?"

Even though he was dressed for a trek in the woods, he looked appalled at the idea.

"It's not as bad as it looks," she said. "You can't see it from here, but there's a deer trail about twenty yards in. We can follow it almost the whole way there."

Now he looked more surprised than appalled.

"Wait a minute, Sarah. You mean you've been here before?"

"Several times." She saw indecision work its way into his expression. "It's the middle of the day and perfectly safe, if that's what you're worried about."

"What if somebody sees us?"

"Where we're going, we could be a hundred miles from civilization. Trust me, just a few yards in and you won't even be able to see the road."

She saw him smile uneasily.

"Okay," he said. "My life is in your hands."

The path was a little tougher than Sarah had remembered it. The semiskeletal trees were knitted tighter than they'd looked from the road, growing in prickly thickets, their branches enmeshed, and the terrain was anything but flat. The leaf-littered forest floor was crisscrossed with shallow gullies and hidden depressions, and the husks of fallen trees formed regular hurdles. By the time they came to the narrow deer trail zigzagging through the woods, Gary was huffing and puffing.

"Tell me you didn't mention this to anyone," he said as he came up beside her. "Especially the police."

"What?"

"Coming here. They wouldn't look kindly on this kind of behavior, Sarah. I mean, it's not exactly a normal thing to do, is it? And I'm almost sure it's illegal."

"Don't worry. We're not breaking any laws."

"All the same, it feels like we're trespassing on sacred ground. Was it absolutely necessary we meet out here?"

"I have my reasons. You'll see. And, no, I didn't tell anyone. This is our little secret."

With Sarah in the lead, they began to make their way along the narrow trail, following the slight furrow as it snaked between the trees. It seemed to be more of a rut than an animal track, spongy underfoot and filled with autumn leaves.

"So whose bright idea was this?" Gary asked as he trailed a few feet behind. "Jed's?"

"No. It was all my idea. I don't think Jed would approve."

"How's he doing, by the way?"

"Taking each day as it comes. It's all he can do. Some people cope with incarceration better than others." It was a stock answer in the absence of anything more positive.

The truth was, Jed was having a tough time of things. More so lately. At first, in the aftermath of his confession, he'd been allowed to mix with the other detainees. But as word had spread among the other inmates about the crimes credited to him, he'd been beaten to within an inch of his life, and the authorities had moved him into isolation. It was for his own protection, of course, but Sarah worried about his mental well-being. In itself, amnesia was imprisonment enough. The fact that he was now on his own for most of each day not only compounded his sense of separation, but threatened to have a long-term detrimental psychological effect.

"How about his memory?" Gary asked. "Has anything come back? Any flashbacks?"

"No, nothing. Not yet."

"It must be hard on you, Sarah—him not being able to remember the two of you together."

She nodded, trying to keep her shoulders from rounding.

The truth was, Jed's current recall crash had affected her in ways she hadn't anticipated, and the emotional toll was something she'd struggled to contain. Previously, during the occasional hour or two in which she'd been a stranger to Jed, she'd handled it with an aplomb that came from knowing her lover would return with no harm done. But this was different. His persisting amnesic state had brought about a bigger and much more complex challenge. Although physically, Jed was the same man she'd fallen in love with, psychologically, there were marked changes, and it would be a lie to say these last couple of weeks had been anything but difficult.

"But you're standing by him," Gary said, refocusing her. "I admire you for that. He needs someone strong in his corner. I'm worried he might do something stupid in there."

"Funny you should say that, because he's worried you might do something stupid out here."

"How so?"

"You haven't visited."

"I can explain. I've been meaning to. It's just that—"

"Jed thinks you've abandoned him."

"No," he said, brushing a branch aside. "I've just been busy, is all. This deal with Xian Airlines, it's been gobbling up every waking hour and keeping me up all night. I kid you not, Sarah, my head is up my ass right now."

Sarah pushed aside an overhanging tree branch, holding it back so that Gary could pass. "How's it going, the deal?"

"Let's just say the current state of affairs is best described by the word 'precarious,' coupled with the phrase 'hanging by a thread.'"

Sarah released the branch. "I'm sorry to hear that."

"It's to be expected. Right now, the firm is damaged goods. New clients won't touch us with a disinfected pole."

They continued on their way along the trail, kicking up leaves.

"To be perfectly honest," he said, "it's a miracle the Chinese haven't reneged on us altogether. I don't know what's keeping them. After all, you'd think Chang wouldn't want anything to do with us, knowing Jed killed his daughter."

Sarah flinched at the comment but didn't let him see it. "Do you believe that?" she asked.

"Unfortunately, I do. It sounds awful, doesn't it? Like I'm a traitor or something. I didn't want to believe it at first. God knows, I didn't want to think my best friend was capable of such a thing. Who would? But then the more I thought about it, and the more I pieced things together, the less innocent he began to look."

"Is that why you haven't visited him?"

"I guess. And let's be clear, I'm not proud of the fact. Jed and I go way back. He's like a brother to me. We've had our fair share of life's ups and downs, and we've always stood by each other, through thick and thin. But this . . ."

He didn't need to say it; Sarah knew. Something this horrible was hard to put into words, let alone wrap your head around.

The crux of it was, no one wanted to believe that someone close to them could turn out to be a cold-blooded killer—not just because it was an undesirable thought, but because it meant their confidence had been violated.

"So, what about you, Sarah?" he asked. "You're the expert here. Do you think Jed is capable of what they're saying?"

"Never in a million years. Jed has his hang-ups, like the rest of us, but he's no killer."

She didn't add that she knew that some psychopaths were so adept at controlling both themselves and their environment that they could blend in and pass undetected in society. One paper she'd read had even postulated the theory that all of the world's high-functioning career-successful superstars were closet psychopaths, and it was their aberrant brain chemistry and not their intellect that had propelled them into the public stratosphere. They reminded her of unexploded bombs, harmless until something activated the trigger.

"You've seen the same news I have," she said. "The way this killer lashes out at his victims, it points to him being driven by a deep-seated hatred of women."

"Is that your professional opinion?"

His question sounded derisive, but she chose to ignore his tone.

"I believe rage is his underlying motivation," she answered instead. "It's his driving force, possibly stemming from a traumatic pubescent episode involving a member of the opposite sex."

"You make him sound like a psychotic maniac."

"That's because the real killer is."

They came to a fallen tree cutting across the trail, and they switched tack, crashing through the tangled undergrowth until they caught up with the path again. It seemed a little wider here, wide enough for them to walk side by side.

"Did the FBI speak with you yet?" Gary asked as he came up next to her.

"They did."

"Was it productive?"

"It was interesting. I have another sit-down with them tomorrow. They want to go through my calendar, cross-reference when I was with Jed against the times they know the abductions took place."

"Good luck with that. They did same with me. I have to say, it was a nerve-racking experience. I had no idea there were so many black holes in my week, where I couldn't account for my own whereabouts, never mind Jed's. Try as I might, I couldn't conjure up a single alibi for any one of the times those poor girls were murdered. Not that it would've made any difference if I had. He confessed to everything."

"Under duress, and without legal representation."

"Even so, he admitted to the murders, Sarah."

"It doesn't make him guilty. It makes him vulnerable. Besides, he was in an amnesic state when the police interviewed him. His confession won't be admissible in court. They'll throw it out."

"You don't know that. They found hard evidence to back it up."

"Evidence that could have been planted."

"What?"

She glanced at him. "I think the turning point will be when Jed's memories do come back. I have a bunch of treatments in the pipeline. But right now, I'm jumping through hoops with the Federal Bureau of Prisons and the US Attorneys' office, trying to convince them that we need to implement these new treatment plans as a matter of urgency. The trouble is, I'm Jed's only voice."

"I hear you, Sarah."

"I'm sure if he can remember just one verifiable alibi, it'll blow the case wide open."

She saw Gary come to a stop, and she turned to face him.

"So," he said, "what you're saying is, without you and these radical treatments of yours to bail him out, Jed's as good as sunk?"

"Just about." She pointed off to their right. "That way."

They followed the terrain as it sloped upward, and then came to a sudden stop as they reached the summit.

Yellow-and-black crime-scene tape was looped around the nearest trees, with more of it running off to the sides and circling around to form a large corral at least thirty yards in diameter. In stark contrast to the rest of the forest floor, the ground in this area was dark, the black soil plowed up and mounded.

"This is why I wanted you to meet me here," Sarah said. "I wanted you to see this, to feel it. It brings it home, doesn't it? Shakes you up on the inside." She looked at his stricken expression, watching his eyes grow larger as he scanned the extensive dig site. "Come on," she said, ducking under the tape. "There's something I want you to see."

He followed her—a little reluctantly, she noted—as they made their way over the uneven ground, their footfalls deadened by the upturned soil. They were deep in the heart of the woods now, with nothing but hundreds of trees in every direction, silent fractal branches holding up a colorless sky.

They came to a large tree standing in the middle of the site, its branches bristling with rust-colored leaves.

"See these," she said, pointing to a series of notches carved into its rough bark, most of them weatherworn. "The police believe the killer did this. One strike for each of the victims he buried here."

"Okay," he said. "So you've successfully creeped me out. Can we please go now? This place is giving me the heebie-jeebies."

"Grow a backbone, Gary." She touched a finger to one of the notches, sensing him flinch as she did so. "See how they all lean slightly to the right? The FBI's forensic handwriting expert believes they were carved by a left-handed person."

"Great. The killer's a southpaw. Can you get to the point?"

She turned to face him. "Jed's right-handed."

"Okay. And?"

"And I read the coroner's reports for Song Chang and Paulina Gonzalez, the killer's last two victims. Guess what the ME found? The same rightward-leaning cuts, confirming the killer is left-handed."

For a moment, his face was a mixture of mockery and bewilderment, as though she were talking gibberish. But then, as she stared back at him, her own expression stony and challenging, his expression changed.

"Exactly what are you trying to say, Sarah?"

She drew a shaky breath, her heart suddenly beating so hard and so fast that it made her light-headed. "That you framed Jed for these murders."

"Me?" Now he laughed, but it sounded forced. "You're saying *I'm* the killer?"

"You're left-handed."

"So is ten percent of the population! It doesn't make me a mass murderer." A sneer snagged on his face, twitching, like a scrap of litter caught by the wind. "And besides, why would I even do such a thing?"

She grabbed another shaky breath, gesturing at their surroundings. "Because someone came across this, your dump site. And the FBI was called in. You saw it on the news like the rest of us, and you panicked. Maybe because you thought they'd find your DNA here, or some other piece of incriminating evidence, I don't know. So you took advantage of Jed's amnesia. You planted the knife and the dress with the blood on it in his car—to stop the police from looking any further. And then you prayed that his amnesia would be his undoing."

His sneer disappeared. "Jesus, Sarah. Can you hear yourself? I know these last two weeks have been hell, but I think the pressure's finally gotten to you. Me, a killer? That's ridiculous."

"Is it?"

"Of course it is! Anyone who knows me will tell you it's sheer fantasy. I'm the epitome of placid. And even if it were the case, that I stashed those things in Jed's car like you say, how would I know he'd implicate himself at just the right moment?"

"You wouldn't."

"I rest my case."

Sarah resisted the urge to smile with irony. Not yet. She had more to give, and she wanted to make sure she said everything she had to say while there was still time.

She put her back to the tree. "Jed implicating himself happened out of luck. My guess is you were planning on making an anonymous tip.

But then, in all his innocence, Jed went to the police himself with the bloodied dress, and he saved you the trouble. That's why you won't visit him, Gary. Because you can't bring yourself to face him."

"Thanks for the analysis." He began to back away. "But excuse me if I don't stick around and listen to any more of your psycho-baloney. I have better things to do."

She saw him turn and begin to retrace their steps across the black soil, allowing him a few yards before saying, "I'm going to the police with what I know."

He stopped and turned back to face her.

"Which is what, Sarah? What is it you think you know?"

"I know you had a traumatic childhood, Gary, prior to Jed's parents giving you a home. I know your father abandoned you when you were young. I know your mother was a drunk. I know she abused you, in terrible ways. I know you found it difficult to form relationships, especially with girls. I know you feel like society owes you a favor. Jed told me everything. I looked into it. He's telling the truth."

Gary's face was a slab of chiseled stone.

"It doesn't prove anything," he said. "Least of all that I'm responsible for killing all those women."

"You're right. On its own, it's just the sad story of an abused child with a damaged way of looking at the world. But when you couple it with this"—she put her hand in her pocket and brought out a memory stick, holding it up in her trembling fingers so that he could see it— "that story becomes the pathetic account of a coward who took out all his mommy issues on other defenseless women."

He frowned at her latest revelation. "Really? Am I supposed to be scared at this point?"

"Oh, you will be." She swallowed down the nerves clutching at her throat, and wagged the memory stick at him. "This contains a recording. It comes from the security camera in the parking garage where Jed parked his car on the morning of his most recent recall crash. You see, it occurred to me that if you were going to plant incriminating evidence in Jed's car without him knowing it, then the garage would be the ideal place to do it. You can imagine my glee when I saw you doing exactly that."

Gary's eyes had shrunken to pencil-line slits.

Sarah allowed herself the smallest of smiles. "You didn't know there was a security camera, did you? You thought you'd covered all your bases. But even psychopaths make mistakes. How does it feel knowing you're just as infallible as the rest of us, Gary?"

She saw him take a step toward her, his fingers flexing.

"So why bring me all the way out here? Why not go right to the police with this?"

She dropped the memory stick back in her pocket. "Because I have a selfish fascination, I guess. Like you, I have something inside me that needs satisfying. I'm a psychologist at heart. I want to know what makes you tick. I want to understand the process that turned an innocent child into a bloodthirsty monster. Call it a professional curiosity."

"Even if it gets you killed?" He started toward her.

It was a move she had anticipated, and part of her wanted to run and to keep running all the way back to the highway. But she had committed herself to this long before coming here, and in any case it was too late to back down now.

She saw him reach inside his padded jacket with his left hand, and she took a step back, her shoulders coming up hard against the tree trunk behind her. His fist came out brandishing a jagged blade, and he was on her in a heartbeat, pinning her against the tree.

"You made a fatal miscalculation, Sarah," he said, putting the tip of the knife against her throat, "coming here and failing to let anyone know about it. The sacrificial lamb whose own stupidity is about to make her pay with her life."

Sarah shrank from the blade, fear blossoming in her belly. "Please. I just want to know what made you kill all those women."

"How about I show you?"

With his right hand, he yanked at her coat, pulling it open and then down over her shoulders so that she couldn't move her arms. Then it was her shirt's turn to be torn apart, the buttons springing off as the fabric ripped away.

Sarah's heart was beating fast in her chest, every one of her senses on overload. Her instincts were screaming at her to run, but her legs had become as immobile as if they were made from stone.

She felt the blade follow the contour of her throat, moving down to her breasts, knowing it left a line of blood behind it. "Please," she said against the pain, her breath coming in rapid gulps, "I need to know."

Gary brought his face to within an inch of hers, looking directly in her eyes. She could smell his breath, feel it on her lips, sense the raw energy in his body.

"You'll like this one," he said, twisting the knife so that the tip nipped at her skin. "It'll give you something to think about while I slice you up."

Then he whispered in her ear, her whole body tensing and quaking as he unveiled his dark truth.

Epilogue

"No more meds," I say as I put down my coffee cup emphatically, as though it's a judge's gavel, finalizing my decision. Sarah looks at me like I have gone insane, her own cup poised halfway to her mouth.

We are at a popular restaurant in Central Park, overlooking the boating lake, with its picturesque backdrop of autumn gold and russet red. It's the middle of November. There's a definite winter nip in the air, and the ducks seem to be complaining about the dip in the water temperature.

Without taking a sip, Sarah lowers her cup, giving me three whole seconds of a wide-eyed stare before saying, "Wow, Jed. Where's this coming from?"

"I've been thinking it through. Long and hard. And I've made up my mind. For better or worse, I don't want to go back to being the man I was. That episode of my life is over. It's been boxed up, placed in storage, and I've thrown away the key."

She blinks. "Okay."

"You're not sure."

"It's not that. It's just . . ."

Her hand touches mine, and even after spending virtually the whole last week in her company, still my basic instinct is to withdraw. It's a problem, I know. My insecurity. But I fold my fingers around hers, reminding myself that this is what I want, and it's not a decision I have made lightly.

Those sleepless nights in jail provided me with plenty of time to reflect, to focus on the few positives in an abundance of negatives. The previous version of me had made hundreds of bad decisions in his time, based, for the most part, on personal benefit. I was hard-pressed to find any redeeming life choices.

But I did find one.

"It's me," Sarah says, holding on to my hand. "I'm still getting used to this altered version of the man I fell in love with."

"You prefer the old me?" It's an undesirable thought, and something I can't ignore. After all, she fell for him, not me. "I guess if pushed, I could always try a few more of those cutting-edge therapies of yours, see if we can bring back the guy with all the hang-ups and the border-line personality disorder."

It's meant as a joke, but I see her struggle with finding an answer that is accurate enough to describe her feelings and yet subtle enough not to offend mine. It's a tricky balancing act, and I decide to cut short her torture.

"Ignore me," I say, squeezing her hand. "Like I said, I want this to be fair, for both of us. No pressure. I'm fully aware you could have walked away back there and left me to rot in jail. You went above and beyond for me, Sarah. I owe you my life."

"Is that why you've decided to give *us* another try?"

"No!" The remark triggers a slanted smile on my face. "Well, maybe a little bit. I'm kidding! Remember, this is all new to me. Understandably, I'm still pretty screwed up. It's going to take a while to reconstruct my worldview. But I want to try. These last few days we've spent together—they've given me a taste of what could be, and I think I can get addicted to the flavor. More than anything, I want *this* to work."

"I want it to work, too." She smiles, but the strain of the past few weeks shows in her eyes.

None of this has been easy on her, I know. Despite the emotional roller coaster, she stood by me, even put herself in harm's way—for me, for *us*, she says. It's clear her feelings for me are real, and in spite of his errant ways, my former self also felt something toward her. Although I don't remember the depth of those feelings, I do sense an undeniable connection between Sarah and me, and I want to explore the possibility of rekindling what went before.

"Besides," I say, "the last thing I want is to put you under any kind of pressure. I know a good thing when I see it. I'm happy to take one day at a time, see where things go from here."

She sits back, her hand leaving mine. "No more meds."

"It's the only way I can stay being me. Call it self-preservation. I like who I am these days. Amnesia has given me a chance to start over, not just with everything else, but with you. Every way I look at it, it's a godsend. How many people get the chance to go back and live their lives again, with the benefit of hindsight? This is how Lazarus must have felt when he was raised from the dead."

"Everyone deserves a second chance."

"Exactly. And I want you to know I'm serious about this. I'm committed. I want to do the right thing this time around. Let's be clear about that. Total transparency. No secrets between us. We've had more than enough bad surprises for one lifetime."

I see her fingertips caress the hairline scratch on her neck, and although she's smiling, I know she's putting on a brave face.

So far, we haven't been able to broach the subject of her encounter with Gary in the woods without both of us breaking down into emotional wrecks. A great deal has happened in the last week, and there's a lot that has remained unsaid. Some of it for good reason. Our nerves have been tried and tested, and today is the first day in which neither of us has had to work the front line. Sitting here, in this public place, with the cool breeze swooshing through the trees and the happy chatter of people dining all around us in the open air, the horror of the last few weeks seems a world away. Now seems like the right time to bring it up again.

"It was a very close call, wasn't it?" I say, nodding at her scar.

"It's nothing that won't heal." Sarah looks away, perhaps hoping that I won't notice her wilting smile.

"You didn't have to do it."

"I had no choice." Her gaze comes back to me. "I wanted to make sure they got his confession on tape."

"And if he'd slit your throat before you'd said the safe word?"

It's at this point in the conversation that emotion usually gets the better of us. I see her draw an unsteady breath, and for a second I think she's going to evade again. But then she sits a little straighter, saying, "It was a risk I was willing to take."

Her voice is slightly choked, and she doesn't add *for you*, but we both know it's why she did it.

That day in the woods, a second from being sliced by Gary's knife, Sarah gave the prearranged signal, and the FBI rushed in from all directions, presenting an overwhelming show of force. Gary surrendered without a fight, and Sarah escaped with her life, plus a victory that led to my exoneration the next morning.

"Besides," she says, "I wasn't in any real danger. There were armed FBI agents hiding in the undergrowth all around us. Probably, one or two with sniper rifles. Even if I hadn't screamed for help when I did, someone would have taken the shot."

She smiles hesitantly, mostly to reassure me, and I let her see that I'm okay with it, even though we both know she played a dangerous game and things could have turned out very differently.

"I still can't believe you had a microphone in your earring," I say, picking up my coffee. "It's like something out of a spy movie."

What was even more incredible was that the FBI had listened to Sarah's suspicions about Gary. After all, they had their man. *Me.* I'd confessed, although stupidly, albeit under the suffocating weight of evidence. Until, days later, a specialist at the FBI determined that there was a high likelihood of the killer being left-handed, no one had been looking at anyone else for the murders, especially not at Gary.

The deal breaker came from an unexpected source.

A week or so after my arrest, when Sarah was allowed to visit me, we spoke more about the knife and the bloodied dress I found in my car. Right away, she asked a question I hadn't asked myself: Who else had access to the car, and did the parking garage have security cameras? After that, it was a matter of checking the tapes, confirming Sarah's suspicions, and then alerting the FBI to the footage of Gary planting the items in my car.

On the back of that discovery, Sarah convinced Agent Escobar to let her help trap Gary, her reasoning being that a psychopath like Gary would be unable to resist spilling his secrets to a potential victim, and especially at a location so meaningful to him. The sting operation captured Gary's confession on tape, and a subsequent search of his apartment yielded a treasure trove of trophies—an item of bloodied clothing taken from each victim, stored in vacuum-sealed bags in his closet. Following the find, a broader search of the location in Central Park where Song Chang was attacked resulted in the recovery of a pocket-knife lodged between two rocks. Blood on the blade matched Song's. And a fingerprint on the handle was a perfect match with Gary's left thumb.

Gary was charged with multiple counts of homicide, and I was released with an apology.

I drain the last of my coffee and place the cup on the table, running a finger around the rim. "I still can't believe Gary is the Central Park

Slasher. It's still absolutely dumbfounding to me when I think about it. I mean, in my present state, I don't exactly know him. Not with this amnesia of mine getting in the way. But I did, and for practically my whole life. Apparently, I knew him better than anybody. Knowing what's he's done, it makes me feel, I don't know, *weird*."

"Betrayed."

"Not just that. More like I've been duped."

"No matter how close we get, we never really know someone."

Her comment isn't referring solely to Gary. It takes into account my other self's sordid activities. In a way, I duped Sarah, too, hiding that part of me from her, so effectively that she never saw it.

"Love is blind," she says with a faint smile, as though reading my thoughts. "And no one's perfect. We all have flaws."

"You missed mine."

"Correction: I chose to look past them. Don't go getting all hung up on your mistake-ridden past, Jed. You're not a bad person. And you weren't before either. Right from the get-go, I saw you had a heart in there. That slightly creepy side of you—it's not your fault. Your whole life, you were allowed to do exactly what you wanted without anyone keeping you in check. Character defects were unavoidable."

I smile. "Sounds like something I should have printed on a T-shirt."

"The important thing is, you're learning. And that's great, for both of us. Besides, the essence of you that I fell in love with is still the same, only much closer to the surface."

"I don't deserve you."

"Sometimes we get what we need."

My smile falters. "Either way, I can't help wondering if the other me had suspicions about Gary, you know? Or if he had his head buried in the sand."

"Well, unless your memories come back in full, I guess we'll never know. It's possible Gary hid it well. He's a master manipulator."

"But we grew up together. We lived in the same household for years, went to the same college. He told me we were like brothers. Practically inseparable. You'd think I'd notice something even a little out of the ordinary with him, especially if he was a psychopath. I think I would have picked up on that. Don't adolescent psychopaths kill animals for fun?"

"Some do. But it's not a hard and fast rule. And, anyway, you're not Gary's keeper. You never were. What he did, that's all on him. In no way are you responsible for anything he did to those women. Don't beat yourself up over it. Everyone harbors secrets. Like I said, it's impossible to know every detail about a person."

"And the devil is always in the details, right?" I stop playing with the cup and sit back. "I guess what's eating at me the most is the thought that if I *did* know what he was doing, I did nothing about it."

I look at Sarah, and I can see in her eyes that it's crossed her mind, too.

"Let's think positive," she says. "All things considered, we did well, didn't we?"

I let out a tremulous breath. "I'm not sure this applies to you, but I came out of the whole thing in about as good shape as possible. One pretty vicious beating and a bunch of sleepless nights. But no visible scars. All charges dropped. A chance to get my life back on track. I swear, for a while back there, I was convinced I would be spending the rest of my days vegetating in a cell. Thank God the police decided not to pursue the stalking angle."

She picks up her cup again, warming her hands around it. "The least said about that, the better."

"I thought psychologists were supposed to encourage candid conversation?"

"Only when it's in the best interests of the patient and not detrimental to the psychological well-being of their lover."

Now it's my turn to smile. "I'm lucky to have you."

"Yes, you are. Don't blow it."

She drinks some of her coffee, and not for the first time this week, I notice her. Not like noticing something unimportant in passing, but in the way that makes a man sit up and beg.

"I let her go, you know?"

"Who?"

"Cassie. Or, rather, my misplaced obsession with her. That second night in lockup, after the beating, I came to my senses. But not before doing an awful lot of soul-searching. I made a big mistake, and I'm sorry for what I put you through."

"It's okay."

Sarah reaches out and touches my hand again. This time, I don't even have to think about my reaction.

We entwine fingers and swap smiles.

Even so, we both know it's not all okay. This is what we say to get past something, or to put it to bed until we're in a better place to wake it up and face it. No matter how I look at this, my best friend was a serial killer, and the other version of me was a stalker. Both are fact, and it isn't a stretch to think that my other self might have been influenced by Gary. And if that is the case, what other secrets am I yet to uncover?

Before Sarah can sense the sweat starting to prick out on my palm, I let go of her hand. "Anyway, the long and the short of it is, you'll be proud to hear I've learned to recognize my unhealthy obsessions when I see them."

"You're a quick study."

"Trust me. Being stuck in a cell for twenty-three hours a day is a great way to stimulate introspection. I came face-to-face with my demons and I didn't back down. As soon as they rear their ugly heads, I run a mile."

"No more Cassies."

My smile tries to falter, but I keep it hiked up. "No more anything even remotely seedy. From now on, I'm on my best behavior."

She raises her cup, making a toast. "I can drink to that." Then she finishes her coffee.

Mine is already gone, with just the dregs darkening the bottom of the cup. "Another?" I ask.

"No, thanks. That concludes my daily caffeine allowance. I'd like to sleep tonight, preferably with you. But not until after we've made love."

I can't help my smile from broadening. "Wow."

"What?"

"Your frankness scares me."

"Life is short, Jed Allen, and we're not getting any younger. A woman approaching her middle years needs to say what she means and mean what she says." The corners of her lips are curved upward, but there's suddenly an edge of uncertainty in her eyes. "Are you sure you'll be okay?" she asks. "Without your meds?"

"Sarah, I'll be fine. Put it this way, I can't be any worse. I've come to terms with what I was and who I am. Honestly, I'm settled inside. It's given me a whole new outlook and a kind of inner peace I didn't have before. I'm actually beginning to like the new me, and I don't want to lose it." I pause, noticing a change in her expression. "What?"

"It's just that your 'inner peace' reminds me of Gary," she says. "When he had the knife to my throat, I asked him to explain why he killed all those women with such brutality."

"What did he say?"

"That it was the only time he ever felt tranquility."

"The calm at the center of the chaos."

Now she laughs. "You should go into psychology."

"Seriously? Give me a break. I need to keep a big distance from everything that starts with the word 'psycho.' Starting now."

"Including me?"

I show her my grin. "There's always one exception to every rule. I'll prove it to you. Later."

She pushes her chair back, getting to her feet. "Hold that thought. Meanwhile, I need the bathroom. Can you take care of the check?"

"Sure."

I sit back, watching her as she weaves her way between the tables. I have no doubt that Sarah Merrick is the best thing to ever happen to me. She has demonstrated an unwavering loyalty, risking her life to save mine, sticking with me when others tried to pry her loose. She has forgiven the error of my ways, and she wants to be with me for who I am. It's something money can't buy. I owe it to her to keep my demons at bay and to make good on what we have. Together, I'm sure we can build ourselves a wonderful life, if I don't screw up.

As Sarah disappears into the restroom, I raise a hand to attract the waitress's attention. She sees me waving, smiles, and comes over.

She's a tall brunette with possibly the bluest eyes I have ever seen.

"How was your meal?" she asks.

"Great. In fact, perfect. The lasagna was to die for. Can I get the check?" I peer at her name badge. "Savannah."

"Sure thing."

"Thanks. Nice name, by the way."

She smiles and then goes over to the register. And I watch her, fascinated with the cute way her front teeth nibble at her lower lip as she brings up our order on the touchscreen.

While she's distracted, I pick up my phone from the table, opening up the camera app. Then I pause with my thumb over the button.

What am I doing?

I'm a changed man.

I've been through hell and come out the other side.

I have a new life now, and a new love interest to explore.

I'm at the pinnacle of my game, with everything I want at my fingertips.

I have been given a second chance.

I don't need *this*.

Like it's radioactive, I drop the phone back on the table.

Then I stare at it as it lies there on the white cloth, innocuous, innocent, taunting me.

All at once, there's a whirlwind of conflicting feelings inside me. And I'm sure everybody in the restaurant can hear the thoughts screeching in my head.

At the center of my focus, the register is printing out the check, and Savannah, the waitress with the bluest eyes ever, is about to come over.

It's now or never.

I pick up the phone again.

One harmless photo won't hurt . . . will it?

Acknowledgments

For your steadfast support, your honesty, your truth. For your endless words of encouragement, your positivity, your patience. For giving me your time, your thoughts, your love. For being my muse and for being my wife.

Thank you, Lynn—for without you, I am just a dreamer.

My family is the most important thing in my life—so an extra-special thank-you goes to my lovely daughters and sons-in-law, Gemma and Sam, and Rebecca and Ruben. Fondest grandpa cuddles go to my four wonderful granddaughters, Willow and Perry, and Ava and Bella, for never failing to impress me with your uncluttered wisdom. And warmest hugs go to my mum and dad, June and Bill, and to my dearest mother-in-law, Lillian, for always being there with smiles and with humor and with as many cups of tea as it takes.

Together, you are my world.

Thank you, Emilie Marneur, editorial director at Amazon Publishing, for your continuing faith in my writing, and for your patience when it comes to my pace. Thank you, Charlotte Herscher, my developmental editor, for reminding me that no matter how many times I take a hammer to it, a square peg will never fit into a round hole. Thank you to Elizabeth Johnson, my eagle-eyed copyeditor, for smoothing out the wrinkles and helping Americanize my work. And thank you also to Erin Cusick, my proofreader, for the final polish that left things gleaming.

Thank you to all my loyal readers worldwide, new and old, and especially to those who have been with me since the start. Your kind e-mails and your social media support is always sincerely appreciated, and often makes me smile when I need to smile the most.

Lastly, thank *you* for reading my book. I hope you enjoyed it.

Keith Houghton, England, June 2017

About the Author

Ask Keith Houghton what he writes about and he won't say crime or murder, even though these are major themes in his work. Instead, he'll say contrasts and extremes.

When it comes to storytelling, what interests him are life's polar opposites, both internally and externally—what pushes us to reach for the moral high ground or pulls us deep into our psyche. Moreover, his stories aren't simply concerned with good versus evil, but also with the crossover between the two—the gray area where the line between right and wrong is often blurred. It's not surprising, therefore, to see his good guys turn out to be half bad and his bad guys half good, all the while being drawn in opposite directions along plot lines split equally between denying truths and embracing lies. In the world of Keith Houghton's imagination, not everything is black and white—sometimes it's blood-red.

Keith Houghton is the author of the stand-alone psychological thrillers *No Coming Back* and *Before You Leap,* as well as the four Gabe Quinn thrillers: *Chasing Fame, Killing Hope, Crossing Lines,* and *Taking Liberty.*

To read more about Keith and his writing, please visit www.keithhoughton.com.

Printed in Great Britain
by Amazon

41187988R00168